THE
INFINITY GUARDIANS

S. M. WILSON

USBORNE

For my three heroes: Kevin, Elliott and Rhys Bain

First published in the UK in 2022 by Usborne Publishing Ltd., Usborne House,
83-85 Saffron Hill, London EC1N 8RT, England. usborne.com

Usborne Verlag, Usborne Publishing Ltd., Prüfeninger Str. 20,
93049 Regensburg, Deutschland, VK Nr. 17560

Text © Susan Wilson, 2022

Cover illustration by Steve Stone. Copyright © Usborne, 2022

A CIP catalogue record for this book is available from the British Library.

ISBN 9781474987004   06041/1   J MAMJJASOND/22

Printed and bound in Great Britain by CPI Group (UK) Ltd, Croydon, CR0 4YY

CHAPTER ONE

A sh Yang looked down at the view beneath her and took a deep breath. Silence. From the vast array of ancient artefacts in the Library to the dark space littered with stars above her head, she was surrounded by silence.

Sometimes she had to pinch herself to believe she was actually here. The Library at the End of the Universe was the storage place for the Infinity Files – a range of artefacts and antiquities from throughout the universe, all taken from planets that were either on the brink of extinction and about to be lost for ever, or from places that were about to destroy themselves with war. Some artefacts would be held permanently in the Library, and others would be returned when the time was right.

Ash's eyes scanned the cavernous room below. She'd been here for six months and still knew only a fraction of what was stored here. In one display lay a bright-orange scroll with brown inscriptions. It had caused centuries of fighting on a distant planet, before she'd retrieved it with her team on their most recent mission. In the mission before that, they'd acquired a tiny microchip, thinner than a strand of hair, that contained coordinates of every major city across numerous continents on Veroagus – allowing them to be targeted with weapons that would wipe out millions. It was now in a safe within the Library walls.

Some aspects of the Library still made her head swirl. Particularly now Orius was no longer here to guide her. All she knew for certain was that, as Guardian, the responsibility for all the artefacts was hers. And only hers – now that Orius, the holographic Keeper of the Library, had finally disintegrated after nine hundred years of service. She hadn't realized just how much of an ache she would continually feel in her chest after he was gone. The space he'd left behind was immense.

From the first day she'd stepped into the Library – on its tiny, lonely moon – he'd guided her work and taught her the roles and responsibilities of the Guardian, in his own unique way. At times Orius's teaching methods had felt like "sink or swim" or "less is more". But Ash had found her feet. She'd battled to save the Library from a former Guardian named Aldus, who'd gone rogue, and then fought to save her own solar system from an endless war based on theft, misunderstandings and the will to survive.

All along the way she'd learned. On each planet she'd visited as Guardian, Ash had found a Friend, a person to assist her with the task of either retrieving an artefact or returning it. One was here now, helping her in the Library.

Amara was a Callean from Columbia 764. It was a planet that had two distinct species – one Human-like and one lizard-like, the Calleans. Amara stood upright and wore clothes like Ash did, but her forehead was ridged and her skin was covered in a variety of green and brown scales. Her fingers were elongated, with claws instead of nails.

"We've got one," said Amara, as an image appeared in the air in front of Ash's face, along with the sound of its now-familiar hum. This was information around her next mission. Diagrams and written text telling her exactly what was at stake hovered on the screen right in front of her and Amara's eyes.

Ash scanned the details. Her task was to retrieve an artefact – a stolen crystal – before it caused the imminent destruction of a space port. It had strange magnetic properties, but also let out dangerous levels of radiation, and was currently being pursued by a powerful and ruthless race from the other side of the galaxy.

Her hand went automatically to the bangle at her wrist – her usual method of transport for missions. It had appeared on her wrist when she'd first become Guardian, and Orius had let her know it would only disappear when she died. It had been a bit of a shock but it almost felt like part of her now.

Ash smiled at Amara as Trik and Ezra appeared from their room, obviously responding to the familiar low hum of a new Library mission.

Things had changed at the Library at the End of the Universe. Before Ash, the Guardian had always worked alone, blindly following the instructions of the Library, which monitored millions of civilizations across the universe and calculated probabilities every nanosecond. But Ash was sceptical enough to realize that even the almighty Library couldn't possibly know everything, and wise enough to know that decisions often had to be rationalized and talked through. And so she'd invited Amara to join her here, as well as two of her fellow space-academy recruits, Trik and Ezra.

Since they'd helped her to stop the war in their home solar system, and a peace treaty had been negotiated, there wasn't much for a fighter pilot to do at the Star Corporation Academy, so they'd jumped at Ash's offer to join her at the Library. Together they made an unlikely quartet, but they worked well as a team. And it felt better – safer – because while Ash liked to act on her instincts, sometimes she knew she had to listen to other opinions. Being Guardian was a big job, and Ash still wasn't entirely sure she was up to it.

She glanced back at the instructions for their new mission. They seemed simple enough. She pulled her hand away from her bangle.

"Let's try something different this time," she said, with a grin on her face.

"Do we just land?" Trik's voice crackled across the comm from his craft.

"I told you we should use the Proteus circle," murmured Ezra from the craft to Ash's right. "This is already too tricky."

Ash bit her lip, scanning the busy space port ahead of them. Quisquilla wasn't exactly a standard port any more. It had started out that way, but over thousands of years it had developed and now resembled interlocking DNA strands, spread throughout the black space ahead.

"It's like a junkyard," said Trik. "Where do we even start?"

Ash couldn't exactly argue. Over years and years, docks, landing platforms, hangars, extra accommodation and connecting walkways had literally been bolted on to the space port, leaving multicoloured, oddly shaped parts hanging in space. Some sections looked as if they were held together with pieces of wire cable. How could those tunnels be safe? And it did look like junk. Even from here, she could see the vibrations of activity on the station freeing the odd tiny piece of metal from its last fastening bolt, to float off into oblivion.

And yet this place was likely home to houses, shops, meeting places, workshops, enforcement compounds, schools – wait, did this place have schools? Did kids actually live in a place like this? Amara was the brains of their team – she didn't often join the other three on missions, instead finding out as much as she could about each destination and briefing the team, to help them avoid trouble. But details about Quisquilla had been a little sketchy. Ash knew that some of the people who ended up here were refugees from distant planets, who'd landed at the space port after hitching a ride, and had nowhere else to go. So the population was probably a mix of many different species. But that was about all the information they had.

Most of the official port traffic flowed in and out of the space docks in neat rows. But that required landing permissions and identification papers – none of which would have been needed if Ash and her companions had stood on the Proteus circle in the Library and used her bangle to instantly transport inside the port, like they were supposed to do.

But it had been over a month since their last mission. The days had been long and they'd all been restless. Which was why Ash had been tempted to try things differently this time.

Without Orius, what happened at the Library was all down to her. So, what if she and her Academy comrades had wanted to take out the super-fighters they'd found stored under the Library? Maybe Ash hadn't become a fighter pilot, but the temptation to fly through space was still in her bones, in her blood. She missed the thrill. The sensation. Any chance she got to be in the pilot's seat again was something she grabbed with both hands. It wasn't often that a mission was actually close enough to do it. So this had been too good an opportunity to miss.

Something caught Ash's gaze. A variety of spacecraft were dotted all around the main port, but she could see another point in the far distance where the occasional ship seemed to disappear out of sight. There must an alternative landing bay – or at least somewhere to dock.

Ezra must have spotted it too. He sighed. "Do you see that? It's got to be for the smugglers."

She smiled. He knew her well. When they'd trained together for the Star Corporation Academy, he'd always been more cautious than Ash. Skilful, brave, but still cautious. Ezra liked to try and weigh up the odds, which could often be against them. Trik was somewhere in between them both. Full of fire and gusto, he seemed to have been born with an inbuilt enthusiasm for the moment.

They were her friends. Her crew. They were helping Ash navigate the strange new life and destiny that had unfolded for her since she'd been appointed Guardian. And she needed them – even though the decisions were ultimately hers to make.

"Let's go around," she said. "And try not to attract too much attention."

"Smuggling," mused Trik over the comm, as he banked left to follow her. "I'm sure there were some smugglers in my family. Hey, maybe I'll meet some distant relative up here in…"

She could practically see him glancing around them. His voice cut across the comm. "What system are we in again?"

"We're in the Anagos system. Six light years from the Library."

Six light years. How long would that have taken them in a regular ship? In her home planet's technology, it would have taken a few weeks – but only if there were a few wormholes to jump through. With the bangle and Proteus circle it would have taken seconds. But with these ships that they'd found underneath the Library, the journey had taken a little over an hour.

Amara's voice cut across the comm. "Guys, I've found some more information. I know why the Byroneans are so desperate for this crystal."

There was an ominous tone to her voice. "Okay," said Ash, as her eyes scanned the rear side of the space port, watching how the ships seemed to line up at a ramshackle smugglers' dock and then be hooked in by some kind of giant magnetic lure, anchoring them in place while a docking tunnel was attached. "Why?"

"The Infinity Files mention that the crystal can have multiple uses. I can only find details of one, but it's probably the most relevant to your mission."

"I don't like the sound of this," muttered Ezra.

"The crystal is a source of power for the Byroneans," said Amara. "Not only that, when the two in existence come together, it allows the Byroneans to reproduce more of themselves."

Trik started coughing and choking. "Wh...at?"

"They can survive with only one," continued Amara, "but their numbers remain the same. With two, they can reproduce themselves exponentially. The Byroneans are notorious for being powerful and dangerous, with no mercy or empathy. Just imagine the damage they could do across the universe if they could create a never-ending army of themselves."

There were a few seconds of silence as Ash swallowed nervously. "So let's assume they already have one. We'd better find this second crystal quickly."

CHAPTER TWO

A hiss came across the comm.

"*Vessel BC679, what is your landing clearance code?*" said a high-pitched nasal voice.

Ash flinched, knowing that BC679 was the identifier for her craft.

She switched on the screens in front of her, to see Trik raising his eyebrows and Ezra giving the smallest shake of his head. I-told-you-so was written all over his expression.

Amara cut back in. Her voice was smooth and perfectly in control. She was the most unflappable of the team: practical, even when she sometimes had to relay worrying information.

"I have a few you can try, Ash. Sending them through now."

Ash's screen flashed with an array of 44-digit codes. "Where did you find these?" she murmured in wonder.

"I've been scanning channels in and around Quisquilla since you left," she said. "It's a smugglers' haven – and even smugglers need codes. Let me know if they work. If they don't, I'll find you some others."

Ash shook her head. She didn't doubt for a second that Amara would. She'd shown an uncanny ability for finding her way round the Library computers and systems since Orius had disappeared.

"BC769, you have ten seconds to send a code before I blast you into oblivion." There was a hint of amusement in the odd voice – as if blasting random crafts into oblivion was actually the highlight of the speaker's day.

"Ash!" Trik and Ezra spoke in unison.

Ash's fingers worked frantically. She fumbled, her fingers sliding on the control, transmitting all the codes at once.

A few moments later the voice responded. *"Interesting… you wait all day for one code and then twenty come along at once."*

Ash's muscles tightened. Transmitting all the codes had been an error. Now the operator was suspicious. She swallowed, her mouth dry.

Silence seemed to hang in the air of her cockpit as she waited. And waited. And waited.

Finally, the comm crackled back to life. *"BC769, you and your party, docking arm C7."*

Ash breathed a sigh of relief and manoeuvred her craft forward, trying to pretend she had any idea of how things worked around here.

As she edged the fighter towards C7, the magnetic lure clamped to the side of her ship, sending a judder through every part of her. Next, something resembling a desert snake coiled out from the station, and after a few missed attempts finally latched over her cockpit.

"Hold for pressurization," came the command.

It felt a little odd arriving for a mission dressed in her own flight suit. On previous trips, when she'd used the Proteus circle to jump, Ash's whole appearance had changed. Her clothes always altered to help her blend in with the local population, but sometimes her face did too, or her whole body. At times she'd assumed the appearance of another person who actually existed on that planet, but who was safely tucked away somewhere else.

Amara was now able to warn Ash if she was about to change species or form, but Orius had never bothered. He'd let her find out for herself once she'd jumped. And Ash had got the distinct impression that he had enjoyed throwing her in at the deep end.

This time, Amara had been able to tell them there would be no need to change appearance or clothing. Apparently the flight suits they normally donned were routine on a space port like this, so they fitted in well. It was another reason Ash had chosen to use the space fighters. Maybe it had made the start of the mission a little trickier, but things seemed to be working out okay now.

The ship juddered again, followed by a loud hissing noise.

Ash released the hood of her cockpit, subconsciously holding her breath for a few seconds. The tunnel looked decidedly unsafe, with several smaller tunnels leading to all the docking ports. She flicked a switch on the comm. "Everyone okay?"

There were a few unimpressed grunts in response. She slid out of the cockpit and took a few tentative steps down the tunnel, feeling as if it could detach at any second and send her spiralling into space.

Ash emerged into a bustling corridor. It seemed that security at Quisquilla was decidedly lax.

Ezra and Trik emerged separately a little further down the corridor, giving her a brief nod as they walked to meet her. But the traffic in the corridor was too busy for small talk.

The schematics of the space port had revealed it was like a warren: multiple levels, cramped quarters in places and enclosed, dark winding corridors.

"Let's see where we are," murmured Ash, and followed the main flow of people.

She was trying so hard not to stare. She knew that space ports varied. Some were only stopgaps for refuelling across wide solar systems, others were gathering places for travellers, often with extraordinary marketplaces – like Quisquilla.

They followed the stream of people out into a wide-open space with a transparent ceiling, revealing the distant stars in the black space above. This was clearly the main market. The noise was incredible, but they managed to pull themselves over to a small corner with a few overturned barrels, where they could sit and observe. They also had to work out where to start looking for the crystal – the Library hadn't been able to pinpoint its precise location.

Ash looked around. "Wow," was all she could say at first.

Trik shook his head. The market was busy, with an array of items clearly being bartered and sold, but it was the crowd that held their attention. It seemed like the marketplace at Quisquilla was the meeting place for half of the species in the galaxy!

At one market stall stood a tall figure with four arms, pale lilac skin and purple hair that reached his waist. His nose was flat and there was something like gills along his jawline. Ash was mesmerized by the shades of violet – they were stunning, more vivid than she'd ever seen before. She had no idea what planet he came from. He was arguing with a small round figure that was completely covered in fur. Ash couldn't even see any facial features, just some small stumpy arms that were gesturing wildly.

Just a little away from them were creatures covered in thick scales, like armour. They stood on four legs and had faces with large ears. But it was their voices that were most surprising. The bangle on her wrist allowed Ash to hear, speak and understand alien languages, and both Trik and Ezra had universal translators under the skin beneath their right ears, so they could understand just as well as she could. Rich and cultured, the two creatures were arguing with each other, but it was the politest squabble Ash had ever heard.

Trik nudged her. "Middle of the room," he muttered.

She followed his gaze. Three figures – bipedal, with

dark-red ridged skin, elongated heads and wearing white uniforms – seemed to be scoping out the marketplace. Much the same as Ash and her colleagues.

"Who are they?" she whispered.

"I think they're Fidulans," said Ezra. "But I'm not entirely sure."

As they watched, another race appeared from one of the other entranceways to the market. These people were dressed in flowing dark-blue robes; they had three eyes, pale-blue skin and an array of glowing lights hovering above their heads in a floating circle.

"Pantheons," Ash breathed in awe. She'd heard of them – most people in this part of the galaxy had. A race that was part flesh, part light. They were rarely seen, but the stories about their powers were legendary. Ash had no idea how much truth there was in the tales of mind reading, empathic healing and the ability to send sharp shocks.

"Maybe we should leave," said Ezra cautiously.

"Why?" asked Trik.

"Because Fidulans and Pantheons are supposed to be sworn enemies. And we have an urgent mission. Eyes on the prize, people."

But Ash couldn't pass up a chance to learn more about the Pantheons. She whipped round, her brow furrowed. "Enemies? Really?"

She'd barely finished the sentence when there was a loud clicking sound. It was like the entire marketplace filled with static. The background chatter halted instantly. Ash turned back round slowly, in time to see the largest of the Fidulans rise up on his toes, shoulders tensed. The noise was coming from him. It amplified by the second. Rage was painted across his face.

In contrast, the Pantheons' faces were pictures of calm and tranquility, but the look in their eyes was as deadly as any Ash had ever seen. They moved closer to the angry Fidulan. It was almost a glide across the floor, the crowd parting instantaneously to allow them through.

She tugged at the sleeve of Ezra's flight suit. "I think you might be right. We should get out of here."

"I'm gone," said Trik quickly, turning and walking rapidly to the nearest tunnel.

"Where are we even going?" said Ezra. "Do you have any idea where the artefact is in this place?"

"Where would you store a stolen crystal from Byroneus?" replied Ash as they continued to walk. "One that, if it was found on you, would result in your death?"

"Surely its magnetic powers mean that it's got to be attached to some kind of metal?" said Trik.

Ezra threw up his hand. "But this whole place is metal! It hardly narrows the field for us." He glanced at Ash. "Any idea where your Friend is?"

She shook her head. "Amara tried to send a few messages but had no response."

In all but one of the places Ash had been sent to before, there had always been a Friend of the Library to assist the Guardian. The Friend was recognizable because of something they wore – a symbol of some sort, made of the same metal as the bangle round Ash's wrist and the Proteus circle back at the Library. On some planets, the role of Friend had been passed down through generations of families. Amara had been the Friend on Ash's first ever mission as Guardian. They had gelled instantly, and it was part of the reason she was a member of Ash's team at the Library.

Ash turned to say more, just as the noise behind her amplified to a roar and a huge bang from the marketplace hurled them all forward onto their hands and knees.

For a second, none of them moved. Instinct was to freeze. A bang like that on a space port meant some kind of explosion. And an explosion on any kind of platform in space could be deadly. All it would take was one tiny piece of the fragile structure to peel back, sucking the oxygen out, and exposing all the lives inside to the vacuum of space.

Ash had no idea if Quisquilla had any kind of functioning force field around it. From what she'd seen outside, it was not a bet she would place.

Ezra was first to move, grabbing both his comrades by their flight suits and pulling them upwards. "Move!"

Their feet hit the floor not a second too late. Whatever had happened inside the marketplace had initiated the survival instincts in every species present. A multitude of beings started flooding through the exit behind them, causing a bottleneck.

Ash barely had a chance to glance back as Ezra dragged them on, and the tunnels bent and curved, meaning any view behind was quickly lost. But the thudding of feet told her all she really needed to know. Something very serious had happened back there.

Trouble was, they were running with no idea where they were running to. Behind them, some kind of siren started.

"Please no hull breach," panted Trik, as he ran alongside her.

Maybe this whole mission should be abandoned. She'd never failed one before, but she didn't want to risk the lives of her crew if the place was about to disintegrate. There was always too much at stake for her to just give up though. Thousands of lives could depend on any one of Ash's missions.

"In here," yelled Trik as he darted down another corridor to the left, ducking through a door and taking them away from the main flow of traffic.

They stopped, leaning over and resting their hands on their knees, breathing heavily. Running in a space port wasn't like running on an ordinary planet. Every part of the body was pushed in a way it objected to. Even the staff at the Star Corporation Academy had to spend at least part of the season on a planet with reasonable gravity, to allow their bodies to recover.

Ash looked up and pushed her hair out of her face, tucking one wayward strand – pink this week– behind her ear. She sucked in a deep breath. Faces were staring at her, drinks clasped in hands and claws and tentacles. A bar. They'd burst into a bar.

Most of the folks in the bar were on their feet – doubtless because of the commotion they'd heard outside. One had his hand – or claw – on a weapon at his hip.

She locked eyes with him and held up her hands. "Don't ask me," she said with a bravado that was completely false. "We're just getting out of the way."

As if on cue, the siren stopped, meaning the threat of a breach was over. But the rabble and noise didn't end. The ongoing fight was still heading in their direction. Most of the bar drinkers headed to the door and pushed forward down the corridor to watch, or perhaps join in. Ash moved sideways to let them pass.

"Let's regroup and make a plan," she murmured over her shoulder as she walked to a table. Trik and Ezra joined her, and a scowling bar server walked over and slapped a jug of something red down on the table in front of them.

Trik tossed a coin from his pocket to get rid of the bartender quickly and gain some privacy. "Let's be quick."

Ezra leaned his elbows on the table and looked around the bar through lowered lids. Ash was cursing her position. She had her back to the few remaining drinkers in the establishment.

"Almost the same as the market," said Ezra in a low voice. "Hardly two from the same species. Might as well have a sign above the door saying Smugglers' Central. We're probably the only people in here unarmed." He gave a lopsided smile. "Ash, you bring us to the best places."

In the dimly lit bar, Ezra's luminescent skin was more

obvious. On a different mission, that could be a problem. But here? No one was even likely to notice.

Trik picked up the jug, stared at the contents and grabbed some glasses from a shelf on the wall behind them. He poured the contents of the jug into the glasses and pushed one towards each of them. "We've paid for it – might as well drink." He took a quick sip, and then smiled, nodding his head. "No idea what it is, but I like it."

Ezra leaned in closer so their voices wouldn't be heard. "We need to find the missing crystal, and fast. You heard the instructions from the Library. There'll be a raid in the next few hours. If the raiders from Byroneus find their stolen crystal here, they'll blast the whole space port out of existence."

Ash gave an involuntary shudder. "How many people do you think live here?"

Trik closed his eyes for a second. "This place is so spread out I'm not sure I could even hazard a proper guess. Twenty thousand?"

Ash threw back the rest of her drink. "We can't hang around. Amara gave me this, along with a med wand." She pulled a slim grey rectangle from her pocket and handed it over for them to inspect. "She hoped it might be able to locate the artefact once we got here. She suspects the crystal might give off some kind of radioactive particles. Maybe it had some kind of shield round it originally, but that must have been damaged or degraded over the years, because apparently the radiation is lighting up the space port like a beacon."

Trik leaned back. "So we can use this to locate the crystal?"

Ezra flicked on the switch and the screen lit up with a strange green glow. "Let's find out."

The corridors were still busy. A thin stream of smoke was wafting in the air. Whatever the filtration system was on the space port, it wasn't managing to work properly. Several of the people passing had minor injuries – blood of various colours was smeared on limbs and heads.

The temptation to head back and see what had happened was strong, but there was no time. It was enough to listen to the passing conversations:

"How did the Pantheons do that?"

"But what did they do?"

"Did you hear that noise?"

"We're lucky the force field held. The marketplace will need to be sealed for the next few days."

"I'm going to lose trade. Who is going to pay for that? Those Pantheons should be locked up!"

"I heard the Fidulan Commander lost part of his hand. Do you think there will be repercussions?"

Ash and her team exchanged nervous glances. Ezra had the scanner low at his thigh. His eyes watched the screen intently as he nudged Trik in the direction they needed to go.

Time was of the essence. Amara hadn't been able to give them an accurate note of when the Byroneans might appear. Even though they'd only spent five minutes in the bar to make a quick plan, the fight in the marketplace, along with the alarm, had eaten up some of their time already.

"How much longer?" Ash urged.

Ezra tilted the screen towards her. "How do you expect me to know? We seem to be going in circles without actually getting any closer to our destination!" He looked up in exasperation. "Why isn't there a map of this place?" His nose wrinkled. "Are there different levels? Are we walking over or under it?"

Ash grabbed the scanner out of his hand. Instead of focusing on how close they were to the green dot on the weird graph, her eyes focused on the red pulse in the corner of the screen. "Tell me that isn't the radiation bars?" she asked.

Ezra wouldn't meet her eyes.

"How many people have been exposed to this radiation? And for how long?" she hissed.

Trik put his hand on her arm. "Ash, this isn't our doing. We just got here. Most of this is outside our control. Let's just find the crystal, get a force field round it and get it out of here."

She stopped walking. "Am I actually going to take this back to the Library and expose all of us to it? Shouldn't we just jettison it out into space?"

"Aren't we supposed to protect the artefacts and bring them back to the Library safely?" Ezra argued. "Who knows, at some point, what we might think is a piece of radioactive junk might save some other species or planet."

There was a noise behind them. Loud voices. Clicking sounds again. Ezra put his hand on Ash's back.

"Move, people. Let's try and stay away from the trouble. We create enough of our own."

The corridor had narrowed again, meaning they jostled against people trying to go in the other direction. The little green dot on the screen never seemed to get any closer.

Ash was getting more frustrated by the second. "What's wrong with this?" she asked, shaking the device in confusion.

A small Human figure standing in their path, arms folded, answered snarkily: "You're just all too stupid to know how to use it properly."

CHAPTER THREE

Ash froze. It took a moment for her to understand that the person on the other side of the corridor and full of snark was actually a child. On a space port brimming with multiple species, size wasn't always a factor in age.

But the person talking to them was definitely a kid. An angry kid. She had dark messy hair and a mishmash of clothes: a dirty cape that looked like it had once been bright blue, a torn scarf at her neck and a pair of well-worn boots on her feet. But the most surprising thing was the way she was looking at them all – with a glare that emanated both distaste and contempt.

"I'm sure we'll work it out," said Trik quickly, signalling with his eyes that they should all keep walking.

"I wouldn't count on it," came the reply.

Figures were passing between them and the kid. Ezra frowned.

"Do we know you?" he asked.

Another group passed and Ash blinked. The kid was gone.

She sucked in a breath and then started, as the girl's face appeared directly under her nose. Before she could move, the girl had her hands on Ash's bangle. Ash tried to snatch her hand back, but the kid was surprisingly strong. Her fingers fastened round Ash's wrist just beneath her bangle.

The bangle was only worn by the Guardian of the Library. It was made of the same precious metal as the Proteus circle, which they could stand on to transport to other worlds. The metal was decidedly dull and the bangle without adornments so there was nothing to draw undue attention to it.

"What are you doing?" asked Ash in a low voice.

The girl dropped her wrist and looked up again. "Checking," was the reply.

As the kid tilted her chin, Ash could see something nestled round her neck. Hanging from a dirty piece of string was a dull misshapen coin. It was clearly made from the same metal as her bangle.

Ash's eyes widened. They'd just met the Friend on Quisquilla!

Ezra leaned between them both, following Ash's gaze. "You're the Friend?" he asked.

The girl stared at Ash. "You're the Guardian?" She gave a disdainful shake of her head.

"I thought Friends were supposed to be friendly," Trik said, with a glint in his eye.

Ash put her hand on the girl's shoulder. "What's your name?"

She shook off Ash's hand. "Reker. Follow me."

The girl spun and started walking down the corridor at a breakneck speed, dodging between people.

For a second, all three of them stood motionless. "And I'm Ash, pleased to meet you," said Ash, as she watched the girl's retreating back.

Ezra let out a laugh. "Guess we better follow her."

They tried to catch up. It was difficult. Because the corridors were so twisted, they often lost sight of Reker. She seemed to have dodging through a crowd down to a fine art.

Then Trik let out a low whistle. "Did I just see that?"

"See what?" asked Ash.

Trik pointed forward. "Keep watching."

They did, and saw that as Reker turned sideways to slide through a large crowd of chattering visitors, a small hand darted out and lost itself in the folds of the loose garment worn by one of them, pulling out a coin pouch.

It happened in the blink of an eye.

Ezra and Trik exchanged glances. "Impressive," said Trik.

"It's not impressive," snapped Ash. "It's stealing."

Ezra looked around as they entered a larger part of the corridor – it was almost like another marketplace. "Maybe it's the only way to survive," he said quietly. At one glance it was easy to tell who were visitors and who were residents of Quisquilla. No one who was rich lived on Quisquilla. It might be a smuggling haven, but those who made the money didn't actually stay here. They traded and left.

Ash looked down at the screen in her hand. This time the green dot seemed close. The group threaded their way through the crowd just as Reker darted into a hidden shaft. They halted, crashing into one another, as they examined the gap. The dark grey walls melded into one another – they would never have noticed this passageway if they hadn't seen Reker disappear.

"Go on." Trik pushed Ash from behind and they followed the little girl.

By the time they emerged through the other side, Reker was standing impatiently at the entrance to another tunnel, her arms folded again.

She gave one nod and they followed her into it. This corridor was darker than any of the others, and the odour emanating from it wasn't pleasant. It was dank, wet, with doors all along it. There was still some noise, but it was muffled. Shouting. Crying. Ash gave a shudder.

Reker stopped, lifting her hand over a scanner next to one particular door. Etched into the dark metal was her name.

The door slid open, and a smell slid out to them. Damp. Again. Ash tried not to wince.

"Get in," said Reker gruffly. Trik and Ezra stepped in first and by the time Ash crossed the threshold, she realized there was barely space for all of them in the room.

That's all it was – a single room. Slim, with a bench along one wall that looked as if it doubled as a bed. There was a panel in the wall opposite that Ash guessed must hide some kind of bathroom facility, but that was basically it.

Well, that and the mess.

Pieces of clothing were scattered throughout the tight space. A few discarded drinking vessels. Some rubbish. It was the room of an unsupervised kid.

Ash felt a wave of empathy. She'd ended up on her own when she was not much older than Reker. First her sister had died in a bombing, then her mother and father had died in succession. Both had developed health issues, but Ash was sure they'd died from broken hearts.

Ash had been resilient. She'd been focused, with one intention on her mind – to get into the Star Corporation Academy, win a place as a pilot and wreak her revenge on the neighbouring planet they'd been at war with.

But Ash had been lucky to have the comfort of a village behind her. She knew she could knock on any door. Neighbours would appear with cooked food. If a repair had been needed on her old family home, she'd find one of her school friends' fathers doing it, without having to ask.

There was an air in this tiny room that Ash could sense. Neglect. Anger. Isolation.

She glanced at the tracker. Apparently, she was right next to the crystal.

"You can't have it." Reker had assumed her preferred stance of crossed arms and glaring at them all.

There were a few moments of silence.

Trik spoke first. "Maybe I should explain what the definition of a Friend is." He adopted exactly the same tone as Reker as he looked her in the eye.

Fury flashed across her face. "A Friend is a person who gets used by someone they've never seen or heard from before. An unknown who puts their own needs above the Friend's."

Ash breathed in slowly. "This isn't personal, Reker. This is about the greater good. The Library sent me here to retrieve something. I know the consequences if I fail. Quisquilla is going to be raided soon. If the Byroneans find their stolen crystal here, it's likely they'll blast the space port into pieces. Twenty thousand people are on this port. I can't let that happen."

"It *is* personal. That crystal has been in my family for generations. It's ours now. I need it. I won't give it up." Reker glared at Ash. "How do you even know that they'll come? Did you arrange this? Did you tell them? That's it, isn't it? The great Library decided to tip the Byroneans off. That way, it gets to keep the crystal and 'save' us all."

Ash opened her mouth to speak, but Ezra got in there first. "Reker, what is it the crystal actually does? Why do you want to keep it so badly?"

There was a knock at the door. The frown lines on Reker's head deepened. "Go away," she yelled. "Come back later – I'm busy."

There was a low croaking voice at the other side of the door. Reker elbowed her way through them and pressed the button to let the door hiss open.

Ash felt herself pull back. The person at the door was Agoran, a species she'd seen on many occasions. But this Agoran was clearly sick. She was elderly, almost a collection

32

of bones, swathed in blankets. Her skin was loose and wrinkled, her spine cowed, and the proud, colourful feathers that usually adorned the head of all Agorans were completely missing.

"Please," said the old Agoran, her voice sounding pitiful.

Reker put a hand on her thin arm. "I have guests," she whispered. "Come back later, Bina, I'll help you then."

"Just let me use it for a few minutes," the old woman pleaded.

Ash noticed Ezra's gaze had narrowed and his head was tilted to one side. She knew he was picking up on something she was missing.

He spoke softly, almost as if he were thinking out loud. "Reker's a healer. The radiation must have different effects on different species." He glanced at Ash and Trik. "For Humans, we know the effects. But the Agorans? Maybe it does the opposite."

Bina's body slumped a little further.

"Come back later, I'll help you then," said Reker, a catch in her voice. Reker waved at the panel to close the door and turned on them. "You can't have it," she repeated. "I won't give it up."

"You don't have a choice," said Trik. He was clearly becoming annoyed.

"Says who?"

Ash could feel her muscles starting to tense. Maybe it was the close space, but it seemed to magnify all the feelings in the room.

"Reker, are you on your own?" she asked.

Reker twitched as if she'd been stung by some kind of ferocious insect. "What?"

Ash held out her hands. "Here, do you live here on your own? Do you have family here?"

Reker's defensive stance became even more pronounced. "Do you think if I don't have a family, you can push me around? Steal from me?" The last few words trembled as they came from her mouth.

Ash shook her head and sat down – uninvited – on Reker's bed-cum-bench. She was suddenly aware that even though she, Trik and Ezra were likely only a few years older than Reker, the three of them towered over her small frame. Her team wasn't here to intimidate the Friend of the Library, no matter how hostile they were. Reker was just a kid.

The boys seemed to get the gist. Ezra sat down next to Ash, and Trik took a sideways step, leaning against the wall.

"I'm not going to steal from you," Ash said. She kept her voice steady and firm. "But that item doesn't actually belong to you. It belongs to other people. Very dangerous people. And if they find you have it, the consequences for you – and everyone else on this station – will likely be fatal."

The floor seemed to shift under Ash's feet for a second, throwing them all off balance, and a moment later, a distant alarm started sounding. They all shot each other looks of worry, but Ash kept talking.

"I have to take it away. I have to keep you and the people on this port safe."

34

"You'll kill us, you'll kill us all." Reker's response had an air of desperation to it.

Ezra pressed on. "Do you use the crystal?"

Reker's head whipped towards him. "What do you mean?" Her words dripped with suspicion.

"Why was the Agoran woman here? She came to you for help. What do you do with the crystal?"

Reker seemed to freeze – as if she'd been caught in some giant spotlight. For the first time since they'd met her, she actually looked quite young. Vulnerable.

"You can't take it. It's my livelihood. I'm the healer. They come to me." The words started out shaky, but grew fiercer as she continued. "Our family, we've always been healers. This is how I *live*. It's mine." She pressed a hand to her chest. "It belongs to *me*."

Ash's eyes fell on the scanner. She picked it up and turned it round so Reker could see the screen. The green circle was exactly coordinated with their current position. "I know it is here." Then she tapped the red bars that now filled the bottom of the screen. "And, you might not know it, but it's dangerous for you. It's harmful to your health."

Ezra straightened and looked at Reker. He spoke in a slow, steady way. "The Byroneus crystal leaks radiation. We think it was probably shielded before, but over time the original shielding seems to have eroded – that's likely why the Byroneans have been able to get a lock on it. It's why they are headed here. Being around the crystal is dangerous – maybe not for every species, but it is dangerous for you."

None of them said what else came to mind – they had no idea what had happened to Reker's parents, but there was a chance they could have been harmed by the radiation.

He pointed to the scanner in Ash's hand. "Our machine detects the harmful radiation, that's how we're tracking it here. But if we can find it this way – so can others." He lifted his hand and for a moment it looked as though he was going to reach out to touch Reker, but then he laid his palm on his leg.

Ash cut in. "Reker, we brought medicine with us. I have another scanner. Can I hold it next to you? Check you? I think you might need some of the medicine we have."

The port gave another lurch, sending Ash and Ezra a little further along the bench, and Trik and Reker wobbling on their feet. More alarms started to sound.

Trik held out his arms, trying to steady himself. His voice was low. "What was that? Another explosion? Do you think the Fidulans and Pantheons are fighting again?"

Reker's voice was shaking. "That's not an internal hazard. That's an attack alarm."

Ash jumped to her feet. "It's the Byroneans. We have to move. We have to get the crystal out of here now. Away from these people!"

Reker started shaking her head as she wrapped her arms round her body and stepped backwards against the wall. "You brought them here. You brought them here," she kept whispering.

"No!" The alarms were getting louder. People were

36

shouting in the corridors. Ash had to get this mission under control. There were twenty thousand lives at risk right now. The ground lurched beneath her feet again.

"They're firing," said Trik. "What are the defence capabilities of this port?"

Ezra shook his head. "I checked. Not much. But they won't destroy it yet. Not if they think the crystal might be here."

"They're breaking down the defences so they can board," said Ash. "We don't have much time." She looked around the small space again. "Reker, where is it? Where is the Byroneus crystal?"

Even in her panicked state Reker was still determined. "No. How will I live? Healing is the only way I can earn money."

Trik lowered his head next to hers. "None of us will live unless you give it up. Nor will anyone else on this space port."

Ezra grabbed the scanner and started waving it up and down the walls. Ash hated doing this. The last thing she wanted to do was take the crystal by force, especially from a Friend. But as Guardian, she had to protect the rest of the universe from the Byronean army.

Ezra's hand froze as the scanner let out a series of sharp beeps, and he pressed at the metal wall, finally hearing a click. A small panel slid back, revealing a plain-looking chunky piece of rock. It didn't look like any crystal Ash had ever seen, but Ezra scanned again, nodded, then pressed a button. This time there was a *zing* noise and a glimmer in the air around the stone.

37

"Shielded," said Ezra. "Hopefully that will stop them from heading straight here."

Reker leaped forward. "I said no!" She tried to grab the stone, her arms scrabbling in the air, but Trik gave a sigh and held her back.

"This isn't yours, Reker. And if we don't get it out of here, the Byroneans will kill you." His eyes met Ash's. "What about the medicine?"

Of course! Ash pulled a med wand from her pocket and swept the air around Reker's body. The readout made her gulp. The radiation levels in Reker's body were currently toxic. It looked like the low-level radiation from the crystal had slowly caused cellular damage. The med wand could administer some immediate medical assistance, but there was only so much it could do.

She keyed in a few settings and before there could be any protest Ash pressed the med wand to Reker's neck and pushed the button.

Reker jumped back, rubbing at her skin. "What did you do?"

"Damage limitation, hopefully." She pulled a bag of pills from her pocket. These were old-style medicines, emergency supplies. "Take these every day. They could help."

Something tugged at Ash's heart strings. She felt a connection to Reker, and wished she could do more to help. But there wasn't time. She had to prioritize all the lives on this space port over just Reker's.

If they could get the crystal away from the port then drop the shield round it for a few moments, the Byroneans would hopefully notice it was no longer on the port and leave the people here alone.

The next blast took them all off their feet. The previous blast had been from an external attack. This one was from inside the space port.

"Time to go," yelled Ezra. His hand slapped against the door panel, and he stuck his head out into the corridor. Smoke was billowing along the corridor.

"They must have boarded," said Ash. She gripped Reker's arm. "You should get out of here. There might be some residual signs of radiation they can track. Get to someplace busy and hide. Find somewhere to lie low."

Reker moved in the blink of an eye. It was like some little switch had flicked in her brain. She grabbed a few things from the floor and piled them into her arms.

"Wait," said Ezra and he pulled something from his pocket and stuffed it into hers. "Now, go!"

She didn't wait, just bolted down the corridor. There was the sound of gunfire, laser fire, sonic blasts and shouting from the other direction.

"Give me that," said Ash, grabbing the crystal from Ezra before they left. Then they all started sprinting in the same direction as Reker. Ash tucked the crystal inside her flight suit as they ran.

"If only one of us had a sense of direction," muttered Ash, as they turned corner after corner, each corridor looking the same as the rest. Reker had disappeared from their line of sight and hopefully holed up somewhere safe.

Alarms were sounding everywhere, each signifying something different. Along with the alarms came a variety of flashing lights. As they turned to a corridor lit up blue, a Fidulan running at cross purposes screamed, "No!" They halted as a loud, tearing metallic sound came from the end of the corridor. If the look of terror on the Fidulan's face hadn't scared them enough, the sounds certainly did. The group turned ninety degrees and started running again.

The place was in chaos. Every now and then, some kind of laser fire could be heard in the distance.

"Wait!" Ezra skidded to a halt.

"Oooff!" Ash ran straight into the back of him.

He pointed right, at a pale grey corridor, infiltrated with intermittent flashing orange lights. "Isn't that the way to the docking bay? Our ships?"

Trik banged into the back of Ash. He took a few breaths then narrowed his gaze. "There is something kind of familiar about it," he said.

"Let's go," said Ash. "The sooner we get away from this place, the better for everyone."

They'd only taken a few steps down the wobbly tunnel when something shot straight through the wall. Their flight suits reacted before they could: space helmets slid over their faces, and gloves zapped over their hands, leaving no skin exposed.

All three of them froze. A small part of the flimsy tunnel was flapping like paper in the wind as the place depressurized.

"A meteoroid," breathed Ash.

"Or space debris," muttered Trik. His hand was on the side of the tunnel. "I told you this place didn't look safe."

Ash glanced sideways. Pieces of the tunnel wall were being ripped away every few seconds, whirling out into the vacuum of space. Ash wondered about the other end. The end leading straight into the corridors of the space port. Had an emergency compartment door come down to save the immediate surrounding area? If not, people and objects could be sucked out into the void too.

"We'd better move. This whole thing is going to disintegrate." She felt a shove in her back. "Move, people."

The tunnel had felt unsteady before, but now, with the pressure gone, it was even more difficult to manoeuvre along. Ash pressed a button on her thigh, activating her magnetic boots to give her some leverage, then carefully skirted around the hole in the tunnel.

Ahead of her, Trik stretched out his hands to either side of the tunnel, helping propel himself along. Within a few moments he turned off into the connecting passage that led to his ship.

There were two more small holes directly ahead of Ash, revealing the path of another meteoroid or piece of space debris that had ripped clean through the tunnel. The flimsy metal seemed to ripple around her.

"Watch out!" shouted Ezra behind her as a small piece of debris scudded off Ash's visor. A crack formed instantly and it felt like her heart leaped into her mouth.

She pushed forward with her arms, finding strength she

didn't know she had. These flight suits were sturdy. But Ash had no idea how much damage had just been done. There was no oxygen in these tunnels now and the supply in her suit would be limited. A crack could cause what little oxygen she had to rush out into the atmosphere – something she couldn't afford.

"Ash, you okay?" She could hear the panic in Ezra's voice behind her. He wouldn't be able to see the crack.

She didn't even waste time speaking. All her energy was currently in her arms and legs, but it felt like wading through shifting sand, the weightlessness of space fighting against the little momentum her magnetic boots could give her.

Ash's own feeder tunnel appeared. It was undamaged but was still affected by the lack of oxygen and gravity. Her space fighter was in sight now. She kept pushing forward. Ash had to be in her craft, with the hood down, before she could release her helmet again. Already her oxygen supply felt thin. She was panicking. She was taking deeper breaths to keep her muscles working, but she was fighting against herself right now.

Ash opened the hood of her craft and her hand fumbled as she tried to grab one of the straps from her pilot seat, to pull herself into place.

"Watch out! Watch out!" Trik's voice echoed through the comm. "It's a meteoroid shower!"

As his words connected with her brain, Ash's hand grabbed part of her seat harness. There was a raining, ripping noise, something like the sound of the great waterfall she'd seen on Ezra's planet, back in her own solar system.

And for a millisecond she was weightless, floating, her feet no longer having any anchor point. Then her shoulder wrenched so sharply she could swear it was no longer in its socket.

Her fingers tightened, and instantly her brain told her they were the only thing stopping her floating off into oblivion right now.

"Ash! Ezra!" came the shout from the comm in her helmet once more. "Are you safe? Let's get out of here." Trik didn't normally sound so worried. Of them all, he was the most reckless. The first one to start a fight. The one who always had an edge of something waiting to burst out. But now he sounded panicky.

"I'm in," Ezra responded, a little breathless. "My fighter's taken some minor damage from the meteor hits, but I can still fly."

Silence. Ash could feel the tug of space. Her shoulder was on fire. Every cell in her body was screaming at her to let go. To stop the tearing pain. She retched, trying hard to keep her sickness down. Vomiting in a sealed helmet was the last thing she wanted to do.

Her body felt strange, as if a million tiny insects were crawling all over it, prickling her skin. The suit. It must be the suit. These flight suits weren't designed for open space. Not really. They included some basic features to keep pilots alive in an emergency. But for how long?

"Ash! Answer us!" Ezra's voice jerked her thoughts back. Was the lack of oxygen in her suit making her lose her concentration?

The meteoroid storm had taken out the feeder tunnel, so the docking anchor was the only thing attaching the fighter to the space port, but it seemed to be loosening, the craft waving around. Ash was floating at the side of the fighter with only one hand keeping her in place, her other arm and legs flopping around, like a sea creature she'd once seen. She had to do better.

Gritting her teeth and summoning all her courage, Ash made herself pull on her injured arm, trying to get closer to the seat of her fighter. The fighters from the Library weren't too big. Hers was only designed to hold one pilot, but when she and it were floating in space, manoeuvrability was tough.

She closed her eyes and moved her shoulder again, bending at the elbow to try and push her body closer to the fighter. Her other hand caught the edge of the cockpit. Ash held on fast. It was easier to pull from her uninjured side. She clamped her body tight against the craft, grabbing the other part of the harness and taking a breath.

Changing position to swing her legs inside was harder than she thought. She couldn't let go of the harness, not for a second, not until she was firmly anchored in her pilot seat with the cockpit closed. The ripping pain in her shoulder made every movement a challenge. All the while she could hear Ezra and Trik shouting. But her brain was getting fuzzy. She couldn't take the time to reply.

The moment her back touched the seat, Ash wrestled the harness into place, while pressing her feet against the dashboard. Finally she secured it with a click and thumped her hand against the button to close the cockpit.

Ash's whole body sagged into her seat.

She waited a few moments, checking the display ahead of her – ensuring the oxygen supply in the cockpit – before she finally allowed her helmet to slide back.

Ash heaved in a breath, her face slick with sweat and her hair plastered to her head. *Breathe. Just breathe.*

Now her helmet was back from her head, the voices were coming from the controls in front of her.

"I'm free, I'm swinging round to her fighter," came Trik's voice.

"Right behind you," said Ezra. She could hear the concern in both of their voices, but her brain and her vision were still fuzzy.

She took another deep breath, letting her lungs fill as her head started to clear. "I'm here." Her voice was a bit croaky. "I'm here, guys."

Expletives filled her cockpit. "What happened?"

Ash leaned back into her pilot seat and looked out around her. Her craft now looked as if it were dangling by a fine thread. She pressed a button that emitted a pulse to disengage the magnetic docking clamps and fired up her engine, her movements on autopilot.

Ezra and Trik's fighters were alongside hers now, close enough that she could actually see their faces. She could also see the damage to Ezra's fighter. It looked like it had been hit by a huge meteoroid, one side crushed completely.

Her skin chilled. Her friend. Her friend could have been killed because of her. Ezra and Trik were only here because of Ash and her new role.

She breathed out slowly and finally answered their questions. "The tunnel to my ship got hit by hail from the meteoroid storm. It disintegrated around me." She could hear them sucking in their breaths.

"Thank the world for these suits," said Trik in an unsteady voice. "If we'd been back at the Academy, you'd never have survived."

Ash ran her hand across the front of the flight suit. Grey and dark red. Her preferred colours. When they'd first found the star fighters under the Library, they hadn't realized there were special suits. They'd flown in their previous gear. But long hours in the Library had led to some exploring. And the flight suits had been found in the landing hangar. The technology was newer than any of them had ever seen. The suits seemed to mould to their bodies. She hadn't realized quite how important they would actually become.

"Ash, you still have the stone?" Ezra asked.

She patted her flight suit, relieved to feel it still there. "Yeah," she replied, "I've got it. The force field is intact. Should we clear out then?"

They pulled on their controls, lifting above the sprawling space port to head back to the Library. Their view changed, revealing the opposite side of the space port – where the official docking bay was now invisible beneath the hull of a giant dark ship.

A ship that hadn't been there before.

Ash automatically sucked in a breath, and through her comm heard Trik and Ezra do the same.

The ship was black, sleek and enormous. Almost oval in shape, it gleamed in a way she had never seen before.

"What on earth is that made from?" she gasped.

The whole hull was the same – sleek in a sinister kind of way, entirely unbroken and unadorned.

"Where are their weapons? Their docking bays and escape hatches?" asked Trik.

"Their communications array," murmured Ezra. "Or their staff quarters. Doesn't anyone on that ship get to look outside?"

As he finished speaking, they all hissed in surprise as one bright white light appeared across the front of the ship. The light was blinding. But as Ash screwed up her eyes she wondered if the central strip was actually the ship's bridge. She was much too far away to actually see any figures, but still felt too close for comfort. Ash gave an involuntary shudder.

"Someone want to remind me who the Byroneans are again?" said Ezra. "How much do we know about them?"

Ash blinked. It was obvious the immense ship belonged to them. It was the largest spacecraft she'd ever seen. Not only that, but with its dark gleaming hull and one bright white strip along the front, it had an ominous presence. She couldn't even begin to imagine just how many crew a ship like that could hold, or its potential firepower.

"Not much," she said quietly. "The Library didn't have that much information on them."

"I don't like the odds here," said Trik. "We know they've already boarded the space port. Maybe we should just give them their crystal back? They look like they mean business. Do you think we have a chance of outrunning a ship like that?"

"No," said Ash, "but does that ship look like a peaceful presence to you? Imagine they got the crystal back and could replicate more and more of themselves. That could be a serious problem for the rest of the universe. I think the Library's first instincts were correct. We can't let the Byroneans get hold of the crystal, and while it remains here, Quisquilla is at risk."

"They could blast the port right out of the sky," said Ezra.

"Exactly. I think the best thing we can do is get out of here. If they notice ships leaving and can't find the crystal, they might be distracted enough to search for it and leave the port alone. And we could drop the shield round the crystal for a few seconds, so they look to us instead of the port. It's our best chance of saving the people there."

Trik smiled, on the screen in front of her. "Attracting attention by making ourselves the target? Why, Ash, you surprise me."

There was a crackle from the comm and Ash hit the panel, to try and filter out some of the noise.

"We're being hailed. They're asking us to identify ourselves," warned Trik.

"Anyone object to getting out of here fast?" She had a horrible ominous feeling in her stomach as she prayed the Byroneans' technology wasn't currently scanning her ship, or their communications.

Then an even more horrible thought occurred, and her heartbeat quickened. "Ezra, you're damaged. Can your fighter still jump?"

There was the slightest delay in his answer. "Sure I can," he said.

"Then let's get out of here," cut in Trik. A few seconds later his craft vanished.

Ash turned to look at Ezra's ship. The damage wasn't minimal, and his delayed answer made her nervous. "You next," she instructed.

She had no plan to leave anyone behind. Ezra cleared his throat. Although he'd never admit it, Ash could tell he was worried.

Her hand lifted and tugged at the pink strand of her hair. The one she twisted round her finger when *she* was nervous. As soon as she got back, as soon as they *all* got back, she was changing it to pale blue – a peaceful, tranquil colour. Maybe it could be some kind of good omen, a wish for future missions to be less frantic.

"Okay," he replied. She waited. And waited.

And then finally, after a flicker, Ezra's fighter jumped. Ash heaved a sigh of relief.

Alarms started sounding in her cockpit – a sign of a potential attack, her shields automatically falling into place. Her comm crackled again. The Byroneans were demanding she identify herself. Identify herself, or be destroyed.

For a few milliseconds, Ash dropped the shields around her fighter, and the shield round the crystal. The cockpit alarms heightened in pitch. The Byroneans had clearly recognized the radiation signal already.

Her hand left her hair and tightened round the controls. She closed her eyes.

And jumped.

CHAPTER FOUR

Ash couldn't pretend she was anything other than relieved when her final jump landed her in front of the Library and she could see the other two ships already in the landing bay. She manoeuvred her own fighter into place and climbed out.

Trik and Ezra were waiting for her, and without words, they all stepped forward into a group hug.

"How many jumps did you make to shake them off?" Trik asked.

Ash rolled her eyes. "Seventeen. I doubled back a few times, hoping it would confuse them even further."

A few moments later they stood back, not meeting each other's eyes, as if the whole thing hadn't happened. That's how it was between them all. Ash worried about her team. She cared about them, just like she knew they cared for her. But none of them were overly affectionate about it.

She held up the rock with the shimmering shield intact

around it. "Can't believe this little thing could cause so much trouble."

They strolled along the corridor and up to the Library, where Amara was waiting. Her brow was already ridged, but somehow the ridges looked deeper today.

"How did things go?"

They could see a screen behind her. She was still monitoring Quisquilla. The Byronean ship was still there.

Ash stepped forward. "At least the place is still in one piece. How much could you see?"

Amara shook her green head. "Not much. I could only monitor some transmissions and tap into a few internal cameras. But the feed wasn't good." She frowned as she looked at the monitor again.

Trik held up his hand to halt the conversation. "Can we be sure the Byroneans aren't going to blast Quisquilla into the next universe?"

All three of them stared at the display as Amara continued tapping at the screen in mid-air. "I'm getting much stronger readings now. They must be coming from that ship."

"What's it doing?" All three voices asked the question simultaneously.

Amara was still frowning. "It's scanning. The port – and the space around it." She looked up and caught their worried expressions. "I can't find any evidence that they're charging weapons."

A large dark presence moved past one of the external screens. They all watched closely.

"It looks like they're leaving."

"We never even set eyes on them," said Trik. "I wonder if they look as scary as their ship."

"It doesn't exactly strike me as a bad thing that we didn't get up close and personal," said Ezra.

"Their technology looks much more advanced than what we had back in our solar system," said Trik. He tilted his head to one side. "Think they might be able to track us, or the crystal, even with the shield in place?"

Ash shivered. An involuntary movement.

"I take it that means you got it?" Amara cut straight to the chase.

Ash held up the stone. "Safe and sound." As she held it up, it was as if the Library came to life. An electronic tag appeared out of nowhere – a kind of digital file, labelling the Byronean stone, its origin, when and where it was retrieved, and its qualities. The label was red, indicating the hazards around the item, and the fact it should be stored with some kind of force field or shield.

Amara pressed the display again and a second force field buzzed over the shimmer of the first. "There," she said, with a kind of half smile. "Two force fields for the price of one. Surely no technology will be able to track this now."

No one spoke for a second, and though Amara's words were said with assurance, it didn't quite translate to her eyes. She swiped another part of the display and the object disappeared.

"For extra precautions, I've stored it in the special

shielded safe, in a hidden part of the Library. We don't need it on display."

Ash's shoulders finally started to relax a little. Trik shook his arms out, as if he were trying to release the tension in them, and Ezra cracked his knuckles, making them all flinch.

Amara looked at them warily. "So, did you locate the Friend? Did they help?"

The way Amara asked the question made Ash curious. "Why do you ask?"

Amara frowned. "I sent several messages. I never got any response. I was beginning to wonder if the Friend still existed on Quisquilla."

"Oh, she existed all right," laughed Trik. "I'm not quite sure if she was a smuggler, a thief, or some kind of fake medic. A whole big career for a kid who looked about eleven."

"It was a kid?" Amara was clearly shocked.

"Yeah, she was a kid," said Ash. "With a survival instinct like no other. She didn't exactly desire the role of Friend or agree with it, she had just inherited it from her family."

"Has there even been a Friend before who didn't want to be one?" asked Ezra.

Ash and Amara looked at each other. "I have no idea," admitted Ash.

"Me either," said Amara. "But is she okay? You said she was young."

"She was," Ash murmured. It didn't matter that the little girl had survived without their assistance for a number of years. It didn't matter that there had been no room on any of the space fighters. Ash could still picture Reker's young, angry and indignant face in her head. It made her stomach twist.

Something sprang into her mind. "Hey." She nudged Ezra. "What were you doing?"

"When?"

"With Reker. You hung back. You gave her something."

He pulled a guilty face and gave her a smile. "Yeah, about that…"

"About that, what?"

"I might have given her some…kilenium."

Trik had just turned to take a drink of something and half splurted it across the floor. "You what?" A smile appeared across his dark face.

Kilenium was one of the most valuable minerals in the universe. The Library had a stockpile that they'd found during the clear-up after the attack. It had been in a small room, previously hidden by shelves. There were no tags. It wasn't part of an Infinity File. It didn't belong to some other place. But Ash was still astounded that Ezra had taken some.

She wrinkled her brow but didn't have to say the words out loud before he spoke first.

"I thought we might need some currency. We were going to a space port that was primarily a smuggling haven. I wasn't sure exactly how we would get the Byronean crystal back and I knew we likely had a time limit. Seemed important to take something to give us bargaining power."

Ash gave a small nod. "Good thinking."

He kept talking. "And since we were taking the kid's livelihood away it only seemed reasonable to give her something in return."

"How much did you give her?" Trik asked.

The pause told Ash all she needed to know. Ezra gave a mumbled response.

This time it was Amara who let out an expletive. "How much? You'll turn her into the latest smuggling baron, with that kind of money."

He shrugged. "We don't even know if the treatment we gave her will work. If it doesn't, she'll need money for medical expenses. She's probably been exposed to low-grade radiation all her life."

He paused and looked up, meeting all their watchful eyes.

"You didn't see that place, Amara. Or where that kid lived. We don't know what she's had to do to survive. Nothing is free on a space port like Quisquilla. Maybe she can even buy passage off it and get herself someplace where she can thrive. Maybe I gave her more bargaining power than she'll ever need. But her family made a commitment to the Library, so we have a responsibility to her. We've been discussing things these last few weeks, but I think we need to make some rules about what we do in the name of the Library."

Ash was struck by his words. Ezra had obviously been giving this some thought. Everything about this felt right. And she knew exactly where to start. Several times in the past she'd worried about the impact of their missions – not just about retrieving or returning an object – but even about their presence in other environments, and their interactions. Today, with Reker, had just been another example.

She held out her fist.

"I think Ezra is right. And I think we need one overarching rule. First, do no harm."

She looked at her friends, and with a nod Trik held out his fist towards hers. Ezra did the same. Amara took a little longer to tuck her claws into her green palm before making a fist of sorts and holding it out so they all bumped together.

"First, do no harm," they all said together.

Trik leaned back. "Hope you didn't spend all the kilenium. We need to try and do less harm to ourselves too – those fighters aren't going to be easy or cheap to repair."

Ash groaned.

"What happened to the fighters?" asked Amara.

"We got caught in a meteoroid shower," said Ezra. "My ship took some heavy damage."

Amara turned and looked back at her screen that showed some small parts of the space port. She enhanced the images. "Quisquilla looks like it sustained some damage too."

"Can you really tell?" quipped Trik.

"At least it's still in one piece. We're lucky we've got the fighters and could jump away," said Ash. "We should probably try and do some repairs." She leaned on the balcony overlooking the contents of the vast Library beneath them. "Amara, can you check the computers and see if you can find any information on the fighters?"

It wasn't exactly urgent. They'd used three fighters and there were actually twelve in the hangar. But Ash had always liked to take care of what she had. Her parents had instilled that in her, back in their dusty village of Astoria, when they didn't have much at all. Ash had spent hours as a kid building things out of junk – things that other people had thrown away. And she'd always been resourceful. Once she had built something, she took it all apart and started on something entirely new. She'd like to try and fix the fighters herself and learn a little bit more about the technology surrounding her. It seemed like part of her role.

"No problem." Amara nodded.

Ash resisted the temptation to peel the shirt that she wore under her flight suit from her body. The hair at the back of her neck still felt sticky. And her shoulder was aching from earlier. It was time for a wash and a change.

She trudged through to her room, shaking her head when she caught sight of her own appearance. A wave of her transformer wand changed the strand she frequently coloured at the front of her head from pink to pale blue. Ash put her hand over the bangle and felt the familiar tingle. When she opened her eyes the room had changed from muted greys, to violets and purples. Orius had taught her to do this when she'd first arrived and her room iterations had changed with her mood. She smiled as she realized where the purple influence had come from. She was still curious about that unknown race she'd spotted back on Quisquilla.

In the room next to hers, she could hear Ezra and Trik arguing over who could freshen up first. Thankfully she didn't have that problem. She didn't share.

Ash picked up a med wand and aimed it at her shoulder. There was a buzz and she twitched as the healing process started instantaneously. There was an intense warmth, along with small shocks, as if tiny insects were stepping on her skin. She had to hold it there until the med wand switched off automatically. It had been at least ten seconds. The damage had obviously been considerable.

It made something spark in her brain. She'd been injured. The damage to Ezra's ship was considerable. It was clear that he could have been seriously injured or perhaps even killed in this latest mission. The instinct when she'd left Quisquilla had been *Leave no one behind*. Maybe that should be their second rule?

Five minutes later, she had washed the sweat and fear from her skin and her hair, and circled both shoulders as she walked back out to the main Library.

The Library had three levels. The hangar for the fighters at the bottom – which Ash hadn't originally realized was there. The top entrance level, with various rooms, central meeting point, the Proteus circle and all the surrounding Library technology, finished with a balustrade that looked down onto the middle portion of the Library – a huge cavern where all the Infinity Files were stored. It was like a giant maze, filled with numerous artefacts from all over the universe. Scrolls, diagrams, jewels, weapons, armour, books, technology, pottery and a whole host of artefacts that Ash still hadn't had time to determine the purpose of. The entire structure was covered with a large dome, meaning the stars constantly looked as if she could reach out her fingers and touch them. The first sight of the place had taken her breath away.

It still did sometimes.

A short while later the four of them sat round a table, an array of food in front of them. Amara waved her hand and an Infinity File appeared above them. It was the item they'd just retrieved.

"Look." She waved her clawed hand.

They all looked up as the information scrolled in front of them.

"It's like the Library has now filled in the blanks," Amara explained.

She was right. The first tag that had appeared for the object had basically just named the object and its origin. Now, a whole host of other information appeared.

Trik pointed. "So, it *does* have temporary healing powers. No wonder Reker didn't want us to take it. But how can something be radioactive *and* have healing powers? Doesn't this lump of rock know the rules of the universe?"

"That might have been useful information to know before we got there," said Ash thoughtfully. "We could have adjusted the conversation we had with Reker. We knew it was radioactive and needed shielding, but that was all."

Amara sighed. She understood the systems in the Library better than the rest of them, but they still frustrated her. "I can only tell you what's there. It's like the system is not quite where it should be. It seems as if, when an object comes into its possession, a whole new file of information appears from nowhere." She turned to Ash. "You did say that Orius had seemed almost forgetful sometimes."

Ash nodded as she pushed some food around her bowl. "Yeah." She looked up and around at the Library. "Orius was part of the system. So I guess if he was breaking down and forgetting things, it means that the system's not infallible. But it's not just that… I sometimes feel as if this whole place is much more alive than we think it is."

Silence. It kind of startled her and she looked back at her friends. They were all staring at her. Hard.

Trik had a spoonful of food heading towards his open mouth that seemed to have frozen in mid-air. "Say what?"

Ezra's head was tilted to the side. "What exactly do you mean?"

Amara's dark eyes were totally fixed on hers.

Ash wasn't quite sure where to start. Maybe she shouldn't have said anything at all.

She set down her cutlery. "I can't really explain it. It's just a feeling. I think I had it even when Orius was around. Sometimes I wondered if it really was his programming that was failing at the end, or whether the Library had decided to keep things from him – and from me."

Amara shifted in her seat and looked around uncomfortably.

"But the Library has highly advanced technology – some that we still don't understand – do you really think there's more to it than that?" She looked at Ash cautiously.

Trik pulled back, giving Amara a questioning stare. He lifted his hand. "So what? You're telling me this isn't actually a place – it's more like some kind of sentient being?"

Now he said the words out loud it did sound entirely impossible. Ash knew it did. She shouldn't have said anything.

But Ezra's lips were pressed tightly together. She could tell he was thinking. "Sometimes weird things happen here," he said quietly.

"What?" Amara's head whipped round to face him.

Trik gave a nervous laugh. He pointed a finger. "Don't you start, too."

Ezra looked uneasy, but his gaze met Ash's.

"I can't put my finger on it. But I understand what you mean about a feeling… I looked at a scroll the other day. When I eased it apart, a tiny fragment fell off."

He had the good grace to look embarrassed. None of them were supposed to touch any of the artefacts without wearing gossamer gloves. There were items in here that were thousands of years old. Some of them were behind force fields, to keep the air and dust away. Some were stored in sealed cabinets.

Ezra continued. "I went back a few days later, wondering if there was any way to repair it – but when I looked at it again, the tiny piece was back in place."

Amara took a deep breath. "I've never seen anything repair itself before."

Trik stood up and started pacing. "But there's a thousand scrolls in here. You must have got it wrong – looked at a different one by mistake." He was clearly uncomfortable with the way this conversation was going.

Ezra shook his head. "The scroll is unmistakeable. It's the only one from Kora 12. It details the uprising and the attacks."

Amara stood up too. She put her hands on her hips. "But if the Library can mysteriously repair things, then why are there artefacts that have been here for thousands of years, but remain in pieces? The clay pots from Dorian. The bowls from Alyssius 5. It doesn't make sense."

Ezra laughed and leaned back. "Oh, I didn't say it made sense. I just," he paused for a second and met Ash's gaze again, "understand what Ash is saying about…something. A feeling. Even though it sounds unlikely."

They all stared at each other. It was an uncomfortable silence. Was this really an idea they wanted to follow through? There was lots about the Library Ash still didn't understand.

It could be that because Orius, her Keeper, had been reaching the end of his life span when she'd arrived, his training procedures had become more erratic. There might have been things he should have passed on, but just not got around to. He'd always seemed a little mysterious. It had frustrated Ash at times, as she'd thought he was deliberately keeping things from her. But maybe that hadn't been the case at all.

Ash sighed and leaned back from the table, looking at the leftover food.

She held out her hands to them all. "I need your help." She pressed a hand on her chest. "I need to feel, deep down inside, that what we're doing is right. I'm still not sure about what just happened. And if I can't be sure I can trust the Library, we're going to need to make those decisions between us. Did we really protect the people on the space port by taking the artefact away? We know what would happen if the Byroneans got their hands on it – the whole universe could be at their mercy. But what if the Byroneans decide to go back to Quisquilla?"

Her words hung in the air. None of them really knew the answer – this time. But it was important that as a team they all considered the consequences of their actions. After a few moments, the group all slowly nodded their heads. She knew they were all contemplating her new rule: *First, do no harm.*

Ash waited, then held out her fist. Within a few seconds her friends had bumped theirs against hers.

CHAPTER FIVE

Amara folded her arms.

"I'm not exactly sure what you think we can find. It's a volcano. It's going to erupt. The whole population will be wiped out. The Library wants you to retrieve an artefact so all knowledge of the civilization isn't lost for ever. There are no sides, no enemy. Just a horrible, natural, unstoppable event."

Trik had been the most anxious about this mission since it had arrived. It was like he could see a ticking clock above his head. But Ash couldn't explain why she was being so pedantic about researching this entirely, so stubborn. She just wanted to feel *sure*. And she didn't feel that way yet.

She wanted to make sure she was doing no harm. This mission felt different from the others and she wanted to be extra thorough.

Amara was getting impatient too. She shook her head and glanced at a screen. "The Library sensors have predicted the eruption will happen in the next few days. If you go now, you'll have at least one whole day to track down the artefact, maybe even two. You're running out of time." She sighed. "Erasmus is running out of time."

Ash pressed her lips together to stop herself from arguing. She glanced at the display that had stayed steadily in the air since it had first appeared. It outlined basic information about Erasmus and that the planet's giant supervolcano would erupt imminently for one final time. This would set off a series of eruptions throughout the entire planet. The whole population would either be killed by the lava flow, or more likely by the poisonous gases.

The Library wanted an artefact from the planet rescued – the Book of Harmony. Apparently the people on Erasmus lived in some kind of utopian society – the specifics of which were recorded in the so-called Book of Harmony. Saving this item wouldn't save the people on the planet, but it was destined to be used on another planet – one where sparring factions were ready to go to war.

It was the first time Ash had seen an instruction like this. It seemed that the Guardian would be expected at some point to take the Book of the Harmony to another solar system, and save them by revealing how they could live in peace instead of war. The whole idea made Ash feel unusually nervous.

The Library didn't know the book's exact location – it seemed to be a closely-guarded secret – but they did know it was situated in the city, Pelosci, that lay – of course – just at the foot of the volcano. The first place that would be destroyed when the eruption started. Ash would have to explore the city and befriend someone in order to find out where the book was kept, then find a way to get her hands on it before it was destroyed. But was the book really the only thing she should save from Erasmus? Was it fair that one book would end up being the only remnant of a whole planet's population?

Ash had never done this before. She'd never gone to a place, knowing that it and its inhabitants would shortly be wiped out and she was only there to retrieve something to remember them by. It made her distinctly uncomfortable.

She walked over to the balustrade and looked down into the Library. So many relics, mostly retrieved by previous Guardians. Thousands upon thousands of items. She would never get a chance to see them all, in her lifetime. Artefacts. Jewels. Scrolls and carvings. Single items representing entire worlds that were now gone. The thought was too huge – it was like something was erupting deep inside her. There was room for so much more in here.

But was there room for people? Could she even retrieve people from another world? Her throat was scratchy, and she jerked her head from left to right, as if the Library might be listening to her very thoughts.

With a new determined edge, Ash turned round and strode over to the Proteus circle. It had already been decided that she was jumping alone on this occasion. Get in, get out, was the instruction Amara had given her. One person going alone would be simpler and less dangerous than all three.

But she knew they were frustrated with her. Ash's stalling over the last few days had made the boys tense and anxious – if she didn't go now, they'd probably insist on going with her. So she tilted her head back and stepped on to the circle, gripping her bangle with her other hand.

"Wait!" Amara stepped forward. She pointed to the bangle. "I'll try and give you a countdown via the bangle. Let you know how close the eruption is."

Ash frowned and stared down at the bangle. "How can you do that?"

Amara gave a tight shrug. "I'm not entirely sure it will work. But as you run out of time, the vibrations of the bangle should get closer together."

Ash pasted a smile on her face. "Thanks, Amara." She glanced at the guys and gave them a half-hearted smile. "See you all soon," she said as she twisted the bangle on her wrist. Then everything turned white.

Every jump was different. Sometimes the Library seemed to dematerialize around her, at other times it felt as if she were actually whooshing somewhere. This time, there were a few seconds of whiteness.

There were a few sensations that were always the same: the feeling of being punched in the guts and having the air stolen from her lungs. The tingling in her skin. The surge of nausea. But all these side effects had gradually seemed to reduce the more times she jumped. It was getting easier.

Ash blinked, finding herself in a crouched position. Beneath her feet was red clay earth and she was wearing some strange kind of sandals. She stood up and took a few deep breaths. The air was warm and oddly dry.

She wore a long flowing toga in a pale green colour, gathered with a clasp of some sort on her shoulder. As she felt around, she realized the toga had a multitude of pockets. In a few were silver coins. The Library had thought of everything.

There was no Friend on Erasmus. Sometimes the Library had not managed to permeate a society in order to establish the role of the Friend.

In a way, Ash was glad there was no Friend here. How could she explain to someone that their entire planet was going to be destroyed? That seemed too painful for words.

Ash put her hands up and felt her face and hair. She pulled the longer than normal strands forward and smiled. It was long and curly. That was a first. Her hair was tied back with a piece of cloth. She squinted at it. It seemed to be the same colour as her toga. Either she was just a colour-coordinated lady, or colour might be important around here.

Ash glanced about at her surroundings. There were barrels in the corner, and shelves filled with sacks along the walls. Ash had never quite worked out how the Library decided where she should land when she stood on the Proteus circle, twisted her bangle and arrived on another planet. It always seemed quite random.

Right now, it looked like she'd landed in a food store. She

listened for a few moments, waiting to hear if she could make out sounds of other people. But there was nothing, so she stepped through the wide door.

It took her into a brighter room that seemed to be some kind of kitchen. She blinked at the fire in the corner and pulled her toga away from her skin at the sudden surge of heat. Ash kept as silent as she could, moving first down a long hallway, past a number of other rooms, and then out of a doorway and into a street.

She wanted to get her bearings, to try and see if she could work out where the Book of Harmony might be and find a way to acquire it quickly – she knew that time was of the essence here. But something else was eating away at her.

Whoever Ash met on her search, she was going to have to win their trust while knowing that they were about to die. Everything and everyone here was about to be destroyed and they had no idea. Part of her wanted to grab much more than one artefact. And the same thought she'd had in the Library kept playing in her mind: should or could she actually try to save some people?

She took a deep breath to try to steady herself and immediately started to cough. The air was heavy. Smoggy. Several other people in the street were walking with scarfs wrapped round their faces. Ash felt a wave of panic – why did no one seem concerned about the amount of smog in the air? Did no one link it with the volcano?

She pulled her toga up a little further, allowing her nose and mouth to be partially covered by the folds, and let herself calm down. She had a job to do. Amara would hopefully be able to warn Ash if the eruption was imminent. It took a few moments of watching to ascertain which direction she should try first. But several other people were exiting the dwellings around her and all heading in the same direction, so she followed them.

Ash turned back to glance at the house she'd left. It was almost identical to the others in the row. The walls were slightly uneven, made of a mixture of wood, stones and clay. It was relatively well built, with spaces for windows and the doors pinned open. Security obviously wasn't a huge issue around here. As she moved slowly along the street, she was struck by how much everything looked similar. No one dwelling overshadowed the rest. All seemed in good order, and of a reasonable size. The people in the streets were all dressed in togas like hers. But as she rounded the corner into what must be the main square, she was struck by the myriad of colours of the togas everywhere.

She stood back for a few moments, as people in white, black, gold, red, purple, blue, green and brown milled around the marketplace. Laughter rang out around her. The market stalls were well-stocked. Bright fruits tumbled from crates, meat and fish were kept under cloths and the smell of something baking drifted in the air.

People were everywhere and the mood was jubilant. It was almost as if a party was about to start. Maybe it was the constantly moving rainbow-coloured togas that created that atmosphere. But as Ash watched, something struck her as

71

strange. There were no people hurrying past with their heads down. There were no soured faces. No arguments.

She leaned against a wall and kept watching as she considered her next move. Even though mouths were covered with scarfs and the volcano overlooking the city was smoking ominously, people here didn't look desperately worried. Her stomach twisted. This wasn't a city that knew it was about to be wiped out. These people didn't fear for their lives. For them, there was no thought of imminent danger. This was ordinary life. They were clearly used to slight volcanic activity.

The cobbles beneath Ash's feet looked as if they'd been there for centuries. The rows of shops and houses were neat and well-cared-for. The vibe from this place was happy and peaceful. If only they knew what she did. She knew she should rush, but was it wrong she hoped she might get to learn a little about this place and these people before they were wiped from history?

Children played in the streets, all of them dressed in pale pink. Men and women in a variety of shades of red seemed to watch over them. The traders in the marketplace all seemed to wear blue. A puff of dark smoke was coming from another building. The people going in and out of it were all dressed in black and some had smudged faces. The windows in this building were long and lots of people seemed to go up and watch the work inside. Ash edged closer.

A small woman sat on a high chair, delicately forming the orange and black ceramic work of a plate. It was like a processing line. No one rushed her, or hurried her at her task. But as soon as one was finished, it was whisked away from her and headed towards the furnace at the back of the workshop.

What was most fascinating was the smile on her face. This woman seemed to love her work, as did all the other people around her.

Ash spun back round and looked over at the centre again. That's what was so different here. The happiness. It seemed almost magical to her. What were the instructions in the Book of Harmony? What secrets did it contain that every single person here seemed genuinely happy?

She watched as people in gold and purple togas laughed and joked with each other. A man in brown who was sweeping the area stopped to join in, the others welcoming him gladly. A girl with golden hair, light skin and a similar coloured toga to her own gave Ash a smile and a wave and ducked into a nearby building.

What was with the coloured togas? Everyone apparently had a job assigned, but there seemed to be no obvious hierarchy. No clear rulers. She glanced down at her toga again, and then over to the doorway that the girl with golden hair had ducked through. What was Ash's role in society here?

She knew she should try and locate the Book of Harmony, but she didn't really know where to start. So surely the best thing she could do was try and make friends with some people. Talk to them and see if they might answer some casual questions that could point her in the right direction.

And this was her chance to find out a bit more about this world too – so she had more to remember this place by than just a book. She could feed back all the information to the Library for its archive. Shouldn't she take the opportunity?

It was as if Amara had read her errant thoughts. The bangle on her wrist sent a tiny jolt through her system. Ash jumped, automatically rubbing her arm.

"Buzz?" she muttered to herself. "More like a shock."

She hadn't quite believed it would work. She might have preferred it if it hadn't. She looked around again, waiting a few moments to see if there would be another. But nothing happened.

More people had wrapped scarfs round their faces. The air was smoggy, choking. Tiny particles of ash were visible floating in the sky around her. No time for any more hesitation. Ash made her way towards the doorway the girl had ducked into.

Her footsteps faltered. This room was bright. The walls were an off-white colour, with benches round the edges of the large entranceway. It was like walking into a rainbow. A variety of people in different coloured togas sat around the room, chatting amiably.

A few coughed. One man looked distinctly pale. A woman was leaning her head against a friend's shoulder.

The golden-haired girl walked in and beckoned someone through to another room with a welcoming smile. She slung her arm round an elderly man and aided him with his shuffling steps.

"Thank you, Lucia," he said. The girl glanced at Ash's toga and waved to her.

"You must be the new aide. I thought I spotted you outside." Lucia wrinkled her nose for a second. "We weren't expecting you for a few days. Did the *Belluna* dock early?"

Ash couldn't think of a single thing to say, so she nodded. It was the best she could do right now. But the thought of a girl like her travelling here made her stomach squeeze. If the boat did dock in a few days' time it would be bringing people to their doom.

Instead she focused on her mission. She had at least one whole day, maybe two, before the eruption. That should be enough time to find the Book of Harmony, and the only way she could do that was by making friends who could give her information.

"I'm Lucia," said the girl, smiling and putting a hand to her chest. "What's your name?"

"Ash." It came out automatically. She hoped to the stars above that Lucia had no idea of the name of the person who was supposed to arrive. This place seemed technology free, so maybe she'd be in luck.

Lucia just beamed. "Pleased to meet you, Ash. Can you help me?"

Ash hesitated for a second, then moved quickly and slid her arm round the elderly man's waist, taking some of his weight. He was thin and frail, and obviously sick. As Lucia led them down a corridor, it only took a glance in a few of the rooms to realize she was in the equivalent of a medical

75

centre. She stared down at her robe again. This colour must signal medics.

Ash pasted a smile on her face, trying to hide the swirl of panic taking over her. Technology in her world meant that care was often the swipe of a body with a med wand, the screen telling the user exactly what was wrong and how to fix it.

The people on this planet were a long way from that. She guessed their technology was around two thousand years behind that of the planets in Ash's solar system. Ash was ill-equipped to deliver any kind of care here.

She took a breath for a moment as she had the horrible thought that it didn't really matter – in a few days, or even a few hours, these people would all be wiped out.

And the Library only wanted her to save an artefact.

The injustice burned inside her as she looked at these people. They were just going about their daily business, when they should be running for their lives, getting as far away from this place as possible. If there were ships, could some sail away to safety? Should she warn them? It was illogical. She knew that. She knew the fate of this planet, but her nature couldn't help but hope for the people around her.

She blinked back tears as she heard Lucia, with her broad smile and blonde curls loosely tied back, speak gentle, comforting words to the sick man. The Library seemed to have accepted the fate of this planet, the loss of all these lives – but could Ash?

Of course, she couldn't stop a volcano erupting. But could she save some people? Could she save Lucia? And what would happen to her if she did? Was she breaking some unbreakable rule of the Library? Would there be terrible consequences?

Her bangle had only alerted her once. In the meantime, there was only a little ash in the air. Maybe there were more than two days left – Amara hadn't been totally sure, after all. Could she do more with that time than just find the book?

Her thoughts came back to the man she was supposed to be assisting. She could feel the rattle of the elderly man's chest.

"He can go in the healing room, can you help me with the door?" said Lucia.

They sat the man on a stool and Ash helped Lucia open a thick wooden door. As they pulled the door open a gush of hot air and steam rushed out to meet them. A loud blast came from inside the room followed by a spatter of hot drops of water.

Ash stood, bewildered, brushing the water from her face. It took her a moment to realize that the steam was coming from a hole in the floor. Lucia called to her to help the elderly man into the room, sitting him on a bench that lined the wall and covering him completely in a lightweight sheet.

"Try and breathe deeply," Lucia said in a reassuring tone to the man. "The steam will loosen your chest. I'll come back for you once your healing is complete."

The elderly man nodded in agreement, and Lucia gestured

for Ash to follow her back and push the heavy door into place.

"We're leaving him in there?"

Lucia looked surprised at the question. "Of course. How else will his chest heal?"

"But the water. It's boiling."

Lucia laughed and shook her head. "Of course it is."

A geyser. They were using a geyser as some kind of weird steam room. The sheet must be to stop the elderly man from getting burned. It was the strangest idea Ash had ever heard of, but it was also weirdly brilliant.

She wanted to ask a million questions. But, as a trainee medic, it was likely that would appear strange. This was stuff she should already know.

They walked back along the corridor together and she asked the most obvious. "Aren't you worried by the ash in the air?"

"Some honours are talking of moving further over to the coast, just until the mountain quietens," said Lucia as they approached the front waiting area.

Honours? That must be the word they used for the people in charge.

"The mountain will never quieten. It's no threat. We have nothing to worry about," said an old man who'd overheard them, with a wave of his hand. His skin was so wrinkled it had managed to catch small particles of ash in the creases in his face. He coughed into his hand and Ash managed not to cringe.

"But it's got worse. If it keeps up, we won't be able to have the naming ceremony tomorrow," said Lucia.

There were a few shocked gasps. "But we've never had to postpone the naming ceremony. That would be unheard of."

A younger woman leaned forward. "My child has been looking forward to the naming ceremony for months. He'll be devastated if he has to wait another season to find out his role." Her hands were pulled towards her chest as if she actually felt wounded by the very thought.

Another woman coughed next to her. "We'll all just have to cover our faces. I'm sure the naming ceremony will go ahead." She patted her colleague's arm. "We can't leave our young folk waiting."

Ash's curiosity was piqued. A naming ceremony. It sounded like a big deal. It hadn't been mentioned at the Library, which probably meant the information wasn't known. Would the Book of Harmony be used at the naming ceremony? If she didn't manage to locate it before then, she would be sure to attend to see if she could spot, or maybe even steal the book.

There was a boom outside. Everyone in the waiting space jumped, but no one seemed worried. Ash stuck her head out of the doorway. What had made that noise?

It took only a few seconds to realize where it had come from. A black cloud hung directly over the top of the volcano, which was spewing ash and rock high into the sky.

The air quality was already poor; once the rest of this ash rained down, it would be much worse.

There was hardly time to think after that. The ash started to descend over the city and more and more people – or honours – came in for treatment. Ash was kept busy – following any instructions she was given and trying not to look like the imposter she was.

All thoughts of the book had vanished from her head, swallowed by the overwhelming instinct to help ease the suffering of people who would soon be dead.

When the waiting space was finally empty and she finished clearing up the room she'd been working in, Lucia appeared at the door. "Come. It's time to eat."

Ash hesitated. She hadn't managed to find out anything about the book yet. She was already running out of time. But, if she went along, there was always the chance she could ask some questions about the location of the book in a way that wouldn't sound suspicious. It might be her best option.

She was surprised to see all the other medics in their pale green and turquoise togas waiting for them as they went outside. Lucia handed her a scarf of the same colour to wind round her face against the drifting ash, and they made their way through the streets as a group.

She noticed other people all in the same coloured togas heading off together to various buildings. Was this how things worked here? Those who worked together lived together?

They filed into the building Ash had found herself in after the jump, where a large table was now set with food and wine, the benches pulled out, inviting them all to sit.

Lucia patted the empty space on the bench next to her

and Ash slid into place, taking cooked meat, and green and orange items that she assumed were vegetables, from the wide platters that were passed round the table.

"Did you arrive on the *Belluna*?" asked the man sitting next to her.

"Of course she did," Lucia answered before Ash could, then turned to her. "We weren't really expecting you so soon. Usually the journey from the port takes a little longer. I thought you wouldn't arrive for another few days." Her smile and trusting demeanour made Ash feel even guiltier about the horrific knowledge she was keeping hidden from them. But Lucia kept talking. "No matter. Russo's old room is ready and made up for you. I'll show you after dinner. You'll be very comfortable there."

"We hoped for two new trainees," said the middle-aged man to her right. "I'm Elias, the elder here."

Ash nodded in greeting, trying to pretend she understood what that meant.

Lucia leaned forward and whispered in Ash's ear. "Elias? He's my father. But we don't mention it much. He doesn't want to show any favouritism towards me." She nudged Ash. "I was secretly relieved to be named a medic, but don't tell him that."

A man further down the table joined in, "But just wait until tomorrow. After the naming ceremony we may find we have another young medic among us."

The rest of the group nodded and smiled. Ash stared down. The scarf that had been tied round her face was on her lap, thick with ash. Her toga was the same, and she didn't even want to consider what her new curls must look like.

Didn't these people realize the peril they were in? It made her stomach ache.

"I noticed you seemed a little overwhelmed today. I expect your city wasn't quite as busy as ours." There was a sympathetic edge to Lucia's words. She waved a piece of fruit she had in her hand. "Don't worry. You'll catch on." She tucked a curl behind her ear. The bright blonde colour had dulled with the ash intermingled through her strands.

There wouldn't be time for Ash to catch on. And she was trained to be a fighter pilot, not a medic. She wondered if people here were just naturals at particular tasks, and what profession she would have ended up with if she'd been brought up here. It was all so very different to the planet she'd been born on. She shook herself. She had a mission to complete. She was letting herself get pulled into a world she wasn't supposed to be part of.

As conversation continued around the table, Ash tried to ask about the Book of Harmony, but attempting to steer the chat in a way she wanted was tough and her questions were lost.

There was a tremble beneath her feet and Ash sucked in a breath. Several of the others placed their hands on the table as if to steady themselves. She heard one nervous laugh as she watched the little orange and black bowl she'd noticed moments before shiver on the shelf.

After a few seconds, the tremor died away, and everyone started talking again.

She looked at Lucia. "Does that happen often?"

Lucia looked thoughtful for a second. "Yes, most of the time, for as long as I can remember." A frown temporarily creased her forehead. "Maybe a bit more in the last few days," she added. She smiled at Ash. "It's nothing to worry about."

Ash swallowed. These people had no idea that tremors, small earthquakes, or whatever they were, could be a warning sign of something more destructive. She was a bystander. An observer. And soon to be a thief. She was sitting at this table, planning to steal something from this bright, articulate, vibrant community that would soon vanish without a trace. And this was just one settlement. The whole planet of Erasmus would be wiped out in the sequence of events that would follow. Men and women, kids, and teenagers the same age as herself, would never get to live the lives that they should.

Ash knew that back at the Library, Amara, Trik and Ezra would be looking at the time and worrying about her. They had no way of following her. She was the only one with a bangle and the ability to transport via the Proteus circle. If she got in trouble, they couldn't help. All she could focus on was the fact her bangle hadn't buzzed again. She still had time here. Time to complete her mission – and maybe more.

Once the meal was over, Lucia nudged her. "We're going to walk into the hills. Do you want to join us, or are you too tired from your journey?"

Ash stood instantly; she still wanted to learn more about these people and maybe it would be easier to get answers to her questions from Lucia as they walked.

She strolled with the group through the back streets and out into a green space dotted with trees. Lucia was by her side.

"I meant to ask," Ash tried to say casually. "The Book of Harmony, I've always wanted to see it – where is it kept?"

Lucia gave a surprised look and let out a nervous laugh. "Oh, everyone who visits here wants to see the Book. But we keep its whereabouts a secret. We can't have something so important put at risk. What if someone tried to steal it?"

Ash sucked in a breath. She needed to know where that book was. Her mission depended on it. She'd never failed a mission yet, and wasn't about to start now.

The small city of Pelosci was nestled at the base of a mountain range, with the volcano rising on one side and low green hills circling the other. And as they had cleared the streets and left the city behind, the trees, fields of crops and green grass seemed to stretch for miles. Now, as they stood near the peak of the hills, Ash could truly appreciate her surroundings.

In the far, far distance she could see a smudge of blue. Was that the sea?

The air here seemed clearer. The rumbling volcano was at the other side of the city, but there was still a slightly toxic scent.

The group settled on a patch of grass part way up one of

the hills, looking back over the city. Ash pulled up her knees and tugged down her toga, kicking off her sandals and wiggling her toes in the grass. She was seventeen, and this was the first time she'd ever done this. With her childhood spent in a dusty village with virtually no greenery anywhere, and the rest of her time mainly in space, Ash was finally experiencing something that some people in the universe got to do every day.

The grass was slightly damp, even though the air around them was warm, and it kind of tickled. There was something so soothing, so relaxing about doing this. Her visits to other worlds had given her a wish list that she kept only in her head. While she could spend every night staring up directly into a galaxy of stars, she had never fallen asleep listening to an ocean, or swum in a blue lagoon.

The countryside here was beautiful. The view, even with a slightly smoking volcano in the background, seemed tranquil. She wanted to capture this moment and seal it into a bottle and keep it for ever.

If only she had the technology to do it.

If only she had the power to keep this world safe.

CHAPTER SIX

Ash woke with a start, surprised that she'd actually slept at all. Her first thought was the volcano. She leaped to her feet and stuck her head through the open space that served as a window. Their dwelling didn't face the volcano, but she inhaled deeply, trying to figure out if any more plumes of ash had been ejected into the sky.

Apparently not. Ash rubbed her bangle as it gave a buzz. It had done that a few times during the night and she was growing used to the little shock-like sensations. They weren't coming in quick succession yet, so she was taking it as a sign there was no need to immediately panic. She pulled a fresh toga from the impeccably neat pile on a shelf and washed her face and hands using the basin of water in her room. Sliding her feet into her sandals and going back to the main room seemed like a normal thing to do. Normal. Here on Erasmus. Where things were about to be anything but normal.

The excited chatter in the main room was all about one thing – the naming ceremony. All were wondering if anyone would be allocated as a medic.

Ash ran her hands through her hair – or she tried to, the curls catching in her fingers. Her plan was to go to the ceremony in the hope that the book might be there. Even if it wasn't, there was a good chance it might be mentioned, which might give her some idea of where it was hidden. With the rest of the people focused on the ceremony, there might even be a chance to sneak away to where it was stored.

She kept the smile on her face as the rest of the medics appeared and grabbed breakfast. Within a short space of time, they were all making their way back along the streets towards the marketplace. It was even busier than yesterday. Most people weren't wearing scarfs across their faces, as the air was a little clearer. And it seemed like no one in the city wanted to miss the naming ceremony.

There was a deep rumble and instantly the ground moved beneath her feet. Ash threw out her hands to steady herself. Ahead of her, someone tumbled to the ground, and she was sure a pillar holding up the roof on a two-storey building near her swayed slightly. It ended as quickly as it had begun. Others rushed to pick up the woman who'd fallen, helping her brush off her dusty yellow toga. There was some good-natured laughing. People bent to pick up things that had fallen from their hands. Just like the night before, no one seemed overly concerned.

But Ash's stomach flipped as her bangle buzzed again. It had been happening every few hours, but this time it seemed the span between buzzes might have shortened. She needed to find the book.

Ash watched as people naturally stayed in their groups. As they approached the square, she was struck by the volume of colours clustered around. Where the market stalls had been yesterday, now there was a long stage. Along it was a veritable rainbow of people, with every group represented.

Lucia beamed. "There's Elias. Our elder."

Sure enough, the man that had sat beside her at the table last night was there. Except he wasn't exactly old. He looked in his mid-thirties. The only difference between the people on the stage and those in the crowd was the slightly different clasp on the shoulder of their togas. Ash hadn't noticed last night. Where most people had a gold-coloured clasp, the people on stage wore a darker, more intricate looking amulet on their shoulders. There was also a range of ages up on the stage and Ash was struck by the fact that only a few elders were actually old. Her gaze swept round the square. Sure enough, older faces were scattered among the crowd, but there weren't many.

Interesting. She hadn't noticed it before. Erasmus had given the impression of a utopian world, but maybe life wasn't so perfect here if not many people lived to an old age.

One of the elders, a woman dressed in white, clapped her hands and addressed the crowds.

The woman had a deep and powerful voice that carried

across the crowd. "We thank you all for attending our naming ceremony today. It's such an important part of our culture, a fundamental lesson included in the Book of Harmony in order to help us live productive, useful lives," she gave a broad smile, "in perfect harmony!" The crowd let out a round of applause.

At the mention of the book, Ash gave a start and looked around. It brought her back to her mission. Although she was still questioning it. Should she really just do what the Library wanted? After all, the Library had been wrong before. It had thought a previous Guardian, Aldus Dexter, was dead, when he was very much alive and wreaking havoc in another part of the universe. Maybe she should stop the ceremony, tell everyone what was about to happen, and ask them all to join hands, one holding onto her as she twisted the bangle.

But the thought made her stomach twist even more uncomfortably. The bangle wouldn't have enough power. She had jumped back to the Library with her team before, but never more than three people at once. There were hundreds here, maybe even a thousand. She knew just by looking it would never work – and how could she pick just three people to save? What gave her that right to choose?

She tugged at Lucia's sleeve. "The book? Is it around here?"

Lucia scowled. The woman on the stage was still talking. "Why are you so curious?" she said, rolling her eyes as if she were almost bored by the whole subject.

Ash shrugged. She was conscious that every visitor to Pelosci must ask the same questions. She decided to play on it. "Isn't everyone? I'm going to be living here now. Why can't you tell me?"

Lucia looked thoughtful. "It's not that I can't tell you, it's just…" She looked up at the smoking volcano. "When people first come here, they are always curious to see it – and it's not exactly in the most accessible place."

Now Ash was beyond curious. "What do you mean? Where do you keep it?"

Lucia bit her bottom lip and stared at the volcano again. The way she looked at it made Ash's skin tingle. "Later," Lucia whispered to Ash.

The woman on the stage continued. "Nothing makes us prouder than assigning our children to their roles. As you know, we all spend years watching our youngsters closely, in order to match each one to the happiest place for them."

She waved her hand to the right and Ash could see a nervous bunch of teenagers in pale pink, all standing in a line. There was around sixty of them. This could take a while. But Lucia had made it clear she wouldn't say any more about the book right now. She had to try to be patient.

But it seemed the people of Pelosci had the naming ceremony down to a fine art. Each elder in turn held up a new coloured toga and named a child.

A man in dark red was first, his words simple, "Engoro Amassi." The crowd cheered and applauded and a dark-haired teenage boy with light brown skin hurried onto the stage and allowed his new dark-red toga to be placed over his pale pink one before being handed some kind of certificate.

He then left the stage, beaming with pride, and moved towards the group of people dressed in his new colour.

Lucia whispered in Ash's ear. "I always thought he would be a wine maker."

So that's what red meant. Ash continued to stand impatiently next to Lucia as each teenager was called up in turn. "Builder, baker, spinner, artist, ceramic maker, market trader, farmer, fruit picker, street cleaner, barrel maker, dyer, metal worker," Lucia murmured quietly, then held her breath as Elias stepped forward holding up a pale-green toga. Ash noticed Lucia scan the teenagers who were still standing, waiting to be called.

"Maura Rala," Elias announced with a wide grin on his face, and the fellow medics round Ash erupted in pleasure. A beautiful dark-skinned girl with waist length hair stepped nervously up onto the stage, clasping her hands together as Elias put the toga over her head and gave her a certificate. As the applause finished, she practically ran off the other side of the stage then pushed her way through the crowd to join Ash's group of medics. The excitement among the group was palpable. They all rushed to envelop her in welcoming hugs, but what struck Ash most was the mixture of relief and pleasure on the young girl's face.

She watched as the girl ran up to Lucia and hugged her too, waited while Lucia helped rearrange her toga slightly, then thrust her certificate towards the older medic. "Will you look after it for me while I celebrate?" Maura asked, her eyes bright.

"Of course." Lucia grinned, tucking the precious paper into the folds of her toga as Maura ran off.

"Do you remember that feeling?" said Lucia in Ash's ear. "The pure joy of knowing you've been assigned to the job you're meant for?"

Ash shot Lucia a sideways glance. "Do you think we always get it right?"

From a young age, Ash had known she'd wanted to be a pilot and had made it her mission to learn everything she could to give her the best possible chance of qualifying via the Star Corporation Academy.

She could remember the devastation she'd felt when, after acing every other exam, her final test had been a disaster. The horrible ache in her gut as Trik, Ezra, Arona and Castille had all been called out and awarded pilot slots. Now, she fixed her eyes on the last few teenagers waiting to be allocated their role. For all she knew, one of those kids could be feeling the way that she had. Nervous. Sick.

By the time she tore her eyes away, Ash felt a sense of unease. Lucia was looking at her curiously. "Why would the elders get it wrong?" She put her hand on her chest. "I might have pretended I wasn't interested in being a medic – purely because my father was the elder. But in the end, the rest of the elders knew exactly what suited me. They know what suits us all."

Ash pressed her lips together and did her best nonchalant shrug. It was clear she was making Lucia suspicious.

As the naming ceremony came to a close, wine was passed

through the crowds and singing began to ring from the opposite side of the square.

Ash turned back to Lucia. She'd already decided if she didn't get a straight answer this time, she'd have to ask someone else. Her bangle gave two sharp buzzes. That was new. Time was running out.

"Lucia, I've come all this way. Are you going to show me where the Book of Harmony is?"

She tried to keep the tension out of her voice, even though she was conscious of the tingling up her arm. The shocks had seemed stronger this time. The volcano looked suspiciously inactive. Was this the calm before the storm?

Lucia bit her lip. "You know the rules. Once you've stayed here for ten full moons you'll be considered a citizen of Pelosci. You'll see it then." She looked at Ash's determined face and shook her head. "Are you going to ask about this all day?"

"Absolutely. I've heard about the Book of Harmony since I was a child. I can't actually believe I've been lucky enough to come to Pelosci. Of course I want to see it!"

Lucia sighed. Ash hated that she was having to deceive someone who'd only shown her kindness. "Okay," Lucia said, as she grabbed a wine bottle from a passing tray. "But don't tell. I might get into trouble."

They skirted round the edge of the square, moving on to a wide street that was equally busy. Celebrations were continuing everywhere. But Lucia ignored the people and led Ash through the winding streets, into the shadow of the

. The grit under their feet grew darker, along with
, ing else. They were still in the city, but it felt as if it almost merged into the side of the mountain. As they turned another corner, they came up close to the rock face.

Behind them Ash could hear people laughing and singing, clearly drinking the wine that was freely available. Lucia turned round again. "Maybe this isn't such a good idea."

She looked troubled. Ash swallowed. "Why?"

Lucia glanced over Ash's shoulder, as if she didn't want to meet her gaze. "The book is kept somewhere very secure. It's tricky to get to. It can be dangerous. That's how we've managed to keep it so safe for centuries." She licked her lips. "Some people have died trying to see the Book of Harmony."

Ash tilted her head to one side. "What are you trying to say to me?"

This was so important. She still wasn't sure what else she could save from Erasmus, but she had to at least find that book.

Lucia looked solemn. "I don't really know you that well. You seemed a bit tired last night when we reached the top of the hill. You might not be, well, fit enough to reach the book."

Ash was stunned for a few seconds. Lucia thought she wasn't fit enough to get there? How dangerous was this? Was she going to have to scale walls, and leap canyons? At this stage, she didn't care. She just wanted to get to the book. Once she had it, she could decide what else she could save. "I wasn't tired last night. I was stunned. By the view – and all

94

the grass. The place where I lived before had none of that –
and seeing it all for the first time just took my breath away."
She put a hand to her chest. "Believe me, Lucia, you don't
need to worry about my fitness. I'll be fine."

Lucia let out a breath. She seemed relieved. "You will be?
You're sure?"

Ash nodded and Lucia grabbed her hand. "Okay, then
wrap your scarf even tighter round your face and tuck your
hair away. We're about to get very, very hot."

Lucia headed straight towards the mountainside, where
two large men in dark togas were standing guard. Lucia gave
them both a smile and nodded towards Ash. "I'm taking
our new medic to see the Book of Harmony." The ground
shook beneath their feet as she spoke, and all four people
wobbled.

One of the guards shot Ash a suspicious glance. "Don't be
long. And be careful in there. The geysers are very active."

The men moved aside and Ash realized what they'd been
hiding – a narrow entrance into the mountain. She held her
breath as Lucia stepped inside before her, the heat instantly
hitting her.

After following Lucia for what seemed like an eternity,
the slim passageway opened out into a fairly large cave, lit by
burning lanterns.

"You hide the book in here?" she asked incredulously.

Lucia nodded. "Out of the way of any visitors, and the
Book of Harmony is always guarded. It's our planet's most
important possession."

Ash cringed. Their most important possession, and she was going to attempt to steal it. Her hand brushed against the wall of the cave and she pulled it back instantly at the searing heat. "Ouch! Is it normally so hot in here?"

Lucia wrinkled her nose and looked thoughtful, touching a fingertip to the wall and pulling it back like Ash. "Hmmm, not as hot as this." She shook her head as she glanced towards a dimly lit tunnel. "Maybe we shouldn't go any further."

Ash's bangle gave a sharp buzz. "No, we have to," she said quickly. "We're here now. Let me just see it, please?"

Lucia adjusted her scarf further round her face. "Okay," she said, her voice muffled. "Prepare yourself for the next part."

Lucia gathered her toga from her ankles and moved down the tunnel. The torches weren't quite so bright here and steam wafted towards them.

When they emerged into a smaller cave, Ash understood why.

There was water on the floor. Was it a puddle, or was this some kind of indoor lake? Ash had no idea if this water was deep or not.

The surface shimmered and Ash realized it wasn't just water.

Without hesitating, Lucia began jumping between raised stones that were dispersed across the water. They hadn't been entirely visible at first in the dim light. Timing seemed to be key, because every now and then she paused. It took Ash a moment to realize why.

The next second Ash let out a scream as a hot water geyser shot into the air directly next to where Lucia was balancing. Lucia had expected it and turned her back, almost cowering away.

The hot steam and tiny sprays of water burned Ash's skin and she brushed them off frantically. "This is where the book is?"

She couldn't believe it. How could it be safe in here?

But Lucia nodded and pointed over to a dark corner. There was a natural alcove in the rock and, nestled towards the back, Ash could clearly see the outline of a book, covered in some sort of material.

"Be careful," urged Lucia. "You'll have to jump across the stones to get closer."

Ash watched. Lucia was clearly counting, murmuring under her breath, before she jumped the last few stones, narrowly missing another blast of red-hot steam from a geyser.

Lucia turned and faced Ash. "Are you ready?" she shouted. "I'll count and tell you when."

Ash gulped. This was terrifying.

But she could do this. She could. Either that or she would be turned into some kind of steamed dumpling.

"First two," yelled Lucia, and Ash didn't wait a second longer. She jumped, first to one stone, then another. "Turn your back!" shouted Lucia, and Ash spun round just in time for one of the geysers to shoot up next to her. The rush of water was incredible, as was the intense heat. All of a sudden she was glad of the thick toga. Anything lighter would have been no protection at all.

"Concentrate!" shouted Lucia. Ash could hear the worry in her voice. She could see Lucia counting again. "Next two," she instructed.

Ash jumped, wobbling precariously on the first stone, her toes brushing the too-hot water around her. She'd just steadied herself when Lucia shouted again. "Hurry!"

Ash jumped and had barely landed when the blast of another geyser made her wobble all the more. She glanced over her shoulder and saw that the stone she'd been on previously was completely doused in the boiling water. If she'd stayed there a second longer...

Lucia's cheeks were red, but the rest of her skin was strangely pale. Suddenly the whole cave shook, water spraying everywhere. Lucia reached out her hand towards the cave wall to steady herself and screamed as her skin made contact. She lost her footing and crumpled on the ledge where she was standing. Ash didn't wait for any further instructions, just jumped the last few stones and landed next to her, bending to try and pull Lucia up.

"Are you okay?"

Lucia's face glistened with tears. "We shouldn't have come in." She turned her hand over and Ash could instantly see the blisters rising on Lucia's skin. "It's never been as hot as this. We should leave. We should leave now."

Ash nodded in agreement, hating being Guardian right now. She'd put this girl in danger. It didn't matter that she knew all the people on Erasmus were going to die. What mattered was that her actions right now were causing harm to Lucia.

Do no harm, leave no one behind, echoed in her head along with the friends she'd left behind at the Library. What would they think of all this?

She tried to take a deep breath and choked. There wasn't soot in here, like there was outside, but the steam was stifling as she helped Lucia up. Ash then turned towards the book, which was nestled safely at the back of the alcove in its waterproof wrappings.

It was there. Right in front of her.

The palms of her hands itched. She couldn't help herself. Ash reached in and tugged the material covering it away. She breathed slowly, trying to calm her heart which was thudding in her chest.

Lucia was adjusting her toga, the edges dripping with water. She looked up at Ash, her eyes wide.

Ash couldn't believe this. She was next to the Book of Harmony. The most precious item on this planet. The book was large and the cover was a thick red material. The edges of the pages were red too.

Her hands trembled as she reached over and lifted the cover to glimpse inside. The paper was thick and cream, and the writing on it was a language she'd never seen before. Her heart ached a little. She'd hoped a glance at a few pages might have revealed some of the secrets of the Book of Harmony. But right now, in this stifling cave, that was impossible. Maybe, when she got it back to the Library, it would translate the messages in the book for her? Should she just grab the book, twist the bangle, and go straight back to the Library now? Of course, that would be the sensible thing to do.

Three rapid buzzes at her wrist made her jump. There wasn't even a chance to think before there were three more. There had never been a clearer message.

"You shouldn't touch it," said Lucia in horror. "Only the Elders are allowed to."

"It's not safe here," said Ash quickly. She moved to grab the book.

"No!" Lucia was clearly stunned. "What do you think you are doing?"

The ground shifted beneath their feet again and they both swayed. Ash grabbed the book and tugged at Lucia's sleeve. "Let's get out of here. This place could come down all around us!"

"Ash..." But Lucia's words were lost behind Ash as she jumped on to one of the stones.

A geyser erupted right next to her. Then another, and another.

Ash crouched down, sheltering the book against her body, trying to protect it from the boiling water.

She looked over her shoulder again at Lucia's terrified expression. "We have to get out of here. Move!"

Ash made some kind of silent prayer as she jumped from stone to stone. The whole mountain was moving. The stones wobbled beneath her feet, and staying upright was near impossible. As she jumped to the last stone it felt as if the world moved sideways and only luck meant that her instincts allowed her to tuck and roll, landing in the entranceway to the tunnel. Seconds later Lucia landed next to her.

"The book…" she started to say, but Ash just grabbed hold of her arm.

"Run!"

CHAPTER SEVEN

Ash and Lucia ran as cracks started to appear in the rock around them. When they burst into the air outside, they realized that both of the guards had disappeared and a thick layer of soot filled the air.

They kept running, back through the twisting streets.

There was a crash as something slid from the roof of one of the buildings and smashed on the street. Lucia let out a yelp at Ash's side, but her face was pale and her eyes fixed on the book under Ash's arm.

"The Book of Harmony." Her finger was shaking as she pointed, just like her voice. "Give it to me."

The ground moved again beneath their feet and Ash wondered if she should grab hold of Lucia and twist the bangle. She could explain everything later.

The explosion came from nowhere.

A black column of ash and pumice erupted into the sky. Everyone nearby was instantly knocked off their feet. Tiles rained from the roofs above, crashing down on heads and bodies, smashing on the cobblestones at Ash's feet and splintering shards of shrapnel all around.

As she lay on the ground, Ash was sure some of the buildings around her swayed. Lucia was lying in front of a building a little away from Ash, looking dazed.

Something smashed into the villa next to her, as fast as a laser blast, and there was an instant surge of heat. Seconds later a fire started burning inside.

This was it. This was the eruption.

Ash had landed on her side. By some stroke of good luck, the book was still cushioned among the folds of her toga, tucked into her other hip.

Someone yelped next to her and she jerked her head, turning to see fresh red blood pooling on a man's pale green toga. He'd been hit by flying debris.

"Try and take cover," Ash yelled at those around her. It didn't matter that it would do no good. She wasn't thinking about what she knew of their future. She was thinking about the situation she was currently in. Lucia crawled over next to her.

Within a few instants, the air had turned completely dark, the plume of ash blocking out the sun.

The missiles were raining down like meteors from space, destroying everything in their path. The ground continued to tremble beneath her body. Tiles continued to fall. People were trying to scramble to their feet. Some had managed and were clutching nearby buildings. She could hear children crying and animals yelping.

Ash flipped herself onto her hands and knees, the book underneath her belly. She tried to take a deep breath, but the thick ash caught at the back of her throat and she choked and spluttered. Her eyes were watering.

She reached out with her other hand. Lucia had been right next to her. Now she was gone. Panic gripped her chest. She wanted to save people. She wanted to save Lucia. She didn't care what the Library's instructions were. She had the book, but she could also save some of these people around her. She wiped some dirt from her eyes and caught a glimpse of pale green – Lucia was trying to lead an older woman to shelter.

Ash glanced to her right. There was some kind of temple at the end of the street, with long columns at the entranceway. Several people were sheltering underneath. It was like slow motion. Her mouth fell open as one of the columns swayed first gently, then with more force, tipping sideways. It crashed into the column next to it, setting off a chain reaction. The roof the columns were supporting crashed instantly to the ground. A cloud of dust and sand blasted outwards, obscuring her view. But she didn't need to see to know that those people were gone, without a single chance to escape.

Chaos was erupting all around her. Across the street she saw two children – obviously twins – crying, with their hands over their heads as everything collapsed around them. Two little girls, around five years old, clearly terrified. Ash moved on instinct, running to drag the twins away from the danger of the tiles sliding off all the roofs around them. A man lay directly in their path, his eyes fixed and wide open, his head split open by a falling tile. The twins screamed and Ash tugged her toga to try and cover the children's eyes.

She settled them on the floor of a villa, just inside the entranceway and set down the book, too, turning back to try and find Lucia. She had to prioritize. People were more important than any relic the Library could possibly want.

She could save them – Lucia and the twins. "Wait here," she said in a loud voice. "I'll come back for you."

The black ash was thick, the ground still shaking underfoot. Ash could hardly keep upright. She blinked, and looked from side to side, but she could only make out one pale-green toga. It was the elder of the medics, Elias, in the middle of the street. He was clutching at his stomach. Conflict pulled at her. She couldn't leave him unaided. Maybe she could save him too. As she got closer, she could see the blood staining his toga, along with fierce gashes on both forearms.

"Come on!" she yelled, putting her arm round his waist and trying to take some of his weight.

There were sparks of orange all around them. The lava bombs were setting buildings alight. Elias coughed and choked, yelping in pain as Ash helped him to his feet.

He could barely walk. The wound in his abdomen must be severe. As the debris rained down, they kept their heads low, pulling their togas up to try and shield themselves as they hobbled to the nearby villa entrance. They'd barely made it over the threshold when Elias collapsed to the ground. He was wheezing. The twins had pulled their knees up to their chests, arms round each other, both clearly terrified.

"You...must...find...Lucia," breathed Elias.

Of course. His daughter. He wanted her to be safe. "I will," she said instantly.

Ash spun round. She could barely see outside. Her head was so full right now. Should she just grab hold of the book, Elias and the twins, twist the bangle and go? But something wouldn't let her.

Leave no one behind.

Lucia. She had to find her. She had to take her too. She couldn't follow the Library's plan. Ash couldn't just save a book when there were people here who deserved to live. She wanted to save them all, Elias, the twins and Lucia too.

There was another loud boom, louder than the first. Everything shook.

A vase crashed over near the doorway, smashing on the tiled floor. Part of the ceiling fell down. The house opposite collapsed to a pile of rubble, sending bricks and wood splintering across the entranceway of where they were sheltering.

Ash looked out of the doorway once more, trying to decide if the villa truly was safer than the street.

That's when she saw it.

That's when a tiny memory slotted into place in her brain – a tiny memory about volcanoes.

Pyroclastic surge. Something close to a giant explosion – a mixture of debris and gas moving at such a rate that no Human could outrun it. The surge would wipe out everything in its path. It would flatten the entire city. It was unstoppable. She could see the shimmer in the distance. Feel the movement beneath her feet. She had to go.

Above her the strong beam across the doorway cracked and tumbled to the floor. The rest of the ceiling followed it, plummeting to the ground, the momentum throwing Ash out onto the street as everything behind her was lost from sight in the clouds of dust.

She saw a flash of green as Lucia appeared out of nowhere to try and help her father.

"Lucia!" Ash yelled in horror, rolling and reaching out towards her friend. But as Lucia moved, so did the remaining walls of the house next to her. Ash's hands desperately reached out, brushing the side of Lucia's toga and grasping something that crumpled in her hand. But it was too late. The building collapsed in a tonne of rubble, the choking dust smothering Ash's gaze and leaving no trace of Lucia, Elias or the twins. Their coloured togas had vanished from sight completely. Gone. They were gone.

But it was also too late for Ash. As she lay on the cobbled street outside, her heart aching, she turned her head to the right. The dark grey cloud of the surge was racing towards her. Smothering and wiping out every living thing, flattening every building, like a giant hand clearing a table, sweeping everything to the floor, with no thought or care.

Tears spilled from her eyes. Tears for these people. For these families. For the welcome they'd first given her. The memories were like shots in time. Pictures that only she would ever see and remember.

The fabulous view from the hills on the other side of the city. To the faces of the fellow medics who'd welcomed her to their home and their table. To the teenagers anxiously waiting to find out where they thought their lives would lead. To the strange customs and society that she would never be able to explore further, or likely understand.

In the blink of an eye, all of it would be gone.

Ash's heart twisted in her chest. She hadn't even completed her mission. The book was gone, buried under the rubble of the villa. She had nothing. The Library had nothing. There would be no evidence of how these people had existed in their utopian society. All because she hadn't fulfilled her role of Guardian. She'd put her own needs and curiosities in front of the Library's. She'd thought she knew best – but had she?

As the surge approached, Ash curled into a ball and her hand grabbed the bangle and twisted strongly, praying she hadn't left it too late.

This time, the world went black.

CHAPTER EIGHT

"Is she okay?"

"Is she breathing?"

"Where did the blood come from?"

The three voices spoke simultaneously. But they were fuzzy, as if they were some distance away from her. It was like someone had stuffed something inside her ears.

The voices vanished again, ebbing and flowing like a tide.

There was a sensation of being moved. Water being trickled around her lips. A deep sleep encompassing her in a way she'd never experienced before. And all this through a thick smoggy lens.

Slowly the fog started to ease from her brain, and the voices started to become closer, just like every other sensation in her body.

Ash tensed her muscles as her stomach cramped. Her lungs ached. She pulled her knees up and crossed her arms over her stomach, her fingers brushing against the bangle.

The bangle. She arched her back and sat up, gripping the side of the bed as the room swayed. Why was she in bed? Shouldn't she be on the Proteus circle?

"Leave her!" The sharp voice cut through her still muddled brain.

Her brain focused. She was back in her own room. The violet and purples gave her a sense of relief, even if the colours now seemed garish.

Amara cast an angry look over her shoulder and kneeled down in front of her.

"Let me see that arm," she said in a concerned voice, taking Ash's arm in her clawed hand and scanning it with the med autorepair device.

She glanced at the scanner, adjusted the settings and set it to some kind of healing pattern. As the pale blue light touched Ash's skin, she flinched.

"Sorry," said Amara, "but it's full of micro debris. I clean it, and it all reappears. Just cleaning it before I seal it again." Her hand swept back and forward a few times before she rocked back on her heels. "There." Amara set her hands on her lap and kept her gaze fixed on Ash. Something was wrong. Something was very wrong.

Ash lifted her head. Trik and Ezra were standing behind Amara. Both had their arms folded across their chests. Both looked a mixture of annoyed and concerned.

"I said *leave her*." An unfamiliar figure stepped forward, with an unnerving air of authority. She was dressed primly in a neat black skirt and white blouse. Her face was unusual.

Harsh, with sharp features. Her eyes were black and her lips seemed too red to be real. But it was her hair that was the most eye-catching. It seemed to be like a living creature. Leaves and twigs were thickly entwined round her head and even though the air in the Library was still, this woman's hair moved as if there were a constant soft gentle breeze. As Ash stared, she realized that the woman's eyebrows were also tiny twigs.

Ash blinked, her brain trying to make sense of what she was seeing. She wrinkled her nose. "Wh-who are you?"

The woman stared down at her. "I," she paused, her gaze so fierce it almost seared a hole through Ash's head, "am the Keeper."

For a second nothing made sense. Then Ash pushed herself to her feet, shaking her head. "No, no you're not. Orius was the Keeper. He's gone. He's gone now, and there's only me," she waved her hand, "and my friends." Anger started to surge inside her. "I don't know how you got here. Or what you think you're doing but—"

The woman put her hand up, almost completely in Ash's face. "Stop." The word was blunt.

Ezra and Trik were both pulling faces behind the woman's back – as if they didn't like her. But they must also be confused. They hadn't been here when Ash had first met Orius, so they probably didn't know how things worked around here.

"Vedis appeared while you were gone," said Amara carefully.

"Well, she's an intruder. She has to leave."

Vedis's nose wrinkled. "You are a disgrace. You were appointed Guardian of the Library, but your actions are anything but those of a Guardian."

She swept her arms outwards.

"And why are these people here?" Disgust dripped from her words. "This is not sanctioned. Only the Keeper and the Guardian can be in the Library, can know of its position. Every single one of these beings puts the Library at risk."

Vedis started pacing.

"I have been sent to clear up this mess, and to see if you," she pointed at Ash's chest, "are actually the right candidate to be Guardian." Her eyebrows shot up. "Judging from what I've seen so far? That would be a no."

"Listen, tree head, I don't know who you think you are, or what you think you're doing, but things have changed around here."

Vedis lifted her green-tinged hand and clicked her fingers.

Ash, in her pale green toga, was no longer in the Library. She was hovering somewhere in space, in some weird kind of bubble, just outside the clear dome of the Library. Vedis was directly in front of her. She had the tiniest hint of a shimmer around her now. One that hadn't been there when she'd first appeared in front of Ash – but one that had always been there with Orius.

"I am the Keeper," Vedis said haughtily. "And that is how you will address me."

Ash couldn't speak. This had to be some kind of dream –

or more specifically, a nightmare. Maybe she hadn't made it back from Erasmus at all?

This really couldn't be happening. Ash pressed her eyes closed for a second, willing herself back to reality.

But when she opened them again, she was still here. Still hovering somewhere in space above the Library – as if she and Vedis were in a giant bubble. Beneath her, she could see Ezra, Trik and Amara screaming up at her. Trik found a blaster from somewhere and started shooting at the dome in panic. Ezra wrenched it from his hands and Amara ran out of Ash's room and straight over to the central terminals in the Library, her hands pressing as many screens as possible.

Vedis had the hint of an ironic smile on her face. She was still holding her hand aloft. "One more click of my fingers and I leave you here, with no oxygen and no hope of life. Outside of this bubble, you would perish instantly."

Ash looked Vedis clear in the eye. Her brain was starting to make sense of things. She wouldn't let the panic that was building in her chest control her actions.

She breathed steadily. "You are the Keeper?"

Vedis nodded.

Ash clasped her hands in front of her. "Then you work with me, not against me," she said as she twisted the bangle on her wrist.

The effect was instant. She landed straight back on the Proteus circle. In a shimmer, Vedis appeared in front of her. She gave the slightest conciliatory nod of her head.

"Finally, a demonstration of intelligence. What a pity you don't use it all the time." She walked away, with a wave of her hand. "Come, it's time to talk."

They all looked at each other. Ash glanced down at the grimy toga. It was covered in the ash from the volcano. Her skin prickled. She'd never been transported back before in the clothes of the mission. She'd always arrived back at the Library in the flight suit she'd been wearing when she'd stood on the Proteus circle. What was different this time?

Her hand went to her hair. Flat. It was back to her usual straight, short style. She caught the strand that was behind her ear and pulled it forward. Blue. Just like she'd coloured it a few days ago. At least something was back to normal.

"How long was I out?"

Trik exchanged a glance with Ezra. "Two days," he muttered. "You'd collapsed on the Proteus circle. We had to carry you through to your bed. At first we didn't know if you were dead or alive."

"Two days!" Her nose wrinkled, wondering just how bad she smelled right now.

For the first time she noticed all the other med devices lying around. Three. One for each of them. These were only ever out when they were in use. Amara had just patched up one gash when Ash had woken up, what else had they been doing?

Ezra seemed to read her thoughts. "You had a lot of lung damage. We weren't sure it could be healed. We had to focus our attention on that, and," he took a breath, "take shifts."

Ash's legs wobbled. Now she was truly getting an impression of how injured she'd been.

"Guys—" she started, but Trik shook his head.

"Let's go." He nodded his head after the Keeper. "Trust me, Vedis doesn't like to be kept waiting."

Ash gave her toga a shake and a cloud of dust went up around her, remnants of Erasmus falling to the floor. Her words caught in her throat. "Erasmus, did it really…"

Amara put a hand on her arm. "Just like the Library predicted. The first volcano set off a chain reaction." She gave her head a sad shake. "There's nothing left." Then she met Ash's gaze. "No one survived."

Her legs buckled under her as she crumpled to the ground and put her head in her hands.

"Ash!" Trik and Ezra yelled in unison and jumped forward to try and catch her. But she was already on the ground, wrapping her arms round herself.

"Leave no one behind," she muttered to herself as she rocked back and forward.

Trik dropped down onto his haunches, in front of her face. "What's going on? What do you mean, leave no one behind? We're all here, Ash. Are you confused?"

She sniffed and shook her head as tears rolled down her face. "The task. The book. It all seemed so stupid once I got there. I wanted to save people, not things." Her voice started to falter. "Once the eruption started, I tried to save Lucia and Elias and these two little girls. But it was all so confusing, and buildings were collapsing around me, and I couldn't get to them… I couldn't get to Lucia." She sobbed. "They were just kids. They shouldn't have died."

Ash was struggling to take a breath and as she looked up, she saw the expressions on her friends' faces. They were shocked.

Ezra spoke first. "Let's get her cleaned up," he said to Amara. "And take a breath, Ash. Pull yourself together. We'll talk later about this. And don't say a word to Vedis. Believe me, she won't like this one bit."

Amara wiped Ash's face with something, as Ezra did the same to her hands. When they'd finished, Amara pulled her to her feet. "Now, breathe," she said smoothly.

It took a few moments. But Ash realized something. Her friends were distracted. Nervy. Vedis had already said they shouldn't be in the Library. Had the new Keeper threatened her friends in Ash's absence? Did she plan on sending them home?

That gave Ash the kick she needed. She straightened her shoulders and swallowed – she wouldn't let that happen.

The ache in Ash's chest was solid.

Her footsteps faltered as she walked over to the atrium of the Library. Beneath her, all the ancient artefacts were stored. Remnants of lives that were gone. Lives like the people on Erasmus. Except Ash had failed them. She had nothing of theirs.

As she crossed the floor, she realized that Vedis was sitting at the table where Ash and her friends usually sat.

Something flared inside her. Rude. Domineering. Harsh.

That was her first opinion on the new Keeper. It didn't feel like it might change.

She reluctantly pulled out a chair at the table and sat down, still wishing she'd had a chance to get changed.

Vedis waited until Ezra, Trik and Amara sat down too. The telltale shimmer of a hologram floated around her edges. She leaned both elbows on the table – at least she appeared to – and looked at Ash's friends in turn. "Thank you all for your service to the Library. You will no longer be required."

"Stop!" This time it was Ash that put her hand up. "You don't get to make any decisions about my team. I think it's time we established some ground rules."

"*My* ground rules are overdue." Vedis's eyes were cold.

"You can't just suddenly appear and start ordering us around. Where were you?" asked Ash.

"Excuse me?" As Vedis wrinkled her brow, the leaves on her head moved.

"I asked, where were you? If you're the new Keeper, why didn't you appear when Orius left? Where were you when the Library needed help? When Aldus Dexter attacked? You know – the Guardian who the Library said was dead, but had in fact stolen a powerful device from here and used it for his own means?"

Vedis shifted in her chair but her gaze remained cold.

Ash kept going. "Where were you when the Library needed protection? Because two of these people were here and you weren't." Ash put up her hands. "Two of these people risked their lives to save a place they knew very little about."

117

Vedis's face was perfectly straight now. "Do you think programming this complex can be done in the blink of an eye?" she said simply.

Now she'd started, Ash couldn't stop. "You're telling me that I've done some things wrong. Let's talk about the Library. Let's talk about the things that the Library has done wrong. But shouldn't you already know all this? Isn't the role of the Keeper to watch over the Library, know everything that's happened, here and in the universe, and assist the Guardian in their role? At least I assume that's what the Library programs you to do. I already had this conversation with Orius – I'm assuming the previous Keeper's programming becomes part of yours?"

"His experience and knowledge do become part of the new Keeper's programming," Vedis said carefully, then she lifted her gaze to meet Ash's, "but his personality and decision-making does not. Each Keeper is unique. Each Keeper chooses part of their own programming and the identity they wish to assume. While Orius's memories may become part of my own, that's all they are – memories. This is *my* Library now. It is my responsibility."

"Good luck with that then," said Ash as she folded her arms across her chest and leaned back. "This Library seems to have a mind of its own. And it doesn't know everything that happens in the universe – Aldus Dexter's appearance proved that. As did the fact that he stole something from here. Is the inventory of the Library even accurate?"

It clearly wasn't the response that Vedis was expecting.

118

Her facial expressions shifted and a gleam of distaste came into her eyes. She stood up and pressed her hands on the table.

Ash could tell by the looks exchanged between her friends that they were thinking the same thing as her. *Can a hologram actually do that?* At the end of Orius's nine-hundred-year program, his features and outline had started to dull. But one of the most surprising things had been the way that at times, he seemed almost real. Ash could remember the sensation of his fingers almost touching hers. The way her brain had tried to make sense of the improbability. But this hologram seemed even more like a flesh and blood person – and that couldn't possibly be true.

Vedis pointed a finger at Ash. "*You* are arrogant. *You* are irresponsible. You had one task to do. Retrieve the Book of Harmony from Erasmus." Vedis held up her hands. "Where is it? Where is the book? What do we have left to remember the people of Erasmus? A now-lost civilization that had a way of life that could have provided valuable learning for other planets, other people in conflict."

Ash could feel panic in her chest. "I have memories. I learned more in the last day and a half than the Library could possibly have hoped for. More than could ever be written in a book. I talked to the people; I watched their lives. I saw how they organized their society."

"What?" Trik's face was screwed up. "You learned all that in barely a day?"

Ezra leaned forward. "How did that actually work?" Ash

could see him trying to figure it all out in his brain.

Vedis slammed her hand on the table. This time they knew the touch wasn't just imagination. This time they all felt the reverberation through the wood. "Enough!"

She pressed a bony finger into Ash's chest. Ash pulled back in shock. There was no mistaking the feel of the angry gesture. "You had one job. Get in. Get out. And you failed. *Keep to the task, leave no trace.* You risked your life. Actions have consequences. The learning of the people of Erasmus has been lost. It's gone. There will be no other chance of retrieval – the planet damage is too extreme. We could sift that rubble for a thousand years and never find the knowledge that was contained in that book. Gone for ever – because Ash Yang thought she knew better than the Library. Because Ash Yang second-guesses every instruction that she's given."

Ash pushed the chair back and stood up too. She didn't shout, she spoke quietly. "With good reason. I never asked for this job. I got flung in here. I met a Keeper who told me I had a role to save artefacts from around the universe. I was told the Library would brief me before I left on every mission. But the information was…" She tried to search for the right word. "Inadequate, on many occasions. Dangerous at times.

"The Library created a false sense of security around my missions. Sometimes there was information that it should have given me, and it didn't. Sometimes it didn't know, and didn't admit that. The Library isn't all-seeing, all-knowing – not in the way it pretends to be. And it's *that* arrogance that nearly got this place destroyed." She took a deep breath and glanced at Trik and Ezra. "It's that arrogance that led to war in our solar system for our entire lifespans. That led to the death of friends and family. That turned a whole planet into an ice zone which virtually no one could survive on."

Her voice was starting to shake, but she kept going. She moved towards Ezra and put her hand on his shoulder.

"That's why I asked my friends to be here. That's why I asked for other opinions. Now, when the Library sets me a mission, we explore all options, research all the information available. We don't just take the Library's word for it. This is a team effort. My friends will only leave if they want to."

She waited for Vedis to click her fingers again and send them all floating into space. There was a flicker at the side of Vedis's jaw. This hologram was more real than anything she'd ever encountered before.

Vedis made a clicking sound. "Maybe," she said slowly, "you required a temporary arrangement while there was no Keeper to guide you." She straightened her holographic shoulders and stuck out her chin. "But now that I'm here, they are no longer required."

"Yes, we are," said Amara, standing up and walking around the table to stand side by side with Ash.

Trik blinked, then scraped his chair on the floor as he stood up too. "We stand with our friend. She might have made a mistake this time around. We don't know what really happened – and from the look of Ash when she landed back here, she barely escaped with her life. It's sad that she didn't get the artefact. Maybe we should have all gone. Maybe then there would have been a better chance of saving something from the planet. But we didn't. And we'll learn from that."

Ash blinked back tears. They'd seen what Vedis had done earlier. They knew this was risky. But they were standing by her. Supporting her.

She cleared her throat. "You're right, Vedis. I was arrogant. I was selfish. I got there, and I wanted to learn as much as I could. I thought that the more I knew, the more I could bring back and keep a little of Erasmus alive.

"I wanted to keep the people alive, not just the book. Why, why do we save artefacts, when we could save people? The book might have contained the knowledge of living in harmony, but surely bringing back people who knew that way of life would have been much more valuable?" She let a long slow breath out through pursed lips and gave a sad sigh. "At the end, the utopian society I'd admired was gone in the blink of an eye. But," she shook her head as the memories flashed into her brain, "at least I got to understand those people and experience their lives a little."

Trik and Ezra looked confused at her words. Amara tilted her head to the side slightly and gave her a searching glance.

But Vedis seemed completely unmoved.

"People have a lifespan, Guardian. Artefacts do not. Elias, Lucia, Tiela and Rosa..."

Ash flinched as she realized Vedis knew everyone's names from Erasmus. The twins, Tiela and Rosa had been their names. But if Vedis knew that, she likely knew everything Ash had done. Orius had been able to watch some missions from the Library, and it seemed that Vedis could too.

"...Would have lived their lifetime. But none of them could have replicated the details in the book. The children would have remembered little of their upbringing. Elias and Lucia, as two people, couldn't hope to replicate the combined experiences and learnings of an entire population, as was recorded in the book. Don't you think that the secret of living in harmony, preventing war – could have been used in the future to help other civilizations at a point of crisis? What you've lost can never be found again." She paused, letting the weight of her words settle on Ash.

"If my programming had been completed earlier, I could have intervened. It's time that you, Ms Yang, were brought into line." She swung her arms upwards in some kind of grand gesture. "Your role and my role are to serve the Library, and in turn, serve all the beings in our universe..."

Ash interrupted. "But you were programmed for your role, Vedis. You even got to choose your appearance." She gave a half smile. "You'll need to fill me in on that." She placed a hand on her chest. "But I wasn't programmed, I was *selected*." She emphasized the word. "The Library seemed to think that I fitted the bill as Guardian and that I could fulfil that function."

"You should never have been left unsupervised," Vedis snapped in an offhand manner.

Ash shook her head. "Actually, I think it's been the making of me."

"Hardly. You've just agreed that you've become arrogant and selfish. Your actions mean that the artefact for a whole planet, a whole society, has been lost for ever."

For a moment Ash almost faltered. Maybe the Book of Harmony could have stopped a future war – even like the one that had destroyed Ash's own family. The responsibility felt overwhelming. But there was more than this.

Arrogant was a word that could work both ways. "I did. And I'm sorry. I think I've learned. My heart ruled my head. And I can't promise I won't make the same mistake again. But has the Library learned?"

Vedis gave her a look of surprise. "What's that supposed to mean?"

"It means exactly what I said earlier. The Library has made mistakes and at times shown poor judgement. Maybe something's wrong with its algorithms, but it's not as perfect as you think. No process is perfect. There's always room for improvement."

"You don't know what you're talking about."

Ash stepped right up to Vedis. "I do. If I need to learn, so does the Library. And so do you." She raised her hand. "I'll be honest. It's clear we don't like each other. I have the option of leaving. You don't. We either learn to work together, or I leave and you find a new Guardian." She gave Vedis a curious look. "And I'm not too sure that you get to pick. There could be worse than me out there – after all, the Library picked Aldus Dexter."

Ash shrugged her shoulders.

"Now, I'm tired and I'm sore, and I'm pretty sure I smell. I want to get washed. I want to get changed. And I want someone in," she glanced upwards, "the *Library* to tell me why I'm still in these clothes." She shook the folds of the toga and something drifted to the ground.

All eyes widened.

Ash bent down, frowning. The crumpled paper was damaged at the edges, singed, and she carefully flattened it out.

"Maura's certificate," she gasped.

Amara stepped forward, her clawed finger brushing the edge of the paper. "What is it?" she asked.

Ash reached up to her shoulder and touched the clasp on her toga. "It belonged to Maura," she replied softly. "I was there during the naming ceremony when all the teenagers are designated their roles. They all receive a certificate." Her voice faltered. "This is…was Maura's. She was so proud to be named as a medic." Ash swallowed and looked down at the words on the certificate. It was a language she didn't understand. "Maura had given it to Lucia while she celebrated and Lucia had stored it in her toga. I reached for her as the volcano erupted and this is what I grasped." Tears pricked at her eyes. "I…I had no idea."

Her brain flooded back to the terror. The fear. The panic. The faces of Elias, Lucia and the twins. She laid the singed piece of paper down on the main table.

Vedis's voice was clipped. "Well, it looks like your question is answered, Guardian Yang. It seems the Library had a reason for leaving you in your clothes from Erasmus. The Library knows much more than you could possibly imagine."

Ash shot her a hateful glare.

"There it is, Vedis, your artefact from Erasmus. A piece of the people who lived and breathed there. Do with it as you will."

And before anyone else could speak, she turned and walked away before the emotions overcame her.

CHAPTER NINE

The situation at the Library remained more than tense.

Erasmus haunted Ash in a series of unexpected flashbacks. She didn't talk about it. She didn't want to.

Vedis continued to strut about with a permanent look of disdain on her face. Ash even heard her complain to Amara about her.

But the certificate had proved more worthy than first thought. Amara had translated its words. It contained much of the ethos of the society that lived on Erasmus, and how allocating everyone a task and role that was viewed with equal value, added to the community. Amara had also helped Ash record her memories of the people and place, in the hope they could be used to help the warring planet the Library had identified. Both the certificate and the memories of Ash were currently labelled like all the Infinity Files in the Library.

Vedis had made a tutting sound at their attempts to save

part of the memories from Erasmus. "What use can these possibly have?"

Ash had frozen, reluctant to give Vedis an audience. She brushed away the tears that were prickling in her eyes. She hated feeling like she'd failed. She could still picture injured Elias and the twins in her head. The tiny fleeting glance she'd got of Lucia rushing to help. Not that it mattered, as she still knew the outcome for them all. It kept her awake at night.

But Amara was more than a match for Vedis's taunt. She held up the certificate. "This speaks of hundreds of years," she said quietly. "Of a society who had found a way to live in harmony. Of the joy and pleasure the teenagers took in being assigned the role that would mean so much to them, and their way of contributing to their community. It shows that all jobs were held in equal measure, whether you were a street cleaner, a tradesperson or an early scientist." Amara admired the detailed writing on the certificate. "It tells me of a people who took pleasure in being together and living in a way very different to many others." She smiled and slid the certificate back under the glass where it was to be displayed. "But then again," she paused and in the most subtle way ran her eyes up and down Vedis's holographic form, "I can find beauty in *most* things," she said, before turning and walking down the Library, away from Vedis.

Ash's heart gave a squeeze. Amara always had a wisdom to her words – something that Ash often envied.

Vedis vanished, her form vaporizing in the blink of an eye.

Those sudden movements made Ash uncomfortable. Orius had never disappeared like that. Vedis mainly seemed to do it when she lost her temper, but it meant that Ash could never know if Vedis was watching her or not.

She sighed and walked over to the very edge of the dome. All that was between her and the black space outside was the glass seal round the Library. Ash pulled over an old-fashioned chair. It was lumpy, with worn patches, but over the last few weeks Ash had adopted it as her own. She'd found it under a pile of debris after the Library had been attacked. She leaned back on the chair and pressed her feet up against the dome. It felt like she could almost reach out and touch the stars.

Ash closed her eyes. Her brain was questioning everything right now – whether she'd made the right decision to stay in the Library as Guardian – and if she was really fit for this job after all. She'd made a mistake. She had let her emotions get the better of her, back on Erasmus. It had distracted her and she'd failed a mission for the first time. And now Vedis had appeared. The Library had a new Keeper. And it was clear she liked Ash just as much as Ash liked her.

Ash sighed. The atmosphere was affecting her mood. She tried to think positive thoughts, remembering her successes as Guardian. In particular how they'd fought against Aldus Dexter after he'd stolen the infinity crystal and sent her solar system spiralling into war. Defeating Aldus in a space battle, and taking the crystal back to her solar system to negotiate a truce, had been the most terrifying and fulfilling task of her life – and it had been against the Library's instructions. Not every decision she'd made since she'd accepted this job had been bad.

"I have to keep remembering that," she murmured to herself as she climbed the stairs back up to the central point. On her next mission she would follow the Library's instruction first, *then* explore her own inclination, though. Not the other way around. The thought of stopping other wars had been playing on her mind – keeping her awake at night, although she would never admit that to Vedis.

Ash climbed the stairs to the main atrium, where the rest of them were setting plates on the table.

"There you are." Amara smiled. "We were just getting ready to eat."

"Darn it," said Trik with a grin. "I was planning on eating your share."

They had barely sat down when an Infinity File appeared in the air above them. It took a few seconds to realize what they were all looking at.

Vedis's high-heeled shoes clicked on the stone floor as she walked towards them, arms folded across her chest.

"Is that…?" Trik frowned and tipped his head to look at the artefact on the screen above him.

Ezra pulled back, eyes wide.

"Yes." Vedis's voice was clipped. "It's a body."

"I haven't seen one anywhere in the Library," said Amara steadily.

130

Ash couldn't speak.

Vedis pointed at the screen and it changed to the overview of a planet. "This is Capuro 12. The citizens here are a little unusual."

A figure flashed on the screen. The outline was certainly unusual. The person was like a giant-sized bird. Upright, with claws on their feet, covered in feathers, with wings that also included hands. The face was more Human than bird, and the overall effect was startling.

"Wow," breathed Ash.

Vedis waved her hands. "Tens of thousands of years ago, a spacecraft crash-landed on Capuro 12. At that point, the species on Capuro 12 was Human. The species on the spacecraft was Pluzon – a bird-like species, with technology so far advanced the Capuron Humans thought they were some kind of mythical beings." She gave a small smile. "The Pluzons and Humans interbred, with the Pluzon genetic material dominating.

"Over years, it spread throughout the whole planet. Legends were forgotten. The new Capuron species believed they'd always been this way. As they evolved, they realized their land was too damaged to live on and as a species now dominated by bird-like features, they moved to a more natural habitat – the clouds. They forgot who was the original species on the planet and were hostile to any contact from other worlds. The bodies of the original Pluzon crew had disintegrated over the years. But the body of one of the first Humans who had assisted at the beginning was virtually intact, sealed and buried in a tomb that had no exposure to the elements."

Vedis looked at them all.

"More than six hundred years ago, this body was removed from the planet – along with some of the technology that survived the crash. Politics were complicated at the time. There were rumours that every attempted contact from space was from different creatures trying to invade and dominate. It was decided that a discovery of this relic from the past would have caused outrage across the planet. The original Human body would have revealed the origins of the species," Vedis paused and raised her eyebrows, "and not all species are ready to know their origins."

She moved to the side of the screen. "But now times have moved on. Fears have calmed and science is valued again. A discovery of a body of one of the original residents of the planet should lead them to understand how the original species on their own planet merged with another. The first contact they think they've avoided for so long actually happened thousands of years ago."

Vedis pressed her lips together as the leaves on her head trembled. "This is a delicate situation. The density and make-up of the rocks on Capuro 12 mean it is impossible to transport the body and other spacecraft parts straight into place. And the population of this planet still mainly avoid ground level altogether, residing in the clouds – in cities they have built there."

"What?" Amara looked stunned.

"Yes," nodded Vedis. "There are cities in the clouds. The land is porous in many places – dangerous in others. And it has worsened over the years. Indeed, if the species hadn't evolved, it is likely there would be no life left on this planet."

"And that's where the body is to go – on to the dangerous part?" asked Ash.

Vedis nodded.

"I can guess what comes next," said Ash with a sigh. "Orius told me a long time ago that the bangle takes us as close as possible to the place we need to be. But it isn't exact. It's not powerful enough for pinpoint accuracy."

Vedis gave something that was probably supposed to resemble a smile. "Yes, the artefacts have to be returned to where they were taken from. The evolved Capurons still investigate and research the land beneath them. They are anxious to understand the changes – to prevent any more damage being done. The Library can give you tools to help you move the rock blocking the entrance to the tomb and return the artefacts back inside it, but we can't transport you onto toxic ground." She paused for a second. "So you'll be transported to one of the nearest cities in the clouds."

Ash shook her head. She wondered if, in that pause, Vedis had actually been contemplating putting them down in toxic ground. Somehow, it wouldn't surprise her.

Vedis scanned the faces at the table. "On this occasion, it might actually be wise to take someone with you. It's unlikely you would be able to manoeuvre the artefacts on your own."

Her thoughtful gaze fell on Ezra, Trik and Amara. "Or maybe even three," she murmured.

"When we transport, we'll turn into Capurons?" asked Ash. "Bird people?"

Vedis nodded again.

"Not me," said Amara quickly. "Flying in the clouds?" She shook her head. "Oh no."

Trik stood up and looked at the planet again. "The chance to soar like a bird? Oh, I'm in. Absolutely." He gave Ezra a nudge. "We might even get to have a race."

"Wait a minute," said Ash. "I need a bit more clarification. Why has there never been a discovery before? Either of original Pluzon remains, or original Humans? It seems odd they've never found anything to make them question their origins."

"There are none." Vedis started pacing. "Because Capurons, in their Human state, lived on the land, that is where all their remains were buried. But the land is toxic. There are huge areas of quicksand. No genetic material can survive being buried in that ground. Everything that came before has been destroyed."

"But the tomb?"

"The tomb is carved into rock, halfway up a mountain, and away from the toxic earth. The body will be safe if we return it there. The tomb entrance is actually close to one of the cloud cities' bases. During that construction, it was feared the body would be found – which is why it was removed."

Ash sat back down and leaned her elbows on the table. "Are you telling us everything?"

Vedis pressed her lips together for a second, a wicked gleam flitting across her eyes. "I think the transformation process might be a little...uncomfortable this time around, as the changes will be so vast."

Ash shivered. She'd had a visit in the past to a place where she'd been in a species similar to the Capurons. She'd experienced flight. She'd experienced the sheer terror. The transformation process had been more than uncomfortable. It had seemed like every cell in her body was being ripped apart from within. At least this time she might be a little better prepared.

She put a smile on her face. "Guys, you should know that I felt as if I was being turned inside out last time I turned into a bird."

Ezra and Trik exchanged glances. Neither of them apparently wanted to appear afraid.

She pushed herself back up, then looked again at the screen, sweeping her hand to go back to the previous figure and study it a bit harder. If she was about to take on that shape, she wanted to be prepared.

The head shape and eyes were definitely more Human like. But the nose and mouth were combined into a more bird-like beak. Her stomach gave a rumble. "I'm going to eat before I go." Her reaction was automatic. She wasn't quite sure if she'd manage to eat with a beak, and she wasn't even sure what food would be like on Capuro 12.

As Ash reached the food dispenser, she paused and turned back to Vedis. "Does this have a time limit? Do we have to leave immediately?"

Vedis tilted her chin upwards. "You can eat," she said sharply. "But, if you delay, there is always the chance that another job could be assigned by the Library."

Ash pressed a button on the dispenser. "Vetti burgers and kabona leaves."

There was a noisy shudder behind her of leaves and twigs brushing together, and Ash pulled a face at the dispenser. Kabona leaves was something that she ate on a regular basis, but she'd forgotten about Vedis's twig-and-leaves hair, which looked distinctly similar to what was now on her plate. She still hadn't gotten to the bottom of Vedis's appearance. The hologram had mentioned that she'd got to choose how she looked, so she'd obviously based her appearance on a species Ash had never seen before. Part of her wanted to apologize, but she pushed the thought away.

She lifted her plate and took it back to the table. Vedis visibly blanched and disappeared. Ash tried not to smile – it might be a useful way to get rid of her in the future. Trik and Ezra got their favourite foods and sat at the table with her, as Amara pulled up some more information on Capuro 12.

"There's a Friend there," she told them. "Ruffako. I'm sure he'll make himself known to you once you get there."

"How long do you think we'll be there?" asked Ezra.

"Who knows?" answered Ash. "First we'll need somewhere

to hide the artefacts, then I guess we'll need to go and scope out the site."

"I wonder what she's going to give us to move a huge mass of rock hiding the tomb?" Trik flexed his muscles. "What do you think these will look like as wings?"

Ash laughed and exchanged an amused glance with Ezra. "Don't you just love how his brain jumps from one thing to another?"

As they were talking there was a buzzing noise and a large pile of artefacts appeared next to the Proteus circle. One was clearly the body, wrapped in some thick brown sacking, the rest, pieces of the original Pluzon spaceship.

Ash instantly lost her appetite.

Amara narrowed her eyes. "Is it just bones? How could a bit of cloth help keep a body in any kind of reasonable state for thousands of years?"

Vedis appeared again, not looking at the food on the table. She put her holographic finger next to the wrapping and an electronic shimmer appeared.

"I told you the Pluzon technology was far beyond anything on Capuro 12. The body has a protective seal round it. When it was transported here, the Library enhanced that with a force field to try and replicate the conditions on the planet. When you return the body, the Library force field will remove itself. The protective seal will remain."

All four stood and stared for a few seconds.

After another few moments, Ash could hear the rustling of leaves to her side – a sign of agitation from Vedis.

Vedis clicked her fingers and two sleek grey handsets appeared on the table. "One is to aid with the movement of the rock, the other will make your artefacts invisible, until you can move them safely, and also to reapply and remove the force field again."

Ash nodded and slid a handset into either side of her red and grey flight suit.

She took a quick look at her companions. "Are we ready for this? Any questions?"

Trik and Ezra looked at each other then shook their heads.

"Then let's go."

Ash positioned herself on the Proteus circle, with Ezra and Trik behind her, each of them with a hand on one of her shoulders. They had to be touching to transport together. Ash wrinkled her nose, pushing one part of the spaceship remains for Trik to touch, and another for Ezra, then she pulled a face and reached out her leg to touch the body. The force field shimmered again.

"Vedis, take the Library force field off now in case it interferes with our transport. The last thing I want to do is leave this behind."

Vedis looked thoughtful and nodded her head. "Done." A small smile crept over her face. "Happy landing," she said as Ash twisted the bangle on her wrist and the world swirled around them.

CHAPTER TEN

The sensation of jumping this time was entirely different. Usually Ash landed somewhere on her knees, doubled over and, most of the time, had to try to stop herself being sick.

This time she landed flat on her back, staring up at swirling clouds.

Except…it wasn't really *her* back. It was the back of the creature she'd become. And flipping over wasn't exactly easy.

Every cell in her body screamed. The sharp burst of pain took her breath away. For a moment she closed her eyes tightly and just concentrated on her breathing. Vedis hadn't been joking about the transition process being tough this time.

Ash wasn't quite sure how long she lay there. Long enough to allow herself to start to relax a little, for her breaths not to cause pain when she inhaled. She turned her head from side to side, not really able to take in her surroundings.

"Trik? Ezra?"

Her voice felt funny, almost as if her inbuilt translator was struggling to function. And the pitch and tone seemed weird.

She tried to cough, but that didn't really work either, so she started flapping her arms, which of course, were actually more like wings.

Getting her brain round her current state was exhausting.

There was a tug on one of her hands. A giant bird was standing above her.

She blinked, "Trik? Ezra?"

"It's Trik," came the annoyed response. Laughter bubbled somewhere inside her. Trik was ninety per cent bird, ten per cent Human. As a bird he had white and black plumage, he was short, with a large belly and small, angry looking beak. He lifted his arms – or wings – and used the hand at the end to clasp Ash's and pull her, a little too sharply, upwards.

As she moved upright, she swayed. "Whoa."

It was like every part of her equilibrium was out of balance. "This feels weird," she breathed.

"You don't say," quipped Trik.

His dark eyes were running up and down her. "What do I look like?" she asked.

"A bird."

There was a noise behind them and they both turned to see another bird walking towards them, much larger, with brilliant blue plumage.

"You have got to be joking," moaned Trik. "You got that, and I got to be the short, round guy?"

The bird's footsteps were faltering, as if he were trying to get used to his clawed feet.

"This is awesome," said Ezra. He lifted a wing easily, letting them glimpse a range of greens and purples among the blues. "I was sick twice of course, but I left that over there." He gestured with his wing to somewhere behind them.

Ash bent her head. Her neck felt a bit strange. Yellow. She was yellow. It was so bright, it was almost luminous. "So much for being inconspicuous," she said. "Why didn't the Library transform us all into dull browns?"

She looked at her companions. All three of them wore strange slings across their bodies, covered in a multitude of pockets.

Ash found her wing bent easily where a Human elbow would be and she patted her own sling, checking the two handsets were safely stowed.

"Where do you think we are?" she asked and she looked around once again.

The scenery was bizarre. They were standing literally in a cloud, its wisps drifting up around them. But under their feet was a certain squishy feeling.

Trik still looked unhappy. He held out his short, stumpy wings. "I thought I would be elegant. Graceful. Huh." It came out as some kind of snort.

Ezra used his height to try and get a better handle on their surroundings. He spread one large wing. "I can see something in this direction. If we've landed near a city, it looks as if it's this way. We should investigate."

Ash nodded and looked down. Just to her right was the body, and the spacecraft parts. "Let me try this first." Manoeuvring the handset out of her clothing was more difficult than she'd thought. Even though she had a hand, it didn't function quite the way her Human one did. She eventually got the handset out, pressed the buttons and scanned the artefacts. They disappeared in the blink of an eye.

"It works," said Trik in amazement. He lifted his clawed foot and gave a short kick. "Ouch! Yip, definitely still there."

Ash fumbled with the handset, then passed it over to Ezra. "Here, you put it back in one of my pockets."

He looked at her. "So, we just leave them here?"

She nodded. "It's not like anyone can see them."

After a few tries, Ezra finally fumbled the handset away. "Okay, can we explore now?"

Ash nodded her head and took a few steps, then stopped. "I'm guessing we're not meant to walk around."

She would have wrinkled her forehead if she could. Moving and talking in an entirely unfamiliar form was messing with her head a bit. She didn't have legs any more, in bird form it was really only ankles. Her body kept telling her to clench her clawed feet – but there was nothing to anchor on to.

Walking on the clouds was like walking on a giant sponge. She spread her wings and took a deep breath.

"Okay, this is different from the last time I was a kind of bird. Last time was a bit more terrifying, because I just had to jump off the edge of a cliff and hope for the best." She jumped awkwardly on her clawed feet. "So, I have no idea how to actually take off into the sky." She tried to flap her wings, but there didn't seem to be much momentum there.

"Do we run?" asked Trik. His virtually rotund body tried to break into a run. Except it looked more like a couple of hops, with a few dispiriting flaps of his arms, before he lost his balance and fell, rolling on the ground again.

Both Ash and Ezra started laughing. They couldn't help it. Particularly when Trik kept rolling as he tried to get back up. Trik wasn't used to carrying weight and it was clear that balance was an issue. Ash was struck by the fact she must have looked exactly the same a few moments earlier.

Ezra moved, holding out an elegant hand to assist Trik, who took it reluctantly with much huffing and puffing.

"Okay," said Ezra. "Let me have a try at this."

He spread his wings again. When he flapped, Ash could feel the rush of air. Within a few seconds, Ezra was lifting into the air. For a moment they could see the surprise and shock on his face. He flapped a bit more and rose into the sky above them, moving further and further away.

They kept watching as he gradually became accustomed to the experience, his movements becoming more of a glide, the lowering of one wing to turn, and both to slow down.

"I don't remember doing any of that last time," murmured Ash. She wanted to grit her teeth but grinding the edges of her beak together didn't give her the same effect.

"Come on," she said to Trik with a new determination. "Last time around, I had to jump off something to get started."

Trik, who was usually so blasé, gave her a strange glance. "Oh yeah, well that sounds safe."

"We have to get airborne somehow. This is a cloud. It's got to have an edge somewhere. Let's find one and jump off."

They tottered along awkwardly. "Why do I think there's got to be a better way to do this," moaned Trik.

It didn't take long to reach what seemed like the edge of the cloud. They both leaned forward and looked down. Ash narrowed her gaze and tried to see what was immediately underneath them.

"What do you think is down—" Trik's voice cut off. There was a whoosh and a yell as he disappeared, dropping like the round solid black-and-white ball he was.

Ash didn't hesitate. She opened her arms and let herself fall forward. "Ezra…" she yelled as she started to fall, feeling the words get lost in the air around her.

Her eyelids instinctively closed with the rush of cold air against her eyeballs. But it was something she could remember from before. She was reacting like a Human. She forced herself to open her eyes. The effect wasn't what her Human brain believed should happen. The Capuron style bodies were used to this. It was just that her Human brain was telling her this should be unbearable.

She made herself focus. She'd angled her wings behind her, allowing herself to plummet faster, anything to try and catch up with Trik. But his round form and heavier weight meant he seemed to be so far beneath her.

"Trik!" Ash tried to yell, knowing it must be completely useless. She had to spread her wings. It was the only way she could start to control her descent. She had to *fly*.

But every part of her didn't want to do it. If she started flying, it would take her further and further away from her friend.

There was a flash of blue underneath her. For a few seconds she couldn't understand what she was seeing.

Ezra had appeared. Like some kind of missile, he barged into Trik in mid-air. And it was like the sense of attack sparked something in Trik. Instead of staying in his round form, he actually spread his wings. His descent slowed immediately.

Ash opened her own wings, flapping easily, and taking a few moments to learn how to steer herself again. She let herself dip a little. Ezra and Trik were now darting round underneath her. It was like Ezra was giving him instructions.

As the air rushed past, she finally got on the same level as them both.

Ezra was indeed shouting instructions. "Dip your left wing, good, now flap, up, up."

Memories were flooding Ash's brain. When she'd stepped off the cliff edge back on Garouro, she'd had the Friend from that planet by her side. He'd given her constant instructions. If he hadn't been there she would almost certainly have fallen into the sea beneath them both. It made her wonder where the Friend on Capuro 12 was right now.

She glided alongside Trik. "Are you okay? You scared me."

145

"I scared myself," he said, his feathers pushed back from his face.

"You've got this," said Ezra in a confident voice. "Just keep going."

They spent the next few minutes circling round each other, trying to take in their surroundings. Even though Trik had fallen for around thirty seconds, the land was still far beneath them.

The whole ground was a mixture of greys, browns and dark red. Ash could make out mountains, and hills, but there was no green. Her own planet, Astoria, was various colours of sand, but this looked even more barren somehow. As they swooped a little lower, she tried to get a better view.

Parts appeared rocky. There were areas that looked as if they could be the quicksand type areas Vedis had warned them about. But she couldn't spot a cliff where a tomb could be hidden.

They kept circling round. "What do you think?" she asked. "I'm not sure where we're meant to be."

Trik's confidence was clearly building as he seemed to get the hang of the whole flying concept. "Let's explore," he declared. "Let's go back up top and take a look at these cloud cities. We didn't see much. The Library must have sent us somewhere quiet. If we're going to find our Friend, I guess they'll be up there somewhere. Surely they can tell us where this tomb is."

Ash gave a nod. She knew he was right. It was the only thing that made sense. They all flapped their wings a little harder and rose up into the air again, taking advantage of some warm air currents.

The sensation of flying through the light clouds was disconcerting. For a few moments, she literally couldn't see where she was going. Then, they all rose high above the largest cloud.

The sight took her breath away. While the edges of the huge cloud were just cloud, the middle part was a bustling city.

It seemed like an impossible sight. There were no vehicles – only buildings and people, lots and lots of people. The city seemed to stretch high into the sky above them. Everything was made of metal and glinted brilliantly. Some of the highest constructions had open-plan rooms at all levels on their structure. People flew between the rooms from building to building. Some looked like work places, others like houses.

"What is this place?" breathed Ezra next to her.

Trik nodded his head towards another structure that had a wide metal beam jutting out from it. They landed there, and for the first time Ash was instantly glad of her claw-like feet. The beam was much thinner than expected and her toes clamped round it, holding her steady.

"How does this place work?" asked Trik, turning his head from side to side as he tried to take in the sights.

The beam they were standing on was replicated on every structure. Like it was some kind of meeting or resting place – a bit like standing in a corridor back on the Star Corporation Academy, or in the street back in Ash's home town.

They all watched in wonder. Although there was no greenery, the metal structures had some resemblance to giant trees, filled with dozens of nests. The most interesting aspect was the open access and easy movement.

Some of the parts that looked like homes had a bit more privacy. Screens and curtains were in place.

Ezra stared upwards. "Do you think there's permanently good weather here?"

"Why do you ask that?"

He blinked. "It's so open. Imagine these structures in a rain storm, or if there were a snow blizzard. Look at that one over there," he lifted one wing and hand to point. "I think it's actually swaying."

Ash tilted her head to look. "You're right." Watching the other building made her feel instantly unsteady and she held out her hands. "Do you think they all do that?" She actually didn't want to look.

Trik gave her what she thought might be a wicked grin – with a different kind of face it was hard to tell, but she could still recognize the mischievous glint in his eyes. "You mean like this one?"

She gulped, trying to stop herself being sick.

Trik kept going. "I'm sure they're all the same." He glanced downwards. "But maybe in this form, we just don't notice."

He spread his wings wide and tilted his face up to the sun. "You're thinking with your Human brain, Ash. You need to try thinking with your bird brain."

"Like you did when your bird brain almost got you killed?" shot back Ash.

Ezra laughed. Ash and Trik turned their heads in astonishment. Bird laughing sounded *so* wrong. The noise kind of petered out as he became aware of their glares. "Okay, let's not try that again." He shifted his feet on the beam. "We've got more to worry about anyhow."

"Like what?" asked Trik immediately.

A bird swooped past them and they all flinched backwards. The sky was full around them. Flying was the only way to travel here, and being perched on the side of building meant that, at times, they were directly in the path of others.

Ash was struck by how different every bird person was. Then she wanted to shake her head with stupidity. Every person she'd known back on her home planet had been different. Why wouldn't that be exactly the same here?

There were short bird people. Tall bird people. Fat and thin bird people. And the mixtures of plumage and colours were extreme. Some had crests on their heads. Some heads were flat and smooth. Some wings were tipped with a variety of colours, other feathers were short and dull. Wingspans could be giant or so small that Ash wondered how they could fly at all.

She looked downwards and gulped.

"That's what I meant," said Ezra. "How many do you think are down there? Thousands, at least. How on earth are we supposed to find – what was his name?"

"Ruffako," said Ash. The Capurons beneath her were tiny

– like insects – and there were so many of them it was overwhelming, all standing on the surface of the cloud. Every now and then there was a flicker, as one spread their wings and lifted up into the air, but most of the time they seemed to be walking, in a much less awkward way than she had. Ash sighed. "I have absolutely no idea how we're going to find him," she admitted.

"I guess we need to go down there," said Ezra.

"And do what?" asked Trik.

Ash lifted her wing and automatically clenched her hand round a nearby piece of metal. "We need to go where the biggest part of the population is, and hope that he finds us," she said softly. Her eyes were fixed on the scene below. It was so far away the bird people looked like thousands of busy insects. Realizing how high up she was, Ash felt herself sway and Ezra and Trik both made to reach for her.

"I'm fine," she insisted, even though she didn't really feel fine.

"Let's plan," said Ezra decisively. Ash gave him an appreciative look. Whenever they travelled on missions together, as Guardian, they always followed her instructions. But when her head was swimming like this, she was happy for someone else to take charge for once.

She watched Ezra and Trik exchange glances. "It's the altitude," said Trik quickly. "Most times we're this high, we're in a ship."

Of course. Altitude. She hadn't even thought of that.

"What about the market?" asked Trik.

"Or we could try the park," suggested Ezra. "It looks a little less crowded. We might get a better feel for the place and how things function. It's as good a place to plan as any."

"Perfect," said Trik. "Follow me."

He stepped off the beam without a moment's hesitation. It was as if he didn't even remember almost plummeting to his death earlier.

Ash watched as Trik circled beneath her. Ezra had taken off too. In the glinting sunlight his bright blue and green feathers were stunning. Ash inhaled deeply and took off, spreading her wings wide and letting the air currents take her.

The hardest part about flying around here was the amount of traffic in the sky. What she'd really like to do was close her eyes and just...fly. Let the air rush past her, feeling the wind rippling her feathers. Swoop and soar.

Instead, she had to keep her eyes wide open. But it was kind of weird. It was like there was a strange internal radar in her body. Even though she couldn't believe how close some Capurons came to each other, they never seemed to clash.

And for some reason, neither did she, Ezra or Trik. Her right arm twitched, pitching her lower, as black feathers brushed against her nose.

Her heart started racing. She couldn't quite get her head round it. Sure, the Library had transformed their bodies. They'd all experienced that across the missions. But this time there seemed to be something more. Did the people on

Capuro 12 have something inbuilt in their DNA that stopped them clashing in the sky? Like the programming of some space fighters Ash had heard about?

Either way, as they grew closer and closer to the surface of the cloud, the traffic in the sky around them became even busier.

They landed in what resembled a park – a vast space of cloud-ground with bird people all around who seemed to be relaxing. At least that's what she assumed they were doing, as birds didn't exactly lie down. Instead, they seemed to hunch with their feet hidden and their wings tucked close to their bodies as they chatted in groups.

Ezra and Trik gave a shrug. "Let's copy everyone else and watch for a while. We might be able to learn something and it will give us time to plan."

They moved to a space and hunched down. "Once we've found the tomb, how are we going to move the body and the ship parts?" asked Ash.

"I think we're going to have to find a way to strap them to our bodies," said Trik.

Ezra nodded. "I haven't seen a single type of other transport. Just the slings round the bodies."

Ash groaned. "Please tell me I'm not going to have to strap a dead body next to mine."

"Hey," said Trik brightly. "What do you think that is? Is that like a canteen?"

Of course. Trik was prioritizing his stomach. At least some things didn't change.

They watched. People were crowded around a kind of shack which looked as though a thousand thin strands of metal had all been woven together to create it. The two bird people inside were handing out long containers of coloured drinks. The three of them watched as the people dipped their beaks into the top of the clear containers and the level of the coloured fluid seemed to mysteriously go down.

"You think it's some kind of suction?" asked Ash. She was fascinated. Even more so when, before their eyes, the long containers seemed to vanish as soon as the liquid had been drained.

"What on earth?" said Ezra.

"What do you think's in the bowls?" asked Trik.

Ash turned for another look. She hadn't noticed the bowls. But they seemed to be widely dispersed from the shack too.

As they watched, a very small bird – a child? – dropped one of the bowls and a whole variety of insects scuttled from it. All three of them jerked backwards.

"Urgh." Trik gave a shudder.

The kid tipped back their head and let out what must have been the bird equivalent of a wail. A few of the adult birds turned around and another bowl was quickly pushed towards the child's hands. She tottled off, beak in bowl.

"I'd like to give one of those drinks a try," said Trik. He turned to them both. "We're here. Why not?"

"Bugs," Ash and Ezra answered simultaneously.

"No one is asking you to eat bugs." Trik stood up. "And it

might help us to blend in while we try to find a lead on our Friend. Pick a colour," he said with healthy determination.

"Blue," said Ezra.

Ash looked down at her belly. "Yellow," she replied. "Might as well try and keep with the colour scheme."

"Look out for anyone that might have some bit of metal on them. Anything that looks like Ash's bangle." Trik walked easily over to the shack and waited his turn. It seemed that the Library had given them some kind of currency, which Trik found in his sling and handed over.

He came back carrying three long containers. One blue, one orange and one yellow. He handed them out and hunched back down next to them.

For a few moments, they all just stared at the liquids in front of them.

"Okay," said Trik hesitantly. "I'll go first."

Ash and Ezra watched as Trik stuck his beak into the top of the tube.

Nothing happened.

Trik wiggled his beak. Still nothing happened.

He pulled back making an exasperated noise. "What am I doing wrong?"

"Can I help you with that?" came a deep voice. They all started as a dark figure completely blocked out the sun and cast a shadow over them.

CHAPTER ELEVEN

Ash squinted up. The sun was bright and although she could see the large bird figure, she couldn't make out any of its facial features because of the background glare. But the voice was distinctly male.

The figure hunched down in front of them. Now she could see properly. His plumage was glossy black, with the tips of his wings scarlet. But it was his size that made him most impressive – even a bit intimidating.

"Why do you think we need some help?" she asked in as light a voice as she could.

"Because I think you might not be from around these parts."

His eyes were the blackest she'd ever seen. Unnerving. But there was a softness to his tone.

"Why do you say that?" Trik's voice was wary.

"Maybe I've got it wrong. I received a message to look out for someone, but I was only expecting one..." He looked them up and down. "Capuron." He spoke the last word carefully.

The trio glanced at each other.

"Does this mean anything to you?" replied the stranger. He stood up, turned round and spread his wings wide. It took a moment for her to see it. A moment to realize there was something different in among the glossy, black feathers. One wasn't identical to the others. One was made entirely of metal – a dull, familiar metal.

"Ruffako?" breathed Ash.

He tucked his wings in and spun round. "Guardian?"

"Yes," replied Ash in a quiet voice.

Ruffako lowered himself back down.

"Wow," breathed Ash, her eyes still fixed on the metal feather that now glinted among Ruffako's plumage. "How did that get there?"

Ruffako gave a nod to her enquiry. "The metal was implanted into my body as a chick; it melds with the body and grows like any other feather. It just never falls out. It's happened in my family for generations."

Ash nodded in fascination.

"I plan to do the same with my child," he added. "But now it seems I might not need to." He tilted his head a little to the side. "The Guardian only ever visits somewhere once, don't you?"

Ash was surprised. No one had ever asked her that question before. "I haven't visited anywhere more than once so far," she said carefully. "But that doesn't mean it might not happen in the future." She wasn't entirely sure what the rules were. She'd have to ask Vedis when she got back.

"How did you know it was us?" asked Ezra. "There are thousands of people around."

Ruffako gave a smile and pointed his finger to his head. "Messed up sonars. It happens to all of us every now and then, but three together?"

"Wait, what? We have sonars?" It sort of made sense to her. "But how do you know ours are messed up?"

"Because I can hear it," said Ruffako simply. "Every Capuron has a sonar. You were in the air a little while ago, and I could hear your sonars – almost panicking."

Trik looked around the park. "Can everyone hear them?"

"Of course not," said Ruffako, shaking his head. "It's my family gift. I'm sure that's why we were picked as the Friend. Don't you have sonars on your planet?"

"Eh…" Ash wasn't quite sure how to answer. "Tell me more about this gift."

"There are only a few people like us on the entire planet. I can hear when someone's sonar gets messed up. It's generally because someone is very sick, or if they've been injured. Sonars self-heal."

"So, what did you hear from us?" asked Ezra.

Ruffako made a snorting kind of sound. "Just jumble," he said. "Craziness. That, and the fact you can't seem to drink from our tubes, made me assume the Guardian was here."

Relief was sweeping over Ash. They'd found the Friend. The million questions she had in her mind might actually now get answered. After Vedis's criticisms, she wanted to succeed at this mission, particularly after failing on the last one. Hopefully they had a chance of completing this task. "It's a pleasure to meet you, Ruffako," she said. "I'm Ash, the Guardian, and these are my colleagues, Trik and Ezra."

Ruffako gave a nod of his head. He waved his wing. "How about I start by showing you how to drink from our tubes. You must use something different on your planet."

Trik opened his beak to speak but Ash gave him a hard stare. "Yes please," she replied.

Ruffako moved over to the shack and came back with a tube of bright green liquid. "It's simple, put your beak inside, open until both parts connect with the edge of the tube and then inhale."

He demonstrated and, in an instant, the bright green liquid drained and the tube vanished. Except it didn't really vanish. Now they were close, they could see it actually collapsed in the blink of an eye, ending in something that resembled a small coin.

"Amazing," breathed Ash, her brain trying to fathom the science of it all.

"Go ahead," said Ruffako encouragingly.

Trik and Ezra bent their heads, Ash a little more hesitantly. Before she'd even managed to touch both sides of the tube, Trik was coughing and choking. She wanted to slap his back with her hand but wasn't quite sure it would have the required effect. When he finally stopped, he looked over at her, his eyes streaming.

"I guess the word 'inhale' translated more literally than it meant to."

"Let me try," she said carefully. It was an odd sensation, because there didn't seem to be any nerves in her beak. So, when she opened her beak, she could only tell it was pressing on each side of the tube because it couldn't open any further. She attempted to shut off her brain, which was telling herself not to breathe in.

She concentrated, and sucked. The chilly liquid slid into her mouth and down her throat. It was the oddest sensation, because she wasn't consciously swallowing. After a few moments she closed her beak and allowed herself to breathe.

"What did it taste like?" asked Trik.

Taste? She laughed. "I was thinking so much about not choking that I didn't even notice! Give me a minute."

Ezra lifted his head from his orange glass. "Sweet," he said, giving his head a quick shake. "Very, very sweet."

Ash bent and tried again. This time as the yellow liquid entered her mouth she noticed a definite taste. She couldn't quite put her finger on it. "Cool," she said, even though she knew that wasn't a usual description. "Cool, with a tiny sharp bite."

Trik bent his head and tried his blue liquid again. This time he got the technique right. When he lifted his head, he looked puzzled. "Fresh," he said finally. And Ash got it. It wasn't like drinking water. Because there was something else to it. They just didn't have a taste similar enough to use as a description.

"Are you still drinking out of bowls back home?" asked Ruffako. "How can that be when the Guardian clearly has more technology than us?"

Ash spoke quickly. "I think our technologies have just moved in different directions." She looked around at the busy park. "We really need to talk. I need your help in order to fulfil the mission for the Library."

"What is the Library?" asked Ruffako. He waved a wing again, the scarlet tips catching admiring glances from others around the park area.

It seemed an odd question from someone who had come from a generational family of Friends. But Ash had no idea how the message had been passed along over the years. It wouldn't be the first time that some information had been lost in translation.

"What did your family tell you?" she enquired gently.

"That our Capuron ancestors created our world," Ruffako said proudly, his chest puffing out. "Also that one of them lived in a special place which gathered special objects, and their descendant would return one day to our planet. My family line was chosen to aid the descendant – the Guardian – on their return."

He shook his head.

"I never understood why that wouldn't be a day for a huge celebration. The descendant of the first person to leave our planet and return should surely be celebrated?"

"Ahh," said Ash carefully. This was clearly going to be more complicated than they'd initially thought. "We can talk

160

about this later," she said. "First, there are some places I'd like to see on this planet. Would you be able to show me the dead lands?"

Ruffako stood up proudly. "Of course. But why would you want to go to the dead lands? No one goes there."

A few heads turned towards him and Ash cringed. "Let's talk and fly," she replied, with more assurance than she felt.

Ruffako hesitated. "You want to go now?"

She tried to make her eyes smile, since her beak couldn't. "No time like the present."

CHAPTER TWELVE

Ash was trying to make sense of the situation on Capuron. It wasn't the Library's fault that family messages about the Guardian had changed over hundreds of years. But she wondered if Ruffako was ready for the information he was about to receive. He'd practically puffed up when he'd mentioned his ancestors. How would he feel when he found out his ancestry was entirely different to what he imagined?

This was the problem sometimes – the Library looked at planets and populations, not individuals. And individuals had diverse thinking, all over the universe. Ash felt certain there would be some bird people who'd welcome the discovery and some who would hate it. But the tiny feathers round her neck prickled. What if Ruffako was one of the ones who hated it?

They took off into the sky. Ezra flew alongside Ruffako and she could see him making an attempt at conversation. It was clear Ruffako wasn't happy though. Ash wanted to get a better look at the site, then return to the clouds to make plans to transport the body and equipment. First she needed to make sure the gadgets the Library had given her would work. She'd hate to get all the artefacts down there only to be met with a rock face that wouldn't move.

Ezra turned his head back towards Ash and Trik, then dropped back. "The journey might be a bit longer than we expected."

Ash nodded. She knew the Library would have landed them as near to the cave as possible, but her wings were aching already from the unfamiliar movements.

Their journey was mainly in a downwards direction, but it seemed that Ruffako might be taking them on a scenic route. He gestured with his head to one point. "We can't fly too close to the ground here. Toxic gases."

Ash's automatic reaction was to try and hold her breath, but that was hardly going to work. The group moved slightly higher into the atmosphere again while the smooth ground beneath them slipped past, unchanging.

Eventually Ruffako swooped low at some grey cliffs. The cliff face was rugged, and there was a large collection of rocks strewn across the floor of the valley below.

Ruffako circled for a moment and then gestured for them to alight on the rocks. The surrounding land was odd. Dry, brown and arid looking in parts, without even a patch of moss or any signs of vegetation, and gloopy and swampy in others. There were even a few bubbles breaking on the surface of the dark sludge.

He tucked his wings behind him. "These are the dead lands. Try and walk on that surface and that's exactly how you'll end up – dead. Nothing survives in among the quicksand and marshes. Even these rocks will eventually disintegrate."

Trik gave a cough. There was a noxious smell in the air around them. Ash nodded solemnly and looked up at the cliff face. The entrance had to be somewhere up there. It took a moment to extract one of the scanners from the sling across her body.

"What's that?" asked Ruffako. He seemed impatient.

"Give me a minute," said Ash, as she switched on the scanner and swept the rock face above her, hoping it would activate and unseal the entrance of the cave. After a few seconds there was a shuffling noise, followed by a trickle of small stones raining down on them.

"Into the air!" yelled Ezra, his bright-blue wings spreading rapidly.

Everything happened so quickly. They'd just lifted from the rock as there was a huge ripping sound above them. Part of the cliff face was moving – detaching itself. As they hovered in the air, a part of the rock started to slide back, except it didn't happen in a smooth controlled manner. Maybe it had been too long. Maybe the technology didn't match up? But there was a sharp crack, and the rock that was apparently sliding back jolted, then crashed down the cliff, landing in the exact spot they had all been standing a few seconds earlier.

Ruffako spun in the air. "What did you do?" he asked, his voice full of horror.

As a cloud of dust blew up around them, Trik darted down to the opening in the cliff. Within a moment he shouted back up. "It's here! Come down."

The tomb cave was wide. With the stone gone, they could all land easily at the entrance. The air was stale and Ash choked a little.

Ruffako seemed shocked by the instant destruction. "What did you do? What was that thing?"

Ash glanced at the gadget still in her hand. She chose her words carefully. "It's a device from the Library. We knew we needed access to the cave in this rock face. Its purpose was to move the rock."

Ruffako shook his head and stared into the space. Even though it hadn't seen daylight in hundreds or thousands of years, it was clear the cave had been in use at some point. There were marks. Signs of habitation. A few small pieces of metal – obviously debris left behind from the spacecraft that crashed here when beings arrived on the planet. Once they added the pieces they had brought from the Library, the whole scene would remain perfectly preserved in here, safe from the dead lands, until the Capurons found it – because it would be Ruffako's job to tell them of the discovery.

"I don't understand," said Ruffako. "What is meant to be here?"

"A whole new world," said Ash quietly.

Trik and Ezra edged closer. It was like they could sense the tension in the air.

"The Library removed artefacts that were hidden in this cave thousands of years ago. Artefacts that it thought the people on this planet weren't ready to see or understand." Right now, Ash wanted to lick her lips. Her mouth had turned dry, but licking her beak didn't quite have the same effect.

"Now, it's time. Time for the Library to return what it took. Your planet has evolved. Your people have evolved. They are at a stage in their understanding where they will be able to embrace what they learn, and use it to their advantage."

Ruffako's eyes narrowed. He looked around himself again. "So, these artefacts. What are they? Where are they? Do you have some device that will just magic them back here?"

Ash shook her head. "I wish. No. We have stored the artefacts up in one of the clouds, covered by an invisibility shield to keep them safe. Their size makes them awkward to manoeuvre. How do you move large objects on the planet right now? We haven't really seen any transport system."

Ruffako made a scoffing noise and spread out his wings. "Why have a transport system when you have these. You mean, you find another way to move about your planet other than wings? What would be the point?"

Ash pulled a face. "To move large objects?" she repeated.

"What about the buildings and large structures in the cities on the clouds? How did you get all the materials there?" asked Trik.

It was honestly like Ruffako had never considered the concept. "We fly them in, bit by bit. Build them together. Construction complete."

In her head, Ash could remember birds from back on her own planet, gathering twigs one at a time to thread into a nest. She'd never imagined that whole cities here had been built the same way. One strand of metal at a time...

"What about the beams?" she asked. "The ones at the edge of the building. They must be more difficult to transport."

"Why would they be difficult? They weigh barely more than a few feathers," said Ruffako.

It was clear they were getting nowhere with this conversation.

"Our artefacts might be heavier than that," she said simply. "We're just wondering the best way to get them down here."

"You can't use the bangle?" asked Ezra. "Maybe now the cave is open and you know exactly where it is you're going..." His voice tailed off as they all looked at each other.

She shook her head. "No matter how much I concentrate, I'm not sure I can entirely rely on it. What if we end up on the land underneath – the dead lands?"

Both Ezra and Trik looked outside at the bleak flat landscape. If they hadn't known any better, they might have attempted to land there, thinking it was entirely solid and completely safe.

"You're right," said Trik. "It's too risky. We have to carry the artefacts. Maybe we'll have to make a few journeys."

"Do you think there'll be enough time to do that today?" asked Ezra. "We don't know when the sun sets around here. I'd hate to fly in the dark."

Ruffako gave them all a strange glance. "But you have sonars. The dark doesn't matter. Your sonars seem to have settled now. You will automatically know if you are about to fly into something."

"Let's give it a try," said Ash quickly. "Maybe if Ruffako can see the size of our objects, he can give us some suggestions on how to move them."

"Let's fly back. I think I can remember where we left everything," said Trik. His eyes twinkled. "Nothing like falling off a cloud to imprint it in your memory."

Ash nodded and they took off before Ruffako could ask more questions.

The journey was long and when they first set down on the slightly damp cloud, Ash wasn't entirely sure they were in the right place. But Trik was confident.

"Wave the sensor, remove the invisibility cloaking," he said, and she did.

"Wow." Ezra leaped forward. The artefacts were now teetering at the very edge of the cloud. They'd moved, and one of the large pieces of ship was at a dangerous tilt, ready to fall.

Ezra grabbed the end and leaned back, tipping it away from the edge.

"But how…?" asked Ash as she stared in bewilderment.

Trik moved closer. "Clouds move, don't they? Constantly transform."

"But how do the cities stay in one place? Why don't they collapse?"

Ruffako was staring at the sheets of metal from the wrecked spaceship, along with a few component parts. The metal was clearly different from any he'd seen before. The control panels and technology confused him, but as his eyes fell on the closely wrapped body he shivered. "What is that?"

"It's one of the artefacts. Part of what we need to transport."

Ruffako turned from the body and moved to the metal. He tried to pick up a part and blanched at its weight. "Why would anyone use this for construction? It's way too heavy."

Ash nodded. "You're right. But this is what we have to move."

"Give me a moment," said Ruffako, and he took off into the sky.

They all stood and stared at each other.

"Do you trust him?" asked Ezra. "He seems a bit… hostile."

"I get that vibe too," said Trik.

"He has a role," said Ash, as if she were trying to convince herself. "He's the designated Friend. He should assist. He should help."

"He also has the power of free will. Not everyone is such a good Friend as Amara, are they? What about our little

Reker, back on Quisquilla? Maybe the Library hasn't experienced Friends that don't want to be Friends before."

Ash groaned. "Oh, so it's me, is it? Thousands of years have passed with hundreds of different Guardians, and I'm the first to come across the rebel kind of Friends. Guess I'm just lucky then."

"What if it's one of the other things the Library has chosen to keep quiet about?" suggested Ezra. "We have to ask Vedis when we get back. Our trouble is we've only concentrated on our own missions. We haven't looked back at any that came before us."

That hadn't even occurred to Ash. Of course! She hadn't really had time to look back on past missions – or find out if it was even possible. She'd been too busy getting her head round her own. Maybe that was something to consider – but it didn't help her in the here and now.

A speck appeared in the distance, black with distinguishable red tips on the wings. Ruffako was trailing something behind him as he flew; it fluttered in the strong winds. He landed beside them and untangled the items from his foot, dumping them on the cloud ground in front of them.

"Here. Tagoras. The only things we have for transporting larger items."

It looked like a giant harness made of some lightweight material. Ash gave it a tug. "Is this strong? I'd hate for the metal to punch a hole in it."

"It's as strong as we've got," said Ruffako bluntly. It was clear he still wasn't entirely happy.

"Let me give it a shot," said Trik as he picked up one end and shot Ruffako a suspicious glance.

Ezra grabbed the other end and between them they wrestled it around the largest remnant of the spaceship. The material was an open weave, but as they pulled it around, it clearly had some stretch.

At either end, Trik and Ezra tried to lift the artefact between them. It was still a bit of a struggle.

"How do we fly with this?" asked Ash.

Ruffako plucked one end from Trik's grasp. "You wear it like this, on either side." He slung part of the harness across his body and pulled a strap to hold it tight. If he noticed the weight of the artefact, he didn't say anything.

Ash gave a small gulp. "Ezra, do you think you can manage the other side?"

She could tell Trik was annoyed. But the truth was Ezra's frame on this planet seemed more muscular – it looked as if he were more likely to be able to bear the weight.

Ezra positioned the harness, giving it a good tug to yank it into position. It was the oddest image – two giant bird people with a large piece of metal slung in a harness between them.

"Should be good," Ezra said with another tug. His voice didn't sound entirely convincing.

Ash glanced around and picked up the other harness. "Will we try this one with…" – she nearly said "the body" but stopped herself just in time – "with this artefact," she said to Trik.

The body would be much lighter, at least. She wasn't quite sure that they would have been able to manage the spaceship part.

Ash and Trik pulled the tagoras round the body, both slightly averting their eyes. It was still a bit weird being so close to a body that had been dead and preserved for thousands of years. Trik gave a visible shudder, then looked over at Ruffako.

"Any hints for how to fly in unison?"

"Don't get left behind," said Ruffako, as he lifted into the air. Ezra was shocked for the briefest of seconds before flapping strongly to keep in time. Flying in unison was important. Flying underneath, or behind, would mean getting left with most of the weight.

Ash took a deep breath. "We can do this. We can do this," she said quietly.

"Are you trying to convince me, or you?" quipped Trik. He'd bent his wings and Ash thought that if he were in his Human form, he'd currently have his hands on his hips and likely his eyebrows raised.

She shook her head. "Let's get this over with. Ready?"

He nodded.

"One, two, three…"

After a momentary false start, they took off into the sky. Flying in unison was harder than Ash could ever have imagined. Every extra flap of a wing took one of them in front. And because the body was an average size, their wings kept clashing in the middle and throwing them off balance.

"Steady!" Trik shouted at one point.

After a few clashes, he looked over at her. "Should we try and fly faster – get this over and done with?"

They'd started at a steady pace. They knew the site was some distance away, and to be truthful, the sooner they got there, the better.

"Let's give it a try." Ash nodded in agreement.

They did their best to speed up and cover the distance more quickly. Ezra and Ruffako were already spots in the distance. The traffic in the sky around them was busy. There were so many different flashes of colour. At first, her yellow plumage had seemed a bit conspicuous to Ash, but it was apparent she was only one of thousands.

Every now and then – as a flash of gold went past, or a streak of silver – Trik muttered, "Why couldn't I have got that?"

"Next time," Ash reassured him, even though they both knew they had absolutely no control over what appearance the Library gave them, and they would probably never revisit Capuron.

Sweat was beginning to pour from Ash, and the heat from the sun above, coupled with the exercise, made her dehydrated. She should probably have attempted to drink more earlier. They all should have.

There was still another journey to make after this, to fetch the last bit of the ship.

Ash was starting to tire. She normally considered herself fit, but her wings were beginning to ache. "How you doing?" she yelled to Trik.

He rolled his head – "No problem" – then made a choking sound. "Who knew that being a bird was such hard work!"

They both started laughing, meaning their wings went out of sync and the body seemed to twist and turn in the harness.

"Eeek!"

Ash's automatic reaction was to reach out her hand and grab it to try and steady things. But her hand was attached to a wing, which meant she sent them careening off to one side.

"Pay attention, Ink!"

Trik's shout made her head shoot back up and focus on what lay ahead. Ink. Her call sign. The thing she'd always longed for, as a kid who wanted to be a fighter pilot. When she'd failed the final test at the Academy, Ash had thought she'd never have one. But when her friends had joined her on the battle to save the Library, they'd given her a call sign. Ink – after her village back home, Inkosata.

"Pay attention yourself, Punk!" she yelled back, reverting to his call sign too.

"After all this, you owe me a drink," Trik replied. His feathers were as damp as hers.

"I owe you more than one," she agreed.

Finally, the cliffs were in sight. For the whole journey they hadn't caught sight of Ezra and Ruffako again, and as the pair landed breathless and tired in the cave, they could tell immediately that the situation was tense.

Ezra and Ruffako were glaring at each other. The panel of metal was sitting in the corner, the tagoras lying carelessly on the floor of the cave.

"Everything okay?" asked Ash, as brightly as she could while trying to catch her breath.

"What is that?" snapped Ruffako, pointing to the metal. She knew automatically that they'd had some time to kill waiting for Ash and Trik to arrive. From his tone of voice she guessed Ruffako had been demanding answers for a while, and Ezra had probably been avoiding giving any. If she'd thought beforehand, she might have done things differently.

"It's part of a ship," she said carefully.

"A ship? What's a ship?"

"It's a mode of transport."

"Metal is a mode of transport?" He moved over, reaching out his large hand and pressing parts of the panel. "And these, what do these do?"

She touched her hand against his. "Why don't you and I go and get the last piece, and then I can explain it to you before we leave?"

Trik jumped in. "You're exhausted. You won't be able to take the weight."

"It will be fine," she said in a determined voice. Somehow, Ash knew she needed some time alone with Ruffako, to try and make this whole process easier on him.

Ezra stepped forward. "Let me." He looked at Ruffako. "We managed before, we can manage again."

There was hostility in his voice – so unlike Ezra. What had gone down between them?

"It will be fine," Ash said, keeping her voice steady.

175

"I'm the Guardian, and Ruffako is the Friend of the Library. It's right that we do this final part together."

She could tell exactly how uncomfortable Trik and Ezra were.

"You two wait here." She didn't add the words, *We can transport straight back*, but they knew exactly what she was implying.

"Come on then," said Ruffako grudgingly.

The absolute last thing Ash wanted to do right now was fly back to the city and then back to the dead lands again. She didn't even know if her wings could take it. But what was the alternative? All the artefacts needed to be returned to the cave. And part of Ash worried that Ruffako might destroy them in a fit of rage if she actually told him what they were right now. She had to try and prepare him a little.

"Let's go," she said as she stepped off the edge and out into the light.

CHAPTER THIRTEEN

Ash did her best to ignore the ache in her wings, her parched throat and the sweat that almost immediately seemed to stream down her back.

"Thank you so much for your assistance today," she said to Ruffako. It was difficult to get close enough to him to speak, his wing span was so broad.

He gave a grunt in response. "Save your energy," he muttered. "You're going to need it."

As they flew, she tried to start a conversation a few more times, but each time he either gave one-word answers or ignored Ash completely. Every part of her was aching. She actually looked down a few times, wondering if there was somewhere they could stop and rest, but for the longest spell there was only the toxic wasteland beneath them.

This time as they climbed, she saw the structure beneath the cloud city. An enormous column, rooted in the ground and made from a strange copper coloured metal, supported the city. The material seemed a little familiar.

"What is that?" she asked.

"The anchor," said Ruffako gruffly.

"What metal is it made from?"

There was a long silence. Eventually he spoke. "No one really knows. How to make that metal has been lost through time. Today's scientists are unsure how it was originally formed. All that matters is that the dead lands don't seem to affect it. There's no corrosion. They're constantly trying to find ways to replicate it."

Ash squinted at the impressive structure. Because it was in constant shadow beneath the cloud, it was difficult to get a good look at any particular element of it. But as they flew past, a tiny chink appeared in the cloud and a ray of sunlight hit the column. It was only for the briefest of seconds, but it told her what she needed to know.

The column was constructed from the same heavy metal as the spaceship!

Her heart was racing. This was good. At least, it felt good. Maybe that's how she'd start the conversation with Ruffako, to try and get him onside.

They pushed up through some smaller clouds. Ash struggled to rely solely on the inbuilt sonar inside her, instead of relying on her eyes. She constantly worried she would crash straight into something nestled among the clouds. But eventually they landed near the last piece of spaceship.

"That didn't seem quite so long," she sighed. Her body automatically huddled down as soon as they stopped.

Muscles that she'd never had before ached. Ash wasn't sure how this would translate to her Human body when they transported back.

"I took a shortcut," said Ruffako. "No one is supposed to fly near to the anchor, but you looked as if you wouldn't make it otherwise. Wait here."

Ash took a deep breath as sweat ran down her beak and landed on her clawed feet. Weren't birds supposed to be waterproof? It didn't feel like it. Her feathers seemed ten times heavier than before.

Ruffako reappeared, clutching four different drinking tubes. "Here," he said, thrusting two towards her.

This time Ash needed no instruction in how to drink. She finished both tubes in seconds and gave a grateful sigh. "Thank you."

Ash glimpsed the metal at her side and her stomach clenched as she wondered how she would have the strength to carry it back.

Ruffako was already making preparations, slinging the tagoras round it. He stood, with an impatient air, waiting for her to attach her side.

But Ash waited. She needed to have some kind of conversation with him.

It felt ill-judged. It felt ill-timed. But also seemed entirely necessary.

"I wonder," she said slowly, "if you've noticed any similarities between the metal we're about to move and the metal beneath us."

Ruffako gave a snort – she wasn't quite sure how someone with a beak managed that – but then there was silence. It was clear he hadn't considered this.

"You said you were bringing something back to us that had been hidden in a cave on our planet. How can that be the same metal as our anchor? What would be the point of hiding metal that we all see every day?"

She moved over and lifted her side of the harness, doing her best to slide it over her head without wincing at the weight.

"But you've never tried to lift the anchor," she said carefully. "The metals that you use here are very lightweight. The whole purpose of an anchor is to hold something in place. Just like the one underneath the city. There has to be weight to it."

She had an odd feeling. Or maybe it had always been there. A slightly ominous sensation around Ruffako that she was now paying heed to. He wasn't just grumpy. He was angry, and she was starting to wonder what that could mean for her. Ash had wanted to speak to him away from Ezra and Trik, but her team was important to her. They had her back. Always. And right now, she felt as if she needed that. The conversation she'd planned could wait until she was back with her team.

"Let's get it back to the cave and then we can talk further."

The Capuron didn't even speak, just took off.

The harness yanked at Ash's whole body, almost pulling her clean off her feet. Her wings started flapping frantically in an attempt to keep up.

Within minutes she was panting. "You'll need to slow down," she yelled, with what little breath she had left.

Ruffako shot a glare over his shoulder. It was almost as if he were doing this on purpose. Had he been like this with Ezra? Perhaps this was why the atmosphere between those two had been so tense.

No matter how much she tried to flap her wings, there was no way Ash could keep up. She was constantly being dragged behind and finding herself with the bigger proportion of weight. At this rate, she might not survive this assignment. Dropping down onto the dead lands below was feeling more and more like a better option.

"Ruffako, you need to slow down." Her voice came out like a croak.

"I would rather get this over and done with."

Ash cringed. What was it with her Friends lately? First, they'd had Reker, the Friend who didn't want to be a friend, and now Ash was having the same issue with Ruffako.

"I would rather get there alive," she shot back. "Isn't your lifelong instruction to assist the Guardian?"

She'd never had to shame a Friend into helping her before. It felt like a low blow. The trouble was, Ash had a feeling she was about to upset him more. Thankfully, for the rest of the journey, he slowed down.

At last they reached the cave. Trik and Ezra were standing anxiously in the entrance, peering up into the sky. They moved back in relief as Ash collapsed to the floor. She'd never been so glad to see them in her life.

They both grabbed the artefact and removed it from the tagoras.

Ruffako was already pacing. Ash slid over and rested against the wall. When they got back to the Library, she was going to bed for the next five days.

Trik kneeled in front of her. "Would you like me to do this?"

Part of her really, really wanted to say yes. But Trik and Ezra hadn't been chosen as Guardian. Ash had. This was her job, not theirs.

She'd love to just jump away from all this. But her own rule was *Do no harm*, and jumping away and leaving Ruffako angry and confused could mean returning the artefacts caused more harm than good. That was never the purpose of the Library.

Ash shook her head and thought about getting back up, but as she pushed one wing against the floor, she instantly changed her mind.

"Ruffako," she said, in as composed a voice as she could. She pulled the other sensor from her own small harness and pointed it at the body, releasing the force field round it.

It buzzed and hovered for a second, just above the ground, before gently resting down.

To Ash, it had always been obvious that the wrappings concealed a body. But for Ruffako the realization was slower, probably because he'd never seen a body without wings before. She slowly pulled the wrappings back.

"Is that…"

"Yes," she said quickly.

"But where are the wings? Did someone remove them?" He looked horrified at the prospect.

"No," she said with a deep breath. "This person never had wings."

Silence echoed around the cave. Trik and Ezra exchanged glances.

"But…how…how can that be? Someone without wings…" He shook his head. "That's not possible. An injury. It must have been some kind of accident."

Ash shook her head. "There was no injury. This person was one of the original people on this planet. He helped the travellers who arrived here."

Ruffako was still shaking his head. "What are you talking about? This makes no sense." His gaze narrowed. "We've never let ships land here. We've always turned them away. We've always wanted to achieve success through our own accomplishments. We don't want outside interference."

She held out her hands, extending her wings again and instantly regretting that action. "The metal. The metal we've transported came from a spaceship. Thousands of years ago, a spaceship landed and was stranded on this planet. The people here," she paused for a second, "were welcoming. The strangers didn't look like them, though. They looked," she met his gaze, "more like you."

Ash kept going. "The land wasn't always like it is now. Once, people lived on the ground. The cloud cities weren't developed until after the spacecraft landed and the people from the craft," she paused, trying to think of a suitable word, "*bonded* with the people on the planet. The original species who landed in that ship were called Pluzons. Their own planet is light years away from Capuro 12."

"This story is rubbish!" Ruffako shouted. "We've always lived in the clouds. That's how we are. That's how we've always been. What is this bed of lies that you are trying to throw at me?"

Ruffako was still shaking his head. She could almost see his pent-up rage rising like a pressure gauge.

His wings swept outwards, blocking out part of the sunlight filtering into the cave as he towered over Ash.

"Enough! Enough of your lies!" Within the blink of an eye his hand was round her throat and she was pinned to the wall. She couldn't speak or breathe. Her hands and wings flapped uselessly and her legs dangled above the ground, failing to make purchase.

She heard a noise to her right. There was a flash of blue. Ezra darted from the back of the tomb, running straight into the side of Ruffako, his body weight and momentum knocking the Capuron from his clawed feet and sending both of them rolling towards the entrance.

Ash fell forward, her body gasping for air.

Ezra was throwing punches, using the muscle the Library had provided in his transformed state to the best of his ability. Ash watched, hardly able to think, as he headbutted Ruffako then used his sharp-tipped beak to tear some feathers from the side of the bird man's head.

Ruffako was no lightweight. He was pure strength and muscle, but Ezra had caught him completely off balance and was fighting as if he were four Capurons instead of one. Ezra had told Ash before that the place where he'd grown up on Hakora had been rough. Trik had said the same. Both of them had talked frequently about all the fights they'd been in as kids. Now it was clear that no matter what form he was in, the memory of how to win a fight was still there.

Ash was still struggling to steady her breathing. Trik glanced between her and the fighting duo, clearly trying to decide who to prioritize.

Ash shook her head. She didn't want him to join the fight.

But Trik ran forward, fists clenched. "GO!" he yelled to Ash. "Just go, you have to stay safe!"

She could see the panic in his eyes as he threw himself into the fight.

"No," she croaked.

"There's only one Guardian and that's you," Trik yelled over his shoulder. It was clear that he and Ezra were having real problems keeping Ruffako on the ground. The Capuron hadn't managed to get back upright yet, but it was only a matter of time. And he still looked furious – if he got free, chances were he would come for Ash again. Should she actually twist the bangle and get out of here?

The thought was in her brain for the briefest of moments. Leave Trik and Ezra behind? Ash couldn't even contemplate it. Not even if she thought she might come to harm. She could never leave one of her teammates behind.

There was a deep throated yell. Ezra kicked out at Ruffako with his clawed feet, the force sending Ezra flat onto his own back and Trik, who was caught in the momentum, to his knees.

It carried Ruffako straight out of the cave entrance and tumbling over the edge of the cliff.

"No!" screamed Ash.

Falling to the dead lands meant death. Trik jumped up and ran forward, peering over the edge, then dropping down to his belly. Ezra was still on the ground. By the time Ash had got herself together, still coughing and spluttering, and limped towards the edge, Trik was extending his hand and wing out to the dark figure of Ruffako beneath.

One wing had caught and twisted as he had fallen. Right now, the Capuron was dangling from the cliffs. As Ash looked closer, she could see that his metal feather – the one that signified him as Friend – was stuck fast between two rocks. It was the only thing saving him from the dead lands far beneath him. But even if he pushed off into mid-air – with one broken wing, Ash didn't have any confidence he'd be able to gain enough height before gravity took hold and plummeted him to the ground.

"Don't move, don't struggle," she yelled down.

As she watched, a few of his black feathers which were caught alongside the metal one fluttered to the ground. They landed below, staying visible for the briefest of seconds before they seemed to be absorbed into the toxic earth. Ash shuddered. She didn't want that to happen to Ruffako, even if he had just grabbed her by the throat.

So many people had been negatively affected by the group's missions recently. Reker, Lucia and now Ruffako. Or maybe other beings were always affected by the missions, and it had just taken Ash some time to realize it. The responsibility of being Guardian weighed heavy on her.

Ezra stumbled over, looked down and shook his head. She could tell that the last thing he wanted to do was help Ruffako, but he lay down next to Trik and stretched out his hand and wing.

"I'm not close enough," whispered Trik. "I can't get hold of him."

Ezra shook his head. "Me neither. How can we do this?"

Ruffako had stopped moving. His whole body and other arm were left dangling in mid-air. His hand with the damaged wing was resting against part of the rock face which was completely flat. There was nothing for him to grab hold of.

Before they could think about anything else, Trik jumped up. "You and me," he said to Ezra.

Ezra looked at him in bewilderment. "You and me, what?"

"Grab the tagoras."

Ash started to think hard. She walked over and lifted the tagoras from the cave floor, while Ezra got to his feet again.

Trik reached out. "Take one end each. We can fly down and hover below while Ash tries to free his feather from the rock face, above. If he falls, we have the tagoras between us. We can catch him before he hits the ground."

Ezra paused for a moment then gave a slow nod. "Wouldn't it be easier just to try and manoeuvre him into the tagoras?"

"In mid-air? With you and me trying not to drop like stones ourselves?"

"I could do that," said Ash quickly.

"No," they both answered in unison.

Trik shook his head. "You've just flown the farthest of any of us. You've no strength left and if he falls the wrong way and misses the tagoras, he could take you with him. You wouldn't survive it. If anyone lands in the bad lands it's him, not you. Leave this to me and Ezra."

The two gave each another a nod. Ash's stomach twisted. The plan was reasonable but not foolproof. But every part of her still ached. They were right, if Ruffako's weight landed on Ash as she tried to unjam the metal feather, there would be no chance for her to save herself. She stared down at the bangle on her wrist. And if she died, then she'd leave her two friends here for the rest of their lives.

Ash nodded slowly. She couldn't let that happen.

It had only been a few seconds, but it felt like much longer. Trik and Ezra moved swiftly, scrambling the tagoras over their shoulders, the giant sling hanging between them. They took off in an uncoordinated sort of unison that on any other occasion might have made Ash laugh. Ruffako was still dangling precariously, having realized that any kind of struggle could dislodge him onto the toxic ground below. Any second now, the jammed feather could free itself. He had a look of panic in his eyes as Trik and Ezra flew towards him.

They positioned the tagoras directly under his feet and body. Ezra was closest to the metal feather. "Ready?" he asked.

Trik nodded. Ash could see the look in his eyes. He was bracing himself for the sudden impact of weight.

Ezra put out one hand towards Ruffako and squeezed his shoulder in reassurance as he kept himself hovering in mid-air. He'd adapted to flying so well. Ash could never have mastered that gesture without throwing her whole momentum out of sync.

But Ezra was calm. He lifted one hand, gave a nod, and then brushed the metal feather with the lightest of touches.

It detached instantly.

Ruffako fell straight into the tagoras and both Ezra and Trik fell too, with the impact of the weight. It happened in the blink of an eye. Ash yelped as all three skirted above the surface of the dead lands for the briefest moment. She darted downwards instantly, grabbing the edge of the tagoras and helping to tug it upwards. She wasn't sure if she actually made any difference or not, but recovery was virtually simultaneous – they flapped their wings furiously, lifting back up into the air.

Ash's heart was in her mouth as she saw just how close Ruffako had been to plummeting to his death and taking her friends with him.

As they all landed back in the cave and hunched down in recovery mode, she leaned against the wall and sighed.

There were a few minutes' silence.

Finally, Ruffako straightened back up. "Thank you."

Ezra and Trik gave a nod but didn't reply.

Ruffako took a few steps into the cave next to the artefacts. It crossed Ash's mind that he might pick them up and just hurl them out into the dead lands, to be lost for ever – but he didn't.

Ruffako spoke quietly. "I don't like anything you've told me, Guardian. I'm not sure I quite believe it." He stared at the metal panels again. "A spaceship, from thousands of years ago, changed the life on my planet? It sounds like a story for the young ones."

"You don't need to like it, Ruffako," Ash replied. "You worry about outsiders interfering with your world, but your planet had become poisoned – much like has happened to many others – and it was outsiders that saved your people. The Pluzons brought technology – the metal that you use as your anchors and columns, keeping the cities in the clouds. If they hadn't brought that, and gifted you all the ability to fly, it's likely there would be no life on Capuro 12 now."

Ruffako looked stunned.

"I know it can be difficult to hear something that contradicts what you've been brought up to believe." She looked at Ezra and Trik. "We've experienced that too."

"How?"

"Our planets were at war with another planet in our system. We thought the people from that planet were the bad guys. We believed they attacked without reason. We realized the reasons behind the attack much later. They had good reasons – their planet had been put into an ice age. We just didn't know that to begin with."

"Are you still at war?"

She shook her head. "We found what had been stolen from their planet. We returned it to them. The hardest part was convincing them that we hadn't stolen it in the first place."

"So, they're out of their ice age?"

She shook her head. "Not yet. It will take years. But they know it will happen. They know there is a future on their planet."

Trik took a step forward. "We'd learned to hate them. Even the name of the planet – Corinez – filled us with rage." He bent his wing and put his hand on his chest. "We'd learned wrong. And it's difficult to unlearn something that is so ingrained in us. It takes time. But we have a duty."

"A duty?" Ruffako's voice sounded broken. "A duty to tell others their history is lies?" He gave the impression the Capurons were a proud species, with a strong focus on their independent achievements. This news would undermine that for them.

Ezra spoke up. "It's not lies. It's misunderstood. The history of your planet is wonderful. A stranded spacecraft and welcoming people? The story of first contact on your planet is probably one of the finest in the galaxy! No wars. No destruction.

"Your planet is living in fear right now of something that happened thousands of years ago. Push that fear away. Embrace your history. Look at the technology and learn from it. Maybe your people will want to try space travel. Maybe you'll want to make contact with the Pluzons..."

Ruffako gave a visible shudder and stood up. "I have a lot to think about." He turned to face Ash. "Guardian, I'm sorry I hurt you."

Ash shook her head. "You weren't ready for the news we brought you, and I'm sorry about that. But I think at least some of your fellow citizens might be. Promise me you'll share the news. Promise me you'll let your people understand where the technology for the cloud cities came from."

She reached out her hand and touched Ruffako's.

"You might not like the true history, you might not feel ready for it. But the reason the people on your planet lived and survived is because the Pluzons landed here and your ancestors – like this man – welcomed them." Ash gestured to the body.

Ruffako bowed his head and moved to hunch back down. She knew he needed time. Part of her wanted to stay and make sure he did everything she wanted.

But that wasn't her role. Her role was to return the artefacts. They'd done that. Now it was time to go home.

Home. It was the first time she'd thought of the Library as home. Home had once been Astoria. But Ash had felt more at home at the Star Corporation Academy, in among the stars, than anywhere else. And that's where the Library was – in among the stars.

She moved into the centre of the cave and nodded to Ezra and Trik. "I think it's time for us to go. Ready?"

Neither of them hesitated. They both moved over to her and held onto wing feathers on each side.

"Good luck." Ash nodded to Ruffako as she twisted her bangle and made the three of them disappear.

CHAPTER FOURTEEN

The transition back home was every bit as painful. The first thing Ash saw on arrival was Amara's feet. Ash, Trik and Ezra were all on the floor, collapsed on top of the Proteus circle. Amara fussed around them all. "Are you all okay? Can I do anything?"

Ash went to move and let out a yelp. One moment there was complete relief she was back in her own body, the next, all she could feel was the scream of her muscles.

Ash looked down at her body. She was back in her flight suit, but the arms were pushed up slightly, revealing angry purple welts on the inside of her forearms.

Moving was a slow process for all three of them. Once they were finally on their feet and seated at the table, Ezra stripped off the top half of his flight suit.

"Something doesn't feel right," he muttered.

He slid his arms out, exposing shades of purple across the skin of his inner arms. Trik followed, pulling down his flight suit and revealing just his T-shirt. His dark skin was equally bruised.

Ash nearly didn't want to do the same. She could only imagine, but as she started to tug at her flight suit, Amara yelled, "What happened to your neck?"

Vedis materialized out of nowhere. She touched Ash's chin, tilting it up to see her neck. For the first time Ash saw a flash of concern in the hologram's eyes.

"Extensive bruising, nasty," she said, before running her eyes up and down Ash's body. She turned one of Ash's arms so she could see fully the extent of the damage.

Ash flinched as she ran her fingers lightly down the inside of her own arm. "How exactly did this happen to us all?"

"Flying," said Vedis immediately. "You used muscles that Humans don't have, but the damage still translates back with the transformation." Her usually smooth forehead creased into a frown as she glanced at Ezra and Trik too. "But I have to say, I didn't expect quite such strong residual problems. I assume you all flew extensively?"

"We had to," said Ash. "The tomb was quite far from where we landed. And we had to physically carry the load." She shook her head and corrected herself – "I mean, we had to fly while carrying the load." Ash was still gently running her fingers up the inside of her arm, trying to take in exactly how bad it looked.

Vedis's gaze moved back to the bruising on Ash's neck. "Did someone try to kill you?" she asked sharply.

Ash's hands went to her throat. "Maybe...I mean, no.

No, it was a misunderstanding."

"A misunderstanding that involved someone having their hands pressed round your throat?" Her dark eyebrow was arched and the leaves were quivering on her head. "You should have left – even if it meant coming back alone."

Ash's eyes locked first with Trik's and then with Ezra's. She shook her head. "Never going to happen. Leave no one behind. Consider that part of our new ground rules." It was so clear in her head. It had been there after the previous mission and now she was finally setting it out. "Do no harm, leave no one behind," she repeated with more certainty.

There was silence for a few seconds, then Ezra gave a small nod of his head. Trik did too and finally Amara. Vedis was staring at Ash with interest. She lifted her peculiar eyebrows, indicating Ash should continue what she'd been saying about the "misunderstanding".

"Our Friend wasn't quite ready for the information we shared with him," Ash said weakly. She really wasn't feeling that good.

"That's a nice way of saying it," snorted Trik.

Ezra was resting back in one of the chairs. "If Trik and I hadn't been there, Ash could have been in real danger."

"Was the mission accomplished?" Vedis checked.

Ezra answered before Ash had a chance. Her throat was tight and she needed some water. "Our part was accomplished. Will the people of Capuro 12 get to find out their true heritage? I guess we'll just need to wait and see."

Ash started talking again. "What you need to see here is

that teamwork made this mission possible. I couldn't have done this task on my own. In fact, the Library's Friend might have killed me. Teamwork is what saved me, enabled us to complete the mission, and likely helped Capuro 12."

Vedis looked thoughtful for a moment. "A hostile or volatile Friend is certainly a factor the Library has never really considered." She gave Ash a look that let her know she was still considering whether Ash was causing the issue or if this could have happened to any of the previous Guardians.

The Keeper pressed her lips together and magicked a scanner out of thin air.

"Let me treat your injuries."

"Leave them," said Ash as she stood back up, walking to the dispenser to get some water. "I'm going to bed. Let them heal naturally." She was tired. All she wanted to do was lie down and try to forget everything that could have gone so badly on their mission. Maybe she deserved to feel aching bones and muscles for a few days.

"But that's not an efficient use of time or resources," said Vedis. "It's pointless to put yourself through unnecessary pain and discomfort when I can treat you in..."

But Ash had stopped listening. She walked along the corridor, flopped into her bed and pulled the covers over her head.

And stayed there for three days.

CHAPTER FIFTEEN

By the time Ash finally left her room, her muscles had just started to stop aching and the purples and blues of the bruising had started to change to an interesting shade of yellow. Mostly, she'd just slept for the last three days.

Trik and Ezra were both slumped at the table. The bruising on their arms was in a similar state to her own. It was clear her team had followed her example and refused the high-tech healing this time around. Ash hadn't even looked in the mirror this morning. She didn't want to see the bruising round her throat.

Trik let out a long sigh as she sat down.

"This has been weird," he said, picking at a bowl of food. "It's like my body can't quite get over the shock of transforming so much."

"I slept for eighteen hours yesterday," Ezra said. "I've never done that in my entire life!" He stretched his arms out in front of him. "I still feel as if I'm getting used to my own body again."

Amara appeared, climbing the stairs from the Library beneath. "Oh thank goodness you're all up."

Ash sat a little straighter. "What? Is there a mission?" It was an instant reaction, but then she shook her head. "I don't know if I can face one."

"No," said Amara cheerfully as she sat down too. "I'm just relieved that Vedis will have four people to pick on instead of one."

"She's still being a pain?"

Amara nodded. "Ooooh yes."

There was a click of heels and Vedis appeared, clipboard in hand. She tutted as she looked at them all.

"Sitting around? There's work to be done!"

"What work?" asked Ash, though she instantly regretted it.

Vedis consulted her clipboard. "Trik, there's an area of the Library that requires some attention. There are still some storage cabinets that need mending after the attack on the Library. Ezra, you can do some repairs to the space fighters in the hangar. I've left a list of instructions down there for you. Amara, you should oversee restoration of the finer artefacts that can't be automatically fixed by the Library. Extra care and attention to detail is required, though it is likely that some are beyond repair. And Ash," she looked her up and down, "you should be doing all of it." She shot Ash a smile. "The Guardian should lead by example."

There was a moment of uncomfortable silence before Ash finally said, "You're right, I should."

She stood up, her chair scraping along the floor noisily. The rest of the team rolled their eyes and dispersed.

Vedis moved alongside Ash, keeping her voice low. "I've been giving some thought to the idea of a team."

Ash tried not to smile. "Really?"

Vedis nodded, her leaves rustling. "You seem to be a tremendously unlucky Guardian. First, the Friend on Quisquilla who didn't want to help..."

"Only because we were stealing her livelihood," cut in Ash. "How is Reker anyway? Do you have any idea? And any word on the Byroneans? Do we still need to worry ourselves about them? Could they trace us to the Library?"

Vedis closed her eyes for the briefest of seconds and gave a visible shudder of annoyance. There was clear impatience in her tone as she replied. "There have been no other disturbances at Quisquilla, and we've heard from unofficial sources that Reker is using her stash of *kilenium*," she emphasized the word, "to become quite the entrepreneur and seems to be investing in several dubious local businesses."

Ash gave a little grin – that sounded exactly like Reker.

"Where did she get kilenium?" asked Vedis. "It's rare. I hardly think she'd come across it on a space port like Quisquilla."

"No idea," said Ash quickly.

Vedis cut back to her point. "As I was saying, you seem to be unlucky, Ash."

Ash blinked. "Just a little."

"The mission to Erasmus wasn't exactly a success either."

Ash didn't reply and Vedis continued. "I've taken some time to review procedures. Aldus was an unfortunate choice as Guardian. The Library," she glanced around her as if she were actually talking to the Library itself, "placed too much trust in him. I'm still picking up on missing artefacts and his…" She paused as if searching for the appropriate word. "Meddling with the systems."

Vedis turned her full attention on Ash.

"But on Capuro 12 you were placed in a situation that could have had an unfortunate outcome." She straightened her spine, holding her clipboard to her chest. "I think the traditional Library procedure needs to be reviewed."

She made a sound as if she were clearing her throat. But why would a hologram need to do that? Ash couldn't help wondering.

"I am also of the opinion that the changes you have implemented should be allowed to continue." Vedis tilted her head to the side as if she were thinking. "Teamwork," she mused, then gave a wave of her hand. "Let's keep it going for now."

Ash was astounded. Had that conversation really just happened? Vedis's heels clipped across the floor then came to an abrupt halt as something appeared in the air.

Ash's feet moved automatically. A screen was hovering in mid-air just in front of her – the way it always did when the Library had a mission for the Guardian. Only this time there was no object, no artefact displayed.

"What's going on?" she asked the Keeper.

Amara appeared too, looking every bit as confused as Ash. She leaned forward, peering at the highlighted planet on the screen in the middle of a solar system. "Konoha?" she asked, then pulled back sharply, looking sheepish.

Vedis turned towards her instantly. She had the instincts of a viper. "What is it?"

Amara gave a very small shake of her head. "I was going through the systems again, trying to unpick something, and I spotted a strange alert for Konoha. Did I do this?"

"No." Vedis shook her head, her leaves vibrating. "You can't have caused this." She held up one hand to the screen. "This is the Library's work."

"What's the mission?" asked Trik, as he climbed the stairs towards them. Ezra was by his side. It seemed they hadn't been that interested in the tasks Vedis had assigned.

"That's just it," said Ash. "There doesn't seem to be an actual mission. Just a picture of a planet along with some information, and a location pinpointed for us."

"What?" They both strode forward, frowning.

Ezra pointed at the screen. "No artefact. So nothing to retrieve, nothing to return. This must be a glitch."

"The Library", said Vedis in her loudest tone, "doesn't have glitches."

Ash folded her arms and raised her eyebrows while the rest just smiled.

Trik shrugged. "Well." He peered a little closer at the planet and the stats down the side of the screen. "If the Library is telling us to go to Konoha, why don't we just go?

Looks like a nice place." They had a view of the planet. They could see expanses of blue water and large forested continents.

Ezra had folded his arms too and fell into place at Ash's side. He grinned. "Maybe, for once, we can go somewhere without someone trying to kill us. Wouldn't that be a revelation?"

Something clicked in Ash's brain. She'd looked up this place before. It had just taken a second for her to realize why the name was familiar. "Wait a minute." She beamed and turned to face Vedis. "This," she said waving her hand up and down. "The species you've based your appearance on. Where do they live?"

There was a long pause. Finally, Vedis gave the briefest of nods. "Konoha," she conceded.

"Can you bring up any information?" asked Ash. She leaned forward as the screen changed in front of her.

Amara pulled up more images.

There was a simultaneous intake of breath.

Konoha was a beautiful planet. A planet of colours. The people there looked similar to Vedis. They all had slightly green-tinged skin. While Vedis had a variety of leaves on her head, others had a sprinkling of blossoms. The whole planet was covered in rich colours: deep greens and bright blues where the oceans were, and trees, plants, flowers and bushes everywhere in shades of red, pink, yellow and orange. But it wasn't only the plant life that was bright. It was also the wildlife. Multicoloured small birds fluttered everywhere.

Animals were grazing the green fields, and they too had brightly coloured hides.

"It looks so peaceful," breathed Amara, her eyes wide.

Trik gave a slow nod. Ash glanced at him. He was a space boy. A wannabe action hero. Would a place like Konoha suit him? But a wide smile was spreading across his face. "I'd get to swim," he said, looking at the blue ocean.

Trik and Ezra both came from the planet of Hakora. Ezra had spent most of his life on the fishing boats, but Trik had been in a military factory, in the heart of one of the continents. He'd admitted to them once that he'd only ever seen the ocean from a fighter jet.

"You'll sink," said Ezra quickly. "And I'll watch."

"Do I get to come too?" All heads turned to Amara's quiet voice.

Amara had generally remained in the Library since she'd first got there. She didn't usually choose to go on any of the missions – although she had been a passenger in one of the fighters on a few occasions when they'd picked up supplies from a space port. For the first time, it struck Ash that the only planet Amara had experienced was Columbia 764, where her people, the Calleans, lived in domes under the sea. Amara had never had the opportunity to experience dry land under open skies. Konoha must look like some kind of paradise to her.

It was Vedis who spoke first. "We haven't decided if this is actually a mission yet," she said sharply, before the expression on her face softened and she gave Amara something resembling a smile. It was clear that just looking at the planet was stirring thoughts and memories for the Callean. "But, if it is, I see no reason why you shouldn't go along. After all, I'm here. I can look after the Library now."

Ezra kept his face straight. "So, if it's not a mission, you're saying it's a glitch?"

"No," said Vedis. She started pacing, her heels clacking on the floor. It was clear that she was just as confused as the rest of them.

All other eyes were still fixed on the views of Konoha.

Trik turned to Ash. "We'd get to breathe," he said quietly.

And she got it. She really did. Konoha looked like a completely unpolluted planet. The planets that they came from might be home, but Human habitation had caused problems on all of them.

"We need to make a decision," said Ash. "The screen has appeared. The Library is telling us something, even if we don't understand it. Should we go, or should we stay?"

For the first time ever, Vedis looked as if she might be lost for words.

"I say we go," said Trik, without hesitation.

"I'm curious," said Amara. "There was definitely something somewhere in the Library system about this planet. I just haven't managed to work out what it is. But this doesn't seem like a dangerous mission."

Ezra frowned and gave a shake of his head. "Every other mission we've been on has been dangerous. Doesn't it strike you as odd that we don't even know what we're supposed to do there? Look at it, the place is beautiful. I really, really want to go. But what if it's a trap?"

"A trap set by who?" asked Ash. "The only race we're worried about right now is the Byroneans. And we don't even know if they're aware the Library exists – let alone if they could disrupt any of our systems."

She paused. There was something off about this, but she couldn't quench the curiosity in her stomach. "Vedis? Do you know anything else about this planet? What's your connection to Konoha?"

Vedis waved her hand and her branches rustled. "It is what it appears to be on the screen – a beautiful, peaceful place. My connection is unimportant, a story for another day."

There was the longest pause and then the hologram made a suggestion that none of them expected. "Maybe this should be a team decision?"

Ash was shocked, but gave a nod of her head. Everyone was already here. "Let's take a vote," she said, and put out her hand with her thumb up.

Trik followed immediately. Ezra hesitated for a second then put his thumb down. Amara gave a nervous smile and put her hand in with the others, with one claw pointing up.

All eyes turned to Vedis.

"Me?" she asked, in surprise.

Ash nodded her head. "You're one of the team, what do you think?"

Vedis moved her clipboard onto her other hip and extended her hand with her thumb down. "My vote was irrelevant anyway." Her laugh was like a trill. "I'll monitor what I can from here. Just be careful."

Ash smiled at her team. "Are we agreed?"

Three heads nodded. She could see excitement written on their faces. Only Ezra looked a little wary. "Great." She smiled. "We leave as soon as everyone is ready." And before the Guardian had a chance to say anything else, Vedis vanished.

The group knew that on Konoha they would have the same sort of bodies they were used to but with either flowers or leaves growing from their heads. Ash's body still had a few aches and pains, but after a few days of doing very little she expected to be back to full strength.

Trik stood in the atrium.

"This feels different," he said. "The bangle and Proteus circle will still change our appearance, and maybe our clothes too, but we don't know why we are going. Will we need anything else?"

Ash shrugged.

"I guess we'll find out. This isn't an official mission. We have no idea why we're going. As far as we know, there isn't anything at stake." She thought back to the first time she'd transported herself to the Star Corporation Academy to visit Ezra. When she'd jumped, she'd stayed entirely the same, even wearing the flight suit she'd adopted for the Library. "I think we might not change clothes." She put her hand up. "But I'll be disappointed if my hair doesn't change."

She tucked the strand that was now coloured red behind her ear.

"After all," she smiled, "we want to blend in."

Amara looked slightly nervous. She touched the green scales on her face and the brown ridges on her skull. "I'm not sure about this. You've all changed before. I've never done it. What if I don't like it? You were all sick the last time."

Trik put his hand on her arm. "Last time around we changed physiology completely. This time," he looked down, "the basics for us all will remain the same. We'll be upright, with two legs and two arms. It's only our skin and hair that will change."

Amara gave a smile and rubbed her smooth head. "Plants on the head! And to think I was sometimes envious of all your hair."

She glanced at the three of them, who all laughed.

Ezra frowned. "Anyone seen Vedis?"

They all shook their heads. She'd been conspicuous by her absence since the team decision less than an hour ago. There hadn't been a single sign of her.

Ash shrugged again. "Well, I guess she doesn't want to say goodbye. Everyone ready?"

They nodded and all moved across to the Proteus circle, assembling themselves easily, all touching another person.

Ash put her hand to the bangle on her other wrist. "Okay folks, let's find out why the Library is sending us to Konoha."

CHAPTER SIXTEEN

"Okay, still not got a clue why we're here. Anyone?" Trik was sitting with his arms folded and staring out across the green landscape, his eyes scanning their surroundings with an air of suspicion.

Ash smiled. "Maybe this is nothing, maybe it's a mistake. Why don't we just take the opportunity to breathe?"

She was dressed in a long red robe she'd bought from a street vendor. It turned out the Library had chosen to cover her head in small red blossoms and she wanted to match.

Amara's head was now very similar to Vedis's. She had a small array of twigs covered in green leaves that rustled in the warm, pleasant winds. Her scales and ridges had completely disappeared and she kept touching the smooth skin on her face with a weird expression of curiosity and disgust. Ezra had a mixture of leaves and small orange blossoms, and Trik had dark-green leaves with white tips.

It took a little getting used to, but their new appearances

actually caused them very few problems. Apart from Amara losing her scales, it was the only significant change from their regular bodies, except for their skin tones, which were now all a pale shade of green.

Konoha was a welcoming place. They'd explored for a few hours and no Friend had appeared to explain why the Library had sent them here. Rather than wandering around aimlessly and being conspicuous, they'd asked about somewhere to stay and had rented this pale wooden shack just outside the edge of a town. It was in need of some repairs, with a roof that had a few small holes. But its best feature was a view of a bright-blue lake and a landscape just like the one they'd viewed back at the Library. They'd dragged some chairs outside so Ash could tuck her bare feet into the grass once more.

The concept of waiting to see why they were there was clearly a struggle for Trik. "Let's go for a swim. Or how about we explore those woods over there? Or we could have a tree-climbing competition." His eyes fixed on a huge tree that soared into the air near the edge of the woods. "I wonder how high that one is." He wandered towards it.

"I have no intention of finding out," said Amara quickly. "This is all enough for me. Just being here, looking out at all this. This is my first time on another planet – one that actually has land that isn't destroyed. I want to enjoy it."

Ash gave her a smile. "It's just a different kind of beautiful. Columbia 764 is all kinds of beautiful too. Remember when I got there and saw the corpereans?"

The flashing silver fish had been mesmerizing. Like fireworks in a dark sky, except the corperean fish moved in perfect synchronized movements. Watching them through the glass dome of Amara's world had been one of the highlights of her visit.

Amara nodded. She held out her hands and took a huge breath. "But this... This is special. You've got to remember I've spent my life in domes, whether on Columbia 764 or in the Library. But this?" Her smile was broad. "This is the most amazing place I've ever been. So green. I've never stood on land before, or grass." She sighed, leaning back into her comfortable chair.

Ash leaned back too and closed her eyes. She swore she could almost hear soothing music playing in the air around them. Between the rustling leaves, singing birds, quiet sounds of other animals and the aromas of budding blossoms and green trees, it was like being hit with a dose of tranquillity. Ash didn't need to look over her shoulder. She didn't need to be constantly thinking. She wasn't plotting revenge. She wasn't trying to ace tests at the Academy. Last time she'd felt this at peace was years ago, back at home with her mum, dad and sister.

The memory punched into Ash and tears pricked her eyes. Maybe quiet time was not what she needed. As she pressed her feet further into the grass and sat forward again, she noticed Ezra was staring straight at her.

"Let's all give it an hour," he said in a low voice. "Then how about we do a bit more exploring? Maybe the Library isn't going to tell us why we're here. Maybe we need to find out for ourselves."

Ash nodded. It was like he could read her mind.

"I'm beginning to understand why Vedis chose to base her appearance on the people from this planet." She wrinkled her nose. "I guess I just didn't associate Vedis with a place so tranquil – so beautiful."

"I sometimes forget she's a hologram," said Amara.

"A hologram who can touch." Ash gave an involuntary shudder. "I still can't quite get my head round that."

"I think it's a mood thing," said Amara. "There's been plenty of times in the Library when she moves things just by looking at them or clicking her fingers. But when it comes to us? I guess she just likes prodding us for fun."

"But is that her, or is it the Library?" said Ezra. He paused. "Are you still curious about that, Ash?"

"Why wouldn't I be? Look what just happened – it sent us here without telling us why we've come. Is the Library really just a building, or is it something more?" She spoke the word she'd been considering for a while: "Sentient."

Amara replied in almost a whisper. "Or maybe even more."

Trik came crashing through the trees to their left and Ash gave him a look of surprise at the gleam in his eyes.

"Hey, do you know what's strange? I just climbed that tree. Fell off, of course, and broke a branch. Walked around for a bit, came back, and guess what?"

He didn't give any of them time to answer. "The broken

branch? It's gone." He waved his hand. "Come closer and look."

They moved over, all staring upwards.

Trik kept talking. "And that would be fine if someone had picked it up and dragged it away. But the spot where it ripped off the tree? There's a whole new branch."

Amara pulled back her head. "What? How is that even possible?"

"Are you sure you got the right tree?" asked Ash. "It is a wood. There's a whole load of them about."

Trik looked around, as if he were considering what she'd said, but then shook his head. "No. It's definitely this tree. I remember these purple flowers at the bottom – I landed on them."

"But I've never known trees or plants that could mend themselves so quickly. Do you think that's even possible?" Amara was staring up, squinting at the tree. She tilted her head. "I mean, does anyone else think that branch looks a bit weird?"

Ash and Ezra looked up too. The sun was streaming through the leaves, so it was difficult to see clearly. But the branch did look a little different from the others. It was the colour – slightly lighter than the rest of the branches.

"I don't know. Maybe?" Ezra shrugged. "Anyway, those purple flowers are round a few trees." He folded his arms. "Bet you got the wrong tree."

Trik looked indignant. "No way. I landed in these flowers. Can't you see the Trik-sized hole?" He leaned forward then frowned at the perfectly intact flowers.

Ezra nudged him. "Guess those flowers healed the hole too. They look fine to me." He waved his hand. "You've got mixed up."

Ash shook her head. "Give it up, guys. I'm hungry. Let's go and see what we can buy at the market to eat, and see if we can work out why we're here." The others nodded and they headed back to the village.

Appetizing smells drifted towards them as they approached. Ezra's stomach grumbled loudly as they came to a stall of some kind of baked goods and he laughed. "Okay, I'm going to get some of whatever that is; you lot see what else you can pick up."

Amara and Ash moved towards some large barrels of fruit. Trik pointed into the heart of the market. "I'm going for a look in there."

They nodded and started moving among the people in the marketplace. Earlier, everyone had looked like a resident of Konoha, but now there were some other species among the crowds. There was a child near them, her head covered in bright-green leaves with yellow tips. She was walking with some sort of frame, her leg blistered and twisted. Ash winced. If they'd been back at the Library, the medic autorepair scanner might have been able to help. But the child moved on, smiling, as Ash continued to move around the stalls.

She was curious and listened to the conversations around her as she bought some red fruit. "Different people from earlier," she mentioned casually to the trader.

"Freighter's just landed," he replied amiably. "Leaves again in a few days."

Ash smiled. "Of course." She couldn't ask any more, it would look odd. Ash was supposed to be a local. She hoped the trader would just presume she was a bit forgetful.

"I wonder where the freighter came from?" she whispered to Amara, as they walked closer to the centre of the marketplace.

"The nearest star system is Lobis," said Amara. "I think there's a wormhole in that system, so these people could come from any place."

Ezra ambled over, holding a net bag full of delicious-looking baked goods. He peered at the red fruits. "Interesting choice." He glanced around. "Are we ready? Where's Trik?"

"Let's start walking back – he'll find us. It's not like we have any place else to go yet," said Amara. She was staring at Ezra's net bag, her mind obviously fixated on eating.

They'd just turned to head back towards the shack when Trik came pacing through the crowd.

His jaw was set, his eyes fixed. Ash could sense the fury emanating from him. "What's wro—"

She didn't get to finish. He grabbed her elbow sharply and pushed her forward.

"Everybody, walk now. Heads down."

Ash didn't have a chance to argue. Trik's momentum was pushing her forwards. She tried to tense her muscles and stop, but something in her brain clicked.

They were in trouble. That's the only reason Trik would act like this.

"No talking," he hissed.

She glanced behind them, watching as Ezra took Amara's arm and spoke quietly into her ear. It was clear that his Academy training was kicking in. Obey instructions, ask questions later.

Ash kept her head down and walked swiftly alongside Trik. They turned into another street and he herded them all into a corner.

His voice remained low as they crowded round. "I think I know why the Library sent us here." He took a deep breath and looked Ash in the eye. "I'm pretty sure I just saw Aldus Dexter."

"What?" It was a natural reaction. Ezra's arm snuck round Ash's waist as she felt herself sway a little. "That's impossible."

She took a deep breath and shook her head. "How can you be sure? You never met him in person."

There was small tic in Trik's clenched jaw.

"I looked him up. And there's every chance he looked all of us up too. If you'd just lost a battle against the Library and its new Guardian, wouldn't you want to know who her wingmen were?"

Of course. It made perfect sense. While she'd still been working with Orius, Ash had been sent to U62, an old planet. Everyone had thought U62 was dead. But what she'd found was a thriving planet, filled with Humans, androids and a mixture of both, ruled by a previous Guardian of the Library. One who was also thought to be dead – Aldus Dexter, an Anterrean with a lifespan of eight hundred years. He'd stolen a device from Corinez, a planet in her solar system, turning it to ice, and used the device to revive U62.

Ash had stolen the device back, leading to a battle at the Library when Aldus had attacked. She and her friends had sent him back through the wormhole, closing it behind him. They'd thought they'd never see him again. She couldn't believe he'd turn up here.

"Did he recognize you?" she asked.

Trik frowned. "I have no idea. I turned round because of the strange conversation. He knows people here. He was talking about the regenerating properties of the planet."

"What?"

They all looked at each other for a moment, reflecting on their earlier conversation.

"This planet has regeneration properties?" asked Amara, her eyes wide.

"I couldn't hear that much. Apparently, everything on this planet regenerates. If a tree or bush is damaged, the planet can make things regrow or replace them," replied Trik.

All four of them automatically looked round – as if they could see it happening in front of them. Trik gave them all an I-told-you-so look, bringing their attention back. "It's like the tree branch. I told you there was something weird there."

"But how does the planet do that?" asked Ezra.

"Please no," breathed Ash. "He's obsessed. Does he think that this planet has a crystal similar to the Kronos device? He's already stolen one before – is he trying to steal another power source?"

"Does this place even have a Kronos device?" asked Ezra.

Trik shook his head. "I don't think so. But Aldus seemed fascinated by the concept. He kept laughing too loudly and rubbing his wrist, saying how it had worked for him before."

"What does that mean?" asked Amara.

"I have no idea," admitted Trik. "But at least now we know why we're here."

Ash breathed deeply, trying to think rationally. "Okay, so he might not recognize us. He won't expect to see us here. I need to see him. I need to check it really is Aldus."

"Do you think that's wise?" asked Amara.

Ash held up her hands. "I have green-tinged skin and red blossoms for hair. I don't look anything like I did back on U62 or when he attacked the Library. And I need to know what Aldus is doing here. He's dangerous. He's unstable. Just the fact he is here makes me feel unsafe. You're right, Trik. This is definitely why the Library sent us here."

"But how did he get here?" asked Amara. "The wormhole collapsed behind him."

Ezra shook his head. "Let's not worry about that. This is Aldus Dexter. If anyone could find a way back from U62, it's him."

Ash straightened herself. "Let's not jump to conclusions. I'm the one that's seen Aldus in the flesh. Let me take a walk – I'll be discreet. We could have this all wrong."

Trik raised his eyebrows at her and folded his arms across his chest. "He's already suspicious of me. I'm not getting under his nose again."

Ash didn't wait. She ducked back out and headed straight

into the marketplace, scanning the crowds for Aldus's tall, lean frame.

Her stomach was clenched, partly hoping she wouldn't see anyone that could even slightly resemble him. But something, deep down, was nagging away at her. Trik's reaction had been too definite. Too strong. When it came to things like this, she'd be surprised if he'd made a mistake.

Ash continued walking; smiling and nodding at fellow Konoha residents as she drifted through the marketplace, all the while her eyes scanning. Every time she saw a group of men she edged a little closer, checking to see if Aldus was among them.

But he was nowhere. She didn't even glimpse anyone who looked like him. There were a few shops around the edges of the marketplace. An eating place. A traditional alehouse. She began to head towards the latter and stopped. No. Going in alone might be too conspicuous.

Ash moved backwards through the stalls, shaking her head as she met her friends again. "I couldn't see him. He might have found some lodgings for the night, or been in the drinking den, but walking in there would just have drawn attention to me."

"Let's go back to the shack and make a plan," suggested Trik. "Or maybe we should just jump back to the Library and decide what to do next?"

They all looked at each other. The idea was tempting.

But something tugged inside Ash and she groaned. "If it is Aldus, we know the reason he's here can't be good. What if we jump back and find out later that he's done something harmful to this beautiful place?" She shook her head. "I couldn't live with that, and Vedis?" She gave a wry laugh. "Just think what she would do to us!"

Amara shuddered. "I don't even want to contemplate that." She looked about. "We know the freighter doesn't leave for another couple of days. Let's go back and make a plan for tomorrow. If Aldus is here, he's up to something. We're bound to see him about. As for the alehouse, we haven't visited there yet. We could all go – tomorrow. It wouldn't be unusual for visitors."

Trik rolled his eyes. "Why do we always do the stupid thing? No, let's not just jump out at the first sign of trouble. Let's hang around and try and land in the middle of it."

Ezra nudged him. "Stop pretending you don't want to know what's going on. You're as curious about this as anyone. And anyhow, the guy tried to kill you – tried to kill us all. If he's up to something, don't you want to mess up his plans?"

"Maybe he's just here for a holiday," put in Amara, a hint of a smile on her lips as they all rolled their eyes.

"Okay," said Trik. "You got me. I don't want to jump back. But not all of us are trained to fight." He met Amara's gaze. "This guy is mean. I don't want any of us getting hurt when we don't need to."

Ash nodded. "He's right. Let's go for now." Her stomach churned as they walked away from the marketplace and back to their shack.

Aldus Dexter was only one thing – trouble.

CHAPTER SEVENTEEN

The next day the group moved carefully.

They split up on their late-morning stroll round the marketplace. Amara headed to the bakery stall, Ash to the clothes, Trik to the fruit and Ezra to the meat. All had the same intention: information gathering.

The marketplace had a few individuals who'd obviously come from the freighter. A red-skinned, large-headed Fidulan, in his traditional white robes. Ash blinked. Last time she'd seen a Fidulan had been back at the space port. There was also a cluster of Nillusions – small creatures dressed in a range of ragtag clothes. They were scavengers at heart, and she could see some of the stall owners eyeing them suspiciously.

There was a collection of androids at one side of the square. At first, Ash thought they were being sold. But as she neared, she realized they weren't being sold at all. They were arguing, loudly, and people had gathered to watch.

Ezra appeared at her shoulder.

"Have you ever seen androids argue before?" he asked, with pure amusement in his voice.

Ash shook her head. "Never. It's beyond odd." Androids were generally programmed to obey orders.

"They must be rogue." Ezra nodded approvingly. "Looks like we're all evolving!"

Ash's curiosity was definitely piqued as she watched a small barrel-like android argue with a spherical droid. They banged against each other, sparks flying. Most of the people around had no idea what they were arguing about, but Ash did. She, and her team, were fitted with universal translators.

She grinned. It was all over a betulan circuit – a tiny power unit that could supply an android like these with enough power to last at least a year. They were scarce. No wonder the androids were arguing.

Ash turned away, leaving Ezra still watching the argument, threading her way through the crowd in the hope of hearing other conversations that might give her a clue as to why Aldus was here. Her time was wasted. She heard about new crop farming on the distant outpost at Farson 271, the shaky government on Kilimeaa, and the war that had broken out in the Maronas solar system. No one was talking about U62. The only relevant information she learned was that Konoha was on numerous shipping routes and, due to its beauty, was a popular rest stop.

By the time she coordinated with the others again, the

sun was high in the sky and the temperature was rising.

"Let's go to the alehouse," said Trik, with a shake of his head. "Hopefully ale will loosen their tongues and we might hear something at least half interesting."

They filed into the nearby alehouse, finding a table in one of the dark corners. Everything about the place seemed old – the dark walls, rough tables and slightly uneven chairs. But as they settled at their table, a screen appeared in front of them all with the drink menu. Amara gave a start, then a nervous laugh. Although they had universal translators for spoken language, they couldn't understand what was written on the screen. She pressed a button randomly and sat back.

"I have no idea what I just ordered, but I guess I'll find out."

They all did the same, and a few moments later, a serving android appeared at their table with four different drinks, which were dumped unceremoniously on the table.

All four of them smiled. "Take your pick," said Ash, waiting for the others to select a drink before she picked up the one that was left – a dark, red liquid.

She took a sip. It was sharp, sweet, with a definite tang.

Amara gave a little choke as she swallowed hers. "Wow," she said as she put it down. "It's kind of forest flavoured – it's a bit overwhelming!"

Ezra lifted his orange drink, sipped and smiled. "Fruits with a hint of bitterness."

Trik went to lift his dark-purple drink and then froze.

He dipped his face downwards and Ash felt the back of her neck prickle. She kept her gaze on the glasses on the table and fixed a smile on her face.

A screen was lit at the table to their right, and as she glanced at the screen she saw the silhouetted figure of a man stride through the alehouse and sit at the table on her left. If she looked up, she would be staring straight at him.

She kept trying to convince herself she looked entirely different. There was no way he could recognize her through this disguise. But she could certainly recognize him.

It was Aldus Dexter, live and in the flesh.

Trik had his back to Aldus and raised one eyebrow. Ash gave the briefest of nods.

A few minutes later, a Konohan man came in and joined him at the table, and then they started talking with heads bowed. Trik automatically leaned backwards in his chair, giving the appearance of relaxing, when actually he was trying to listen to the conversation.

Ash was torn. They needed to act naturally. The last thing they wanted to do was draw attention to themselves. But she also wanted to make sure Trik heard every word. She started chatting nonsense to Amara and Ezra. Not whispering, in case that looked suspicious, but keeping her voice at a level where someone could overhear her if they wanted to.

It was amazing how much nonsense they could talk when they tried. Ezra and Amara cottoned on quick, talking about the variety of items available in the marketplace. Ash pulled up the screen again and they all ordered food. Trik did his best impression of a friend who was very bored with the conversation.

"It's definitely him," hissed Amara under her breath.

"Yip," replied Ash. She was trying not to look in his direction, because looking at Aldus Dexter was filling her head with a whole host of pictures she'd rather forget. The glint in his eye back on U62 when he'd realized who she must be. The technology he'd had that could freeze her on the spot, due to the robotic implants in her transformed body. That time the Library had done too good a job of transforming her body in line with the locals!

Every time she blinked, she saw the space battle outside the Library. The realization that she and her friends might die. The Library being hit by proton torpedoes. The wreckage, the damage, and the glint from the helmets of the androids flying the fighters.

Why exactly was Aldus Dexter here, of all places? It couldn't be for anything good. This man was ruthless, murderous, with only his own priorities. Whatever he wanted to do, he wouldn't care who was hurt in the process.

Ash kept her gaze fixed on her glass. "How did he get out?" she asked, her voice barely above a murmur now. "We closed the wormhole. He should have been trapped back at U62. There's no other way out of the solar system."

"Does it matter?" said Ezra. "He's out. Let's just worry about what's in front of us."

Trik shot them a dirty look. He obviously didn't want distractions from his task right now. Conversation at the table behind them was clearly interesting. He leaned back a little further.

The server appeared, sliding trays of food onto the table. No one really knew what they had ordered. Ash took a taste from her plate and had to stop herself gagging. Unfazed, Ezra grabbed one of the local utensils, gave the food a tentative sniff and swallowed. He shrugged at Ash's horrified face.

"What's wrong? I like it!"

Amara started picking at hers. She nodded. "I like mine too."

Ash eyed the third plate. It was packed with fruits and some strange pots of a gloopy substance. Dare she? The first bite told her she'd lucked out. This was a plate of desserts!

Voices were raised at the other table next to them. Seconds later, two stocky Konohans were on their feet, throwing punches at two Fidulans.

One of the Fidulans flew past their table and collided with Aldus's back. He fell against his table, then stood up in anger, turning round, ready to join the fray.

For the briefest possible second his eyes connected with Ash's. Her mouth dried and stomach clenched. But then he had to duck to avoid the wide body of one of the Konohans being thrown across the bar. Aldus let out a laugh and shouted over to the bartender, "Staron, I see that some things never change!"

He turned his head and said something to the person who'd been sitting at the table with him, then strode out through the main door.

Ash was torn. She wanted to chase after him, but that look, that tiny glance had frozen her to her seat.

What if Aldus came back to the Library? What if he tried to finish what he'd started and destroyed the place completely? And if he decided to attack the Library again, and succeeded, what might he do to her – the current Guardian?

Trik leaned over the table and grabbed her arm. "We need to find someplace else to talk."

But Ezra was shaking his head. "You lot watch where Aldus goes. I'm going to follow his friend, see where he heads after this. We shouldn't miss this opportunity."

Trik had kept hold of Ash's arm and pulled her from her chair. "Catch you later," he said to Ezra as they exited into the bright sunlight.

Her heart was racing. Before she even had a chance to scan the street, Trik sighed. "He's gone. No sign of him. Maybe if Ezra trails the other one, we might find out where they are. Otherwise I'm going back in to ask the bartender what he knows about him."

Ash was struck by Trik's determination. This couldn't be good.

"What did you hear?"

"I'm hungry. I'm going to get something, then I'll tell you back at the shack. I'd prefer to be away from any listening ears."

The queue at the baked goods stall was long and by the time they'd sat down on the steps of the shack, Ezra came jogging

227

back to join them, sweat running between his dark-green leaves and orange blossoms. He wiped his face.

"Sorry." He sat down next to them all. "What have I missed?"

"Nothing." Trik shook his head. "I hadn't started yet." He bit into one of the large buns he was holding. Amara was sitting with her knees pulled up to her chest. It was clear she was uncomfortable.

"Okay," said Ash, waiting for Trik to finish chewing. "Tell us everything."

Trik nodded. "I listened as much as I could. I might have missed a few things – or not fully understood them – but I think I got the gist of the story."

They all leaned forward.

"Aldus has been coming here for a while. I've no idea how he got away from U62, but this is one of many visits. He seems to know most people around here – certainly everyone he wants to do business with and who he trusts."

Ash shook her head. "I still don't get how he got back out of that solar system."

Trik clearly felt the same as Ezra. He pulled a face. "It's irrelevant. What matters is what he's doing here. He's obsessed with this place. He has a lab here."

"A lab?" Ash was shocked.

But Trik held up one hand. "Make that a *secret* lab. He's trying to make some sort of discovery and he thinks he's very close. I'll tell you what's strange though."

"What?"

Trik shook his head and paused for a second. "I think he's been coming here for some time. Longer ago than the Library attack. Much longer than us closing the wormhole. During the course of their conversation, they talked about years, not months."

There were a few moments of silence as they all looked at each other.

"I'm confused," said Amara finally. "Why would someone like Aldus Dexter come here? It's a beautiful place, but he was busy terraforming U62. What did he think he could get from here?"

"The regeneration properties," they all said at the same time.

"There's more," said Ezra. "I followed his partner in crime, and I found their lab. It's a building at the other side of the marketplace. It looks a lot like this place, except it's not at the edge of a lake, and it's at least double the size. It's at the edge of a forest."

"Does anyone know how long it is until the next freighter comes back?"

"Two days," said Trik quickly. "He intends to be on it."

"Aldus travelling on a freighter seems...not Aldus-like at all," said Amara.

Ezra nodded in agreement.

"I have such a bad feeling about this," said Ash. She stared down at her bangle, resisting the temptation to twist it. She hated being afraid, and that's how Aldus Dexter made her feel.

But she could never just twist the bangle and leave. The people of Konoha had no idea how dangerous Aldus Dexter could actually be.

She moved down the steps of the shack and stared out at the lake.

There were some children round the edges, and something struck her as strange.

One of the kids was limping.

Something started linking in her brain. The little girl had green leaves on her head with yellow tips. She still had a stick, but was barely using it.

"Guys," Ash said quickly. "Does anyone recognize that little girl down there?"

They all shook their heads.

Ash pointed at her. "I saw her yesterday. I recognize her hair – well, her leaves. She looked much more injured yesterday, her leg was all twisted. I remember her, because I wished we had our medi scanners to help her. She had a walking frame – something I've only seen on history screens before. But look at her today. She's limping. That's it. She's limping."

Trik frowned. "Listen, you must have made a mistake. There's got to be more than one kid with yellow tips on their leaves."

Ash shook her head. "It's not just that. It's her face. I swear it's her."

"Look, shouldn't we talk about our plan for the lab?" asked Ezra. "We have to find a way to get more info on Aldus.

We need to find out what he's doing and if he plans to harm this place in any way."

Ash sighed. She knew they were right. "And if he is, we need to stop him. Okay, let's sit down and plan."

CHAPTER EIGHTEEN

They all crept out before first light, with Ezra taking the lead. The sky was a dark shade of purple as he slipped through the village. Trik was behind, keeping watch, even though it was pretty difficult to see.

The trouble was, they didn't really know much about the species on this planet. Just because they slept at night, and were generally awake during the day, didn't mean that the people of this planet followed all the same rules as Humans.

As Ezra crept through the streets there was the odd dim light at some of the dwellings. A huge orange furnace was burning in one of the structures near the marketplace. Ash followed from behind. It looked like some kind of kiln.

Her thoughts instantly flashed back to Erasmus, and the ceramic furnace. The people, their faces were still imprinted on her brain, and part of her didn't want to forget them, despite the pain their memory brought.

There was a much brighter light in the distance. Ezra led the way and they crept towards it. He gave a nod of his head.

"That's it. That's the lab."

Her heart sank.

"Do you think they're working there at night?" If so, their plan was ruined. They couldn't exactly sneak into the lab if Aldus and his workers were there.

"We'll just need to go and see," he whispered in a low voice. "Let me do a walk round the building, see what I can find out."

They'd agreed not to do this mob-handed. Stealth and sneaky behaviour had seemed the most reasonable way to progress. None of them really wanted to come face to face with Aldus again. While they were anonymous, they were safe. If Aldus were to discover their true identities, Ash doubted they would be able to breathe easy on this planet again.

He'd wanted to kill her before, and since they'd beaten him and his android forces, she could only imagine that his rage towards her and the Library had built even further.

Ezra started scouting round the building, keeping his head low and moving as quietly as possible. Trik couldn't possibly stay still, so he started circling the building in the opposite direction.

Although the bright white light from the lab was visible, it seemed to be coming from a side window.

Impatience was prickling inside Ash. Yes, they'd agreed to her and Amara staying hidden until Ezra could establish if there was any way into the lab. But already the palms of her hands were itching and she shuffled from foot to foot, anxious to be on the move again.

It took for ever. So long that Ash started to worry the two guys had been caught and were lying unconscious in the dark at the other side of the building.

There was a low whistle. Ash jumped as she saw Trik's face appear at the bottom corner of the building. He gestured them forward with his finger.

"Ready?" she asked Amara.

"Absolutely," was the reply, and in the blink of an eye, she was off.

Amara was proving to be much more adept at sneaking around than Ash had given her credit for. Miraculously, her clawed feet were virtually silent on the dirt and stone ground, and Amara could move lower than the rest of them, keeping to the shadows and recesses of buildings with a skill that impressed.

Ash followed behind, feeling like a clumsy friend. Sneaking about with a head full of bright-red blossoms made her feel conspicuous. Trik had covered some of his leaves with a dark cloth and Ezra had pulled the robe he was wearing part way over his head.

They crept round the side of the building. The bright white light shone out of the window like a giant spotlight. Ezra was at the opposite side from them. They all crouched down.

"Okay," said Trik. "The door is definitely locked. This window is the only way in."

"Can you see anything? Are they in there?"

"We've been watching for a few minutes. If they're in the building, they're not in the lab. Not right now, anyway."

Ash swallowed, her mouth dry. They had to find out what Aldus was doing in there. She nodded her head towards the stream of light. "That's the only way in?"

Before Trik even had a chance to respond, Amara cut in. "I'll go," she said.

"What? No."

Amara turned her head and gave Ash a hard stare. "Why not? How do you choose which one of us goes in there? What makes you think you can do this any better than me?"

Ash was stunned. Amara was always so placid back at the Library; so measured, the voice of reason.

"I say let the girl go." Trik was smiling and there was a gleam of admiration in his eye.

Ash took a breath, and raised herself a little until she could peep into the building. The sight made her gasp.

For a planet where technology didn't seem to be used particularly heavily, the lab seemed completely out of place. Delicate metal machinery, electronic equipment, some kind of magnification technology – Ash didn't even recognize most of the items. Where had Aldus got all this stuff?

Ezra nodded across to Amara. "If Amara's ready, then you both should go, we have no idea what half of that equipment is or what Aldus is doing with it."

"And that's why I need to go inside and read the computer

programs," said Amara, pulling a pair of black gloves over her hands.

"Okay, we'll both go," agreed Ash, then stared at Amara's gloves. "Where did you get them?" Ash asked in amazement as Ezra handed her a similar pair.

"What do you think we do all day?" asked Amara. "Sit around and wait for you to come up with all the brilliant ideas?" She tutted as her glove snapped into place. "There's a reason you recognized that you need a team, Ash." She gave Ash a cheeky grin. "You don't always have the skills you need."

Ezra gave a small nod of his head. "We'll be your lookouts. If we see anyone approach, we'll give you a signal."

Ash pulled the gloves on as Amara turned to Ezra, saying, "Ready," and before Ash had a chance to say a single word, Ezra had boosted Amara up and through the window, without a single sound.

Ash followed a few moments later, blinking at the bright white lab lights.

Amara was already at a terminal, using her gloved hands to sweep screens in mid-air. She was moving at lightning speed, discarding screen after screen. Ash stared into the eyepiece of one of the huge magnifiers in the room, pulling back in shock for a second, then leaning in again, trying to understand what she was seeing. Amara moved for a second and glanced in too.

Ash scanned her gaze over some of the equipment. There was a huge metal box on one of the counters. It looked as if it were surrounded by a range of sensors and probes, more than she'd ever seen attached to a single piece of equipment before. Ash shook her head and whispered to Amara.

Amara stared at the box too, then turned back and flicked screens at an even more rapid pace, as if she were trying to answer a question that had just sprung into her brain.

"What's happening?" hissed Trik, whose head was at the window.

"I know what some of this stuff is," Ash admitted in frustration. "But not everything. He had some technology similar to this on U62."

Trik shrugged and gave a half smile. "Well, if you don't know what it is, there's no chance of me knowing."

Ash returned the weak smile and turned back to the equipment just in time to hear an odd noise.

Ash and Amara froze.

After a second, Ash turned her head to Amara, her eyes wide.

Amara's hands were still in mid-air, and she looked like she was holding her breath.

Ezra could see the panic written on both of their faces. He gestured with his hand, beckoning them towards him, mouthing, "Get out."

But neither of the girls moved. Amara's gaze went to the door at the other end of the lab, as if she expected it to open at any minute.

Ash's heart was clamouring in her chest. She'd put them in danger. She'd let Amara take part when this was her first time away from the Library. She'd put her friend at risk, on her first mission.

But after another few moments, Amara moved her hands, keeping them flat but moving them up and down. Like she was telling everyone to calm down.

She nodded her head towards Ash, gesturing that she should continue.

Amara's clawed finger flicked another screen as she resumed her search of the available information. And then she paused.

Her head tilted to one side, a move that Ash recognized. Amara was probably the cleverest in the team. She only ever did that when she was trying to figure something out.

What had she found?

Ash took a few silent steps closer and looked again at the box. Pieces of the puzzle were starting to slot into place in her brain.

Her hands were poised over one of the panels. Panic flooded her for a second as she started to understand what she was seeing. No, that couldn't be real. Was there really technology that could do this? Back on U62, Aldus had been trying to replicate a crystal. Now, it looked like he was trying to replicate something else. But this kind of regeneration was impossible, wasn't it?

Trik seemed to sense something was going on, and leaned in the window. "What is it?" he whispered.

She heard Ezra's reply. "I think they've found something."

Amara appeared at Ash's side, and Ash heard a sharp

intake of breath. She was almost relieved. Clearly she wasn't the only one putting all the pieces together. This was real.

Amara punched something into the panel, then turned back to her screens and swiped again.

An image flickered in the air. One that made them all catch their breath.

Aldus Dexter.

Except this was a different Aldus Dexter. Thinner, paler and, more noticeably, with only one hand.

They all let out a gasp.

Amara raised a shaky hand to the screen and the image started to flicker again, this time as if it were scrolling through all the saved images.

Ash's mouth hung open as they watched Aldus's hand appear to grow back. It was astonishing. It was impossible. None of them had ever witnessed anything like this before. A limb growing back?

Her voice was gravelly. "That's how he did it."

"What?" Trik asked, from the window. Wasn't he supposed to be their lookout? Staring in the lab was hardly helping.

Her voice was still croaky. "That's how he did it. That's how he got the bangle off."

The horror struck Ash like a tidal wave.

Amara nodded to the magnifier. "I watched the cells regenerating on a slide under the magnifier at a horrifying speed. Now I understand the context."

Amara shook her head and turned to stare at both Trik and Ezra. Both of them had locked their gazes on her.

It was like the same idea had just flooded all their brains at once.

Ash stared down at the bangle and started to shake. It had been one of the first things Orius had told her when she'd arrived at the Library and the bangle had appeared on her wrist. Once she was a Guardian, it was for life. The only way the bangle would come off her wrist was when she died. Well, it seemed that Aldus Dexter had found another way.

"He cut his hand off to get rid of the bangle." Trik's voice was now monotone. He was stating aloud the unavoidable fact that was completely and utterly horrifying to them all.

"No," said Ash as she stepped towards the window. She didn't want to believe it. She didn't want to think that anyone was actually that monstrous. Her hand flew up to her mouth. "He did it to get free of the Library. He did it to trick the Library." She kept shaking her head.

For a few more minutes Ash and Amara examined the contents of the metal box, talking quietly, trying to work out the equations that hovered above the equipment inside, and their meanings.

"Something is missing," hissed Ash.

"But what?" said Amara, shaking her head. "Look, there. He's expecting something in a few days. Is that the missing component?"

There was a noise, a sort of grinding sound. It was closer than last time. This time Ash and Amara didn't freeze. This time they both jumped in horror towards the window.

Amara didn't wait to climb, she just dived head first out onto the dirt and stones, missing Trik and Ezra's faces by a finger's breadth as they pulled back.

Ash went to follow and then stopped. Amara had left the multiple screens open in mid-air – a clear sign that intruders had been in the lab.

Her head flicked back and forth, her heart racing in her chest.

"Move!" hissed Ezra. He looked as if he were about to jump through the window and grab Ash himself.

But she couldn't. She couldn't leave the lab like this. Aldus would know someone had been there. They still needed time to plan what to do next. She darted back the few steps, frantically closing screens as quickly as she could.

Footsteps sounded outside the door at the end of the lab.

Amara had scrambled back to her feet and was looking in horror at Ash's actions, realizing what she'd left behind.

"No," she breathed.

Ash's chest was starting to tighten as she flicked wildly with both hands. Her eyes were half on the door, which creaked and started to open.

Last time she'd encountered Aldus Dexter on another planet, he'd tried to kill her.

At the last possible second, she flicked the remaining screen and in two long strides made it to the window, diving straight outside.

Trik and Amara sprinted ahead round the nearest corner, breathing heavily.

Ezra dragged Ash away and round the same corner, barely giving her the chance to get to her feet.

Whoever was coming into the lab must have seen something, even if it was only a trace of movement.

Trik held up one finger silently. His clothes were the darkest. He moved his head just a tiny bit round the corner and jerked back instantly.

"It's Aldus," he mouthed. "Looking out the window. We'd better move."

It was hard to be quiet. They ran across the street and ducked behind some buildings, crouching down low and trying to quieten their breathing.

Trik kept watch, holding up his hand to keep them silent.

It was clear that Aldus was suspicious. He came out of the building, hands on his hips and stared around, scouring the empty streets.

Ash held her breath as she watched through a tiny gap in the crates she was hiding behind for extra cover. Curiosity swept through her. What did his new hand feel like? Did it feel exactly like the previous one, or was it different, was it strange?

Aldus had used robotic parts on some of the people on U62, making half-Human half-android people. Was a robotic hand not good enough for him? He'd gone the extra mile to grow a flesh and blood replacement hand, right from his own body – something Ash hadn't even known was possible.

After the longest time, Aldus shook his head and went back inside.

They were crouched down low, heads together.

"His hand didn't just heal, it regrew. When have you ever heard of anything like that?" Ash whispered.

Amara spoke in a low voice. "He knew," she said simply. She lifted her head. "It's the only way. He knew about this planet, this place. He came here to get rid of the bangle. He knew he had to cut his arm off to get rid of it."

"Eww," said Trik, shaking his head.

"That's gross," breathed Ash. She twisted the bangle self-consciously on her wrist. There had been a point she hadn't wanted to wear it, but would she actually have contemplated anything like this? Just how much had Aldus hated being Guardian? His actions were unthinkable. But the pictures they'd found were proof.

"Maybe it was an accident – his hand, I mean," Trik suggested.

Amara shook her head. "Nope. It was surgically removed. It's all in the files."

The four of them stared at each other and after a second something occurred to Ash. "That little girl. Her leg. That's why it looked so different today – it's partially healed. Maybe the healing properties here affect more than the landscape?"

Again, they all stared at each other. Ash's mouth was unnaturally dry.

"Is that what people do – come to Konoha because of the healing properties?" She wrinkled her nose. "But how does that even work?"

Trik's voice was steady. "Well, I guess that's why we're here. The Library must want us to find out."

CHAPTER NINETEEN

Ash's brain was racing as she tried to make sense of everything. The temptation to keep talking was high, but the weariness on her friends' faces made her stop.

By the time they got back to the shack it was the middle of the night and they collapsed in their simple beds, exhausted.

"Let's try and get some sleep," Ash said. "We can talk later."

She thought sleep would be hard, but as soon as her head hit the pillow she was gone.

By the time she woke up a few hours later, the children were already down at the lakeside again. She immediately looked for the little girl with the green leaves and yellow tips.

Ezra joined her on the front step.

"She's not there?"

Ash smiled. He knew exactly what she was doing. "Not yet."

She leaned back against the door frame. "Does this place strike you as somewhere with clever, hidden technology?"

Ezra looked across the green landscape and the flat surface of the lake. He gave a wry laugh. "Somebody must be really good at hiding things then."

Ash nodded. "What's going on here is not about tech, is it? I feel like this whole planet is something special."

They sat in silence for a few moments, just waiting and watching. Ash let out a sigh.

"I hate that he's here. I hate that he must have planned this for years. I hate that he's even come to a place like this. It feels like he's ruined it."

"Or that he's about to ruin it." Amara appeared behind them both, rubbing her eyes. "He's got his hand. Why is he back here?"

Trik was close behind, tugging a shirt over his head. He stepped round them and sagged down onto the grass in front of the shack. "Should we just go back to the Library?"

Amara shook her head as she joined him. "Absolutely not! I've been thinking… I couldn't quite understand everything that we saw last night in the lab, probably because we had no context. But now…"

There was a shout from one of the kids down at the lake, and they all turned their heads to watch. The little girl Ash had been looking for had returned. Today, she had no stick. She wasn't running or jumping, but instead walking carefully, steadily. Her legs were bare, and even though they weren't up close, there was no obvious scarring. Her skin looked smooth.

245

This time the team didn't ask questions.

Amara did that head-tilt thing again. "Just being on this planet can heal people."

"Not just people," said Trik. "Plants too. Remember the tree, it grew a whole new branch within minutes."

"Wait," said Ezra. "Is that what you're telling me? Aldus cut off his hand and grew a whole new one overnight? Just from being on this planet? No surgery or technology?" It was just too incredible to be real.

"No." Ash let out a short laugh. "The files in the lab, those pictures of Aldus. They were taken over a month. So this planet definitely has regeneration abilities, but it can't just do things instantly. Look at the girl."

She pointed down to the water, then turned to Ezra.

"Her leg was twisted and blistered. It looks better but not quite there yet. It's been – what, two days so far? At that speed, I would predict that by tomorrow she'll be good as new."

They all stared down at the child. She was playing, still limping a little.

"Wait a minute," said Ezra. "Why doesn't the whole universe know about this place? If this planet really has healing properties, wouldn't every species just come here to get healed?"

"Maybe they do," said Ash. "Maybe that's why the freighter comes every few days."

Trik shook his head. "I don't think so. We've not heard a single conversation about healing since we got here."

"But," said Ash, "if this is just an integral part of this

planet, if this is entirely normal here, why would people talk about it?"

"And I don't think it's widely known," said Ezra. "Otherwise everyone who came off the freighter would have looked unwell. It wasn't like that. Did the other species in the marketplace yesterday look sick to you?"

Trik shook his head. "This place is just a stop-off point. Most of the people on the freighters are only here for a few days. Would people really notice anything in that space of time?"

Amara gave a thoughtful shrug of her shoulders. "Maybe they would just think they had a really good night's sleep, on a beautiful planet." She raised her eyebrows at Trik. "Not everyone visiting a planet for a few hours attempts to wreck the trees."

They all shook their heads at the wonder of it all.

"So," said Ash carefully, "maybe it's not widely known, but some people do know about it. Maybe Aldus found out by mistake. Maybe – if he had a mission here – his Friend told him."

"It's still a huge leap," said Trik, arching his brows. "Aldus finds out about this place, and risks coming here and cutting off his hand because he doesn't want to be Guardian any more?" Disbelief dripped from his voice. "Said it before – boy, did that guy *not* want to be Guardian." He looked over at Ash and gave her arm a gentle slap. "Stop doing that."

She pulled her hand back from where she'd been subconsciously twisting the bangle. It had never really bothered her that much. But now it seemed to be irritating her slightly. It was like a weight on both her skin and on her mind.

"There's more," said Amara hesitantly.

"What else can there be?" asked Trik.

Amara glanced at Ash and bit her bottom lip. That one look made Ash's stomach start to twist and turn. She took a deep breath. "Okay, explain…but I have a horrible feeling I know what you're about to say."

"It's taken me a bit of time to figure out what was going on in the lab. I think we got so distracted by the visuals of Aldus and the timeline that I didn't really process what else I was seeing."

"And?" Trik prompted. "What was in the metal box?"

Ash and Amara exchanged another glance.

"I think I know now," Ash said quietly.

"Aldus came back here for a reason. He's trying to harness the energy from the planet – the healing properties. In a way, he's trying to steal it."

"That's what was in the box," said Ash, with a nod of her head. "His machine for doing that. It took me a while to work out what it was."

"People don't change," said Ezra slowly. "He stole the Kronos device from one planet and took it to another. He's just doing the same thing all over again."

Trik held out his hands. "But is that even possible? If the healing properties are part of the planet itself, how can he steal them? How do you even harness energy like that?"

He folded his arms across his chest and gazed out over the beautiful landscape. "What effect could that have on the rest of this place? Is it this beautiful naturally, or does it rely on a little help?"

Ezra's voice was calm. "How far along is Aldus with his plan?"

Amara gulped. "Quite far. I think he's been working on this for a while. Ever since he stopped being Guardian. The files were going back for a number of years."

"The machine in the metal box," said Ash. "It looks like there's one piece that he's missing, so his work isn't complete yet. He's already drawn some of the energy from the planet. There were calculations there, but it looks like he still needs an essential component – something to hold the energy and store it once it's drawn out."

"Do you think he jumped between here and U62?" Trik shook his head. "Transforming one planet and trying to steal from another... Does this guy ever sleep?"

"Oh no," said Ash, and she sagged down. "Please don't tell me this is my fault." She put her hands on her head. "Did the actions I took back on U62 push him in this direction, make him devote all his time to this?"

Ezra put his hand on her shoulder. "Hey, don't. None of this is your fault. We've already established the guy's a megalomaniac. Amara, didn't you say there was a date on the files? Ash, did you see that?"

Ash took a few breaths, trying to stop the wave of panic she was feeling. She pushed herself back up as she remembered something. "You're right. The date on the files was years old. Long, long before he met me."

"Okay, so I won't pretend to understand the science of everything, but if Aldus succeeds – if he actually manages to harness and steal some of the energy from the planet – what would he do with it?" The leaves on Amara's head rustled as she spoke.

Trik had taken a few steps away. He turned round, looking thoughtful. "If we're talking about Aldus the megalomaniac, I can imagine he's thinking in a direction we might not even have considered. What if this energy doesn't just heal? What if it can do something else? Could it regenerate U62 again? Could it regenerate another planet, just like the Kronos device did? Maybe even at a quicker speed… Let's face it, if it was simply the healing properties he wanted, they'd be his already."

"What do you mean?" asked Ash.

"Well, if Aldus wanted to start his own healing planet, he could just have taken over this one. These people seem pretty tranquil. It wouldn't be the hardest place for him to conquer. Or maybe that's what's next. Maybe he didn't have time to do it before because of U62. Think about it, information about this place is generally kept quite quiet." He put his hand to his chest. "But what if I had a sick family member and I heard about a planet with healing properties? If I had tried all the technology I had, and nothing had helped, wouldn't I do anything," he arched one brow, "*pay* anything to get there?"

A light breeze swept round them. The thought was more than chilling. In some ways, it exactly matched the temperament of Aldus Dexter. Aldus thought he was ruler of all he surveyed. He didn't like to be challenged. And he would glory in the power of it all.

Aldus Dexter would love the ability of picking and choosing who could come to his healing planet – and how much he could charge for it.

And yet he was also planning to harness Konoha's power for some other reason, probably one that was even more despicable. Considering what he'd tried before, it could be a threat to the entire universe, not only this planet.

Ash thought back to some of the calculations she'd seen in the lab and what Amara had said. "We can't let him do this. If Aldus can harness Konoha's power, there's no end to what he might do with it. Knowing him – take over the entire universe. Whatever it is he is planning to do, we have to try and stop him."

"No," said Ezra suddenly. "Not try, we *have* to stop him. No question."

Ash nodded. "You're right. I know you're right. But what can we do? Could we make sure he doesn't get hold of the component he needs?"

"Simpler than that. We blow up the lab," said Trik, with a smile.

The other three turned to look at him slowly.

Trik had his hands folded across his chest and a wicked grin on his face.

His eyes gleamed. "Let's do this."

CHAPTER TWENTY

It was hard to find what they needed. That was the thing about being on an unfamiliar planet. If any of them had been on their own home worlds, they would have known exactly what to put together. But here?

Ash's solution was simple. She stood with her hand poised on her bangle.

"You have to promise me that none of you will go anywhere near Aldus or his lab while I'm back at the Library."

Amara, Ezra and Trik gave solemn nods, but she didn't entirely trust the boys. They were too feisty.

"I'll be there and back in a flash. Don't get up to anything while I talk to Vedis. You're sure none of you want to come back?"

Three heads shook. She had to trust them. They were her team.

So, Ash took a deep breath and twisted the bangle.

*   *   *

Vedis let out a yell as Ash materialized on the Proteus circle. It took Ash a few seconds to realize why.

One of the first lessons she'd learned as Guardian was that when she jumped to another planet, she transformed – face, body and clothes. When she jumped back, she became herself again. This time, as she glanced down and reached up to her head, Ash realized that not only was her skin still tinged pale green and her clothes from Konoha intact, but the blossoms were still on her head.

If it were possible for a hologram to pale, Ash could swear that Vedis did.

"I need help," Ash said quickly. "Have you been watching? There's something wrong on Konoha."

Vedis blinked. "You didn't change back," she said in a voice so quiet it was more like a whisper.

Ash glanced down, distracted by all the other things that were on her mind. "Does it matter?"

Vedis looked as if she was struggling for an answer, so Ash didn't wait, just continued on. "Have you been watching?" she asked again.

"I checked in once or twice," the Keeper replied. "You looked as if you were enjoying yourself. I've been working on some of Library systems. The ones you claim are glitchy."

Ash walked rapidly from the circle to the large wooden table in the middle of the room. She could already sense that Vedis was frozen behind her, so Ash pulled out a chair and sat down. Vedis had never told them why she'd chosen the appearance of someone from Konoha, and now it was time to find out.

The Keeper marched towards Ash, her heels clipping along the floor, and it struck Ash that the straight black skirt, white shirt and heels Vedis wore were unlike anything she'd seen on Konoha. Most of the regular inhabitants of the region wore the loose, colourful clothing that she was wearing now. In fact, they'd found it hard to source darker clothing for sneaking around in.

"Aldus Dexter is on Konoha."

Vedis's voice was tight. "What is Aldus Dexter doing on Konoha?"

Ash's hand went to the bangle on her wrist. "There's more than one reason – and we definitely know why he went there in the first place."

"Why?"

"He cut his hand off to get rid of the Guardian bangle."

"WHAT???"

This reaction stunned Ash. The word seemed to echo around her, as if it were being said by the entire Library and not just Vedis. She swallowed, trying not to allow herself to be scared.

"He has a lab on Konoha. And he has friends. His files showed us that he'd been visiting for many years – before the attack on the Library. He had his hand surgically removed," she slowed and licked her lips, "and stayed for a few months on Konoha, to allow it to grow back." Ash kept her voice steady as she stared at Vedis. "The properties on the planet are quite unique. Almost miraculous. I'm surprised its benefits are not more widely known."

She left the words hanging there, but Vedis didn't reply. The uncomfortable silence magnified.

"Why did you choose the appearance of someone from Konoha, Vedis?"

This time Ash was determined not to fill the silence. She would leave it there until Vedis finally answered.

Eventually, Vedis gave a small nod of her head. "You know that the Library has been here for a long time and there have been a number of Guardians from all across the universe."

Ash nodded.

"Every Guardian leaves a little of themselves behind. They influence the programming in the Library."

Ash shifted on the chair. That seemed unusual. She'd never thought that anything she did would have a lasting impact on the fundamentals of the Library.

"One such Guardian was Gastin. He came from Konoha. He was wise beyond words. When it was time for me to take form, I chose to pay tribute to Gastin."

Ash gave a curious smile. "I don't imagine Gastin wore clothes like those."

Vedis gave a sigh. "No, he didn't. But another Guardian did. Her name was Molly. She was one of the first Guardians." There was a pause. "She came from U62."

"What?" That was the last thing Ash expected to hear. "How could she come from U62? Aldus only just regenerated that planet."

Vedis gave a sad smile. "Molly came from the original U62. The one that was eventually destroyed by its inhabitants polluting the atmosphere."

"The original?" Ash was astounded. "But that must have been—"

"Hundreds of thousands of years ago." Vedis sighed. "Molly had a lowly job on that planet. Menial, unimportant. But the Library could sense what was hidden at her core – a brilliant scientific brain that had never been nurtured. Molly blossomed as soon as she got here. She wanted to stick to her original appearance, though, to allow herself to remember where she came from – a planet that had been destroyed by its inhabitants. The Library was very sad when Molly came to her natural end. It took a long time to find another Guardian that was such a good fit."

It was the first time there had been a suggestion that the Library had feelings. There was so much Ash wanted to explore here, but she would have time for that later.

Ash moved her arm up and down. "So, this...you, is a tribute to both Molly and Gastin?"

Vedis gave a small nod again.

"And you know everything that Gastin did about Konoha?"

Vedis's brow lowered and the twigs on her head twitched. "Why?"

"Because Aldus isn't only there because he needed a new hand. He's up to something. We think he's trying to steal the energy from the planet. Harness it in some way. And if Aldus is doing something like that, it can't be for a good reason."

Vedis jumped to her feet. "But that's impossible! There's no way he could… Draining the energy from the planet would…"

Her words stopped, as if she couldn't continue.

"It's like he's mimicking what he did before, with the Kronos crystal on U62," explained Ash. "He took all the power from that crystal and used it to transform a planet entirely – leaving the place he took it from practically destroyed. He's already tried to extract the healing powers on Konoha, but it didn't quite work. He's missing a key component to store the energy properly, but I think he has plans to get it soon. If Aldus can steal the energy of Konoha, he could return to U62. He hadn't finished his work there. This would allow him that opportunity.

"He planned to conquer every other solar system in the universe – transforming planets to meet his needs. Leaving people at the mercy of his whims. We have to stop him."

Vedis's face remained tight. "How do you intend to do so?"

Ash gave a nervous laugh. "Trik and Ezra think we should blow his lab up."

Vedis looked her in the eye. "Are you absolutely sure Aldus plans to try and steal the power from the planet?"

Ash nodded. "Amara and I both saw the complicated plans. At the heart of them is some kind of device. In the first plan, it looked like the Kronos crystal. But he doesn't have that now – and won't ever get it back. So, it seems that his plans changed. There were star dates and coordinates that neither of us had time to memorize. We didn't even realize what we were really looking at. The first files, all about his hand, threw us completely. The ones after? We didn't have time to see everything. We were disturbed."

"Aldus Dexter knows you were there?"

Ash shook her head. "No, he didn't see us. At least I hope he didn't. But it seems that he's expecting to receive the final component imminently. There's a reason we were sent to Konoha. You must see that now, Vedis. We thought the Library might have made a mistake, with no artefact to retrieve or drop off, but from the second we saw Aldus Dexter, we knew why we were there. The Library knew exactly what it was doing when it sent us to Konoha."

Vedis gave a slow, careful nod. "Blowing up his lab seems...primitive. A transficular pulse, however, would wipe every piece of equipment in his lab. Render everything useless. Stop his attack before it starts."

Ash had tilted her head at the strange word. "What even is that?"

Vedis waved her arms and a dozen screens appeared above her. Her fingers moved rapidly and she muttered under her breath, as if she were talking to someone. The Keeper was tapping one screen, pulling things from screen to screen and doing calculations so quickly that Ash couldn't even pretend to follow. Vedis's forehead was creased in concentration as she worked, and her leaves seemed to curl in on themselves. Ash paced the floor behind her.

"Can you get back into his lab?" she asked over one shoulder as her fingers flew.

"If I need to," said Ash, as her stomach twisted at the thought. It was likely that if Aldus had suspicions of anyone being in his lab, he would have taken extra security precautions. It might not be so easy as climbing through a window next time.

Eventually something materialized in the air next to Ash's head – just like a regular Infinity File. She reached out and grabbed it with both hands, turning it over. It was almost nondescript; a heavy grey box with one small light. Next to it were two other devices that were clearly triggers.

Ash was hesitant. "What does this do? Will it cause any harm to the rest of Konoha?"

Vedis shook her head as her leaves started to unfurl again. "No. It will only affect the technology in the lab space. Not that there is much other technology on Konoha. But nothing in the close vicinity should be harmed."

"How will I know if it has worked?"

"There may be a small pulse. The light on the triggers will change from purple to white. I've created one for you and one for a friend, in case you run into trouble."

Ash's mouth was strangely dry.

"You, however, could be harmed. You shouldn't be near the device when you press the trigger. The pulse will emit radiation at a level that could cause catastrophic damage to any person nearby." Vedis extended her hand and dropped four small clips into Ash's palm. "A protective force field. As soon as you place the four round the lab, the force field will come into effect. It's a secondary protective measure to ensure the pulse doesn't spread beyond the lab."

Ash gave a nod and slid them into her pocket.

Vedis's hand gripped her arm, really gripped it. "Make sure this happens. If Aldus's plan works, and the energy is drained from Konoha, the whole planet will die. You have to stop him. This isn't like Erasmus. That planet was destroyed by environmental issues that we couldn't control. This would be deliberate interference in the natural properties of another planet."

Ash pressed her lips together for a second. "But what if he just comes back and sets up another lab? Tries it all again? I don't think he will ever stop."

Vedis nodded. "You're right. But let's deal with the immediate issue first. We can plan what to do about Aldus Dexter once we've stopped his current attempt to ruin another planet."

Ash took a deep breath and nodded, before walking back over to the Proteus circle and tucking the device and triggers into the deep pockets of her clothing.

As she lifted her head and put her hand on her wrist, Vedis moved in front of her. Her voice was deliberate: "And if you can't plant the device…"

Ash had already started twisting the bangle.

"Find a way to blow him up," were the last words she heard as the Library faded away.

CHAPTER TWENTY-ONE

By the time she got back, the others appeared to have been collecting what they could as part of their backup plan.

"Is this really going to work?" asked Ezra, staring down at the mishmash of items they'd accumulated throughout the day.

"We can do this," said Amara.

Trik nodded. "This will do." He bent over the pile with Amara. "Give us a little time."

They worked diligently, making do with what they had. Ash had shown them what Vedis had given them, but the rest weren't quite as reassured as she was.

Trik pointed to the simple-looking grey box. "It doesn't look that impressive, and we've never tried it before. What if it doesn't work? We can't let him drain the energy from this planet. We need to be certain we have a backup plan in place."

Amara was cursing herself. "We should have paid attention to the dates. I was so busy with the rest of it, and it didn't all make sense at the time. Those dates were probably the most crucial part." She shook her head. "Knowing when Aldus is going to receive his new kind of device was the information we needed most. When does the next freighter arrive? What if he's already received it?"

"We need to watch him. It's another full day before another freighter arrives but I don't trust him," said Ash.

Ezra must have felt the same because he grabbed her elbow.

"Let's go stake out the lab. We need to keep an eye on the place. If Aldus is there, we should try and see what he's doing. If other people are there, we might have to rethink our plan – I don't care about Aldus getting caught in a blast, but we can't let anyone else get hurt."

Ash nodded. "Come and find us later," she said to Trik and Amara.

During daylight hours, the lab was an easy place to stake out. It wasn't too far from the market and had plenty of people passing by. They didn't look suspicious at all. There were shops, food carts and eating places nearby, and Ash and Ezra ambled among them.

A few people did come to and from the lab. One visitor was definitely making some kind of delivery. Another looked like someone who might work there. Aldus came out twice: once to go to the alehouse, once he simply disappeared among the throng of people. At this, Ash hurried round to the window that had been open last night. Today, it was closed but not covered. She peered through.

The lab was empty, but she could see programs running. Lights were flashing at some machines. Her eyes fell on one of the screens and her breath caught. Dates. She could see star dates. More importantly, she could see tomorrow's star date. That must be when Aldus was expecting his final component, the device that would allow him to drain this planet.

Her fingers itched. Ash wanted to get in there. She kept taking things apart in her head. Time was of the essence.

She pulled back from the window. They'd been watching the lab for hours and were certain there was no one else inside right now. The other person who worked at the lab had left. That was good. She wasn't afraid to destroy everything in this place to stop Aldus destroying this planet, but she didn't want anyone else to get hurt.

Amara and Trik joined them and they moved a little away from the lab and back towards the market.

Amara was the only one of the group who had heard of a transficular pulse previously, and she seemed a little wary.

"There's more technology on this planet than Vedis thinks. We need to be a little cautious. What if a ship were coming in to land and the pulse screwed with its controls? The space freighter flight path is directly overhead. Lives could be lost. We need to be careful. And we need to make sure no one is around. The radiation levels are very short-lived, but likely to be harmful."

"I have these." Ash pulled the clips from her pocket. "Vedis said to place them round the building and a force field would be erected to contain the blast."

Amara picked them up and looked closely. "They might work. At least to protect the people. I'm not entirely sure they would be so effective to any passing freighter."

So they had to do it at night – there'd be less chance of space traffic, as all the scheduled arrivals came during the day. And they had to do it when no one was around.

"It needs to be tonight," said Ash. "When I looked through the window, I could see some files running. One of them had tomorrow's date. I think that's when he's expecting the device. We need to wipe out his lab tonight."

All heads nodded then turned as they heard a laugh they recognized. Aldus. Ezra frowned and shot a glare in his direction. Aldus was laughing and joking with one of the market traders.

"Look at him, everyone's best friend. They have no idea that he's trying to steal the essence of their planet."

Ash folded her arms. She hated Aldus. She hated what he'd done to U62 and Corinez, and what he'd tried to do to the Library.

He was a criminal. He had stolen the Kronos device from Corinez. He'd planned it all. Planned to ruin the lives of millions. And now they'd found out he was planning to do something similar again.

Ash nodded slowly as the reality started focusing her brain. She looked up at Ezra. "I hate him. You know I do. The sooner we do this, the better. The pulse should take out the lab. But Aldus will still have the opportunity to try again. And I don't know what to do about that."

"If the pulse doesn't work, we have to blow up the lab." Trik blew on his fingers as they sprung open. "The whole place could be gone in a puff of smoke. Maybe it could take Aldus with it."

Ash's chest tightened. "What if someone else is in there?"

Ezra's jaw was set. "Collateral damage."

She pulled back, surprised at the force behind his words. The boys had been fighter pilots and were used to the concept of taking enemy lives – and there was no doubt that Aldus was the enemy. But Ash had failed the final pilot test. She hadn't been in the same situations as the guys. "I'm not sure I can live with that," she said. "First rule, do no harm."

He sighed and put his hand across his heart. "This is why you have us, Ash. This is why you wanted a team. To help you with the difficult decisions. To second-guess you. To take part of the load – part of the responsibility. To make sure that even if it's a hard decision, it's the right one.

"Perspective, that's what we all need. The man standing down the street from us appears to be a normal, happy guy. But he's not. Not at all. He's a megalomaniac. He doesn't care what happens to this place once he's got what he needs. He would gladly leave all these people to die. He's done it before and he'll do it again."

Ash sucked in the air between her teeth and straightened her shoulders. Her hands reached to touch the blossoms on her head. Every single cell in her body wanted to do whatever she could to protect this planet.

She couldn't save the people on Erasmus, or their planet, but she could save this one.

Ash looked at Ezra and remembered the last comment Vedis had made to her. "I'm the Guardian. If a decision like that has to be made, it's on me." She reached and touched his arm. "But I appreciate your support."

He gave her a half smile. "Come on, let's pull back a little and keep watch. It's getting late. The streets will be getting quieter soon."

They moved backwards into the shadows as a group of children ran past. Or at least some of them did. One of them was the little girl from the day before, distinguishable by the yellow tips of the leaves on her head. She was limping again – badly.

"What's happened to her?" asked Ezra.

"Oh no," breathed Amara. "The healing powers of the planet must have stopped. The energy he stole has already had an effect."

"Are you sure?" asked Ash. "Could it happen that quickly?"

Trik couldn't hide the look of disgust on his face. "We know he'd tried something already. He maybe couldn't store the energy effectively. But he still drained it from the planet. The effect? The evidence is right in front of us."

"But she was getting better," said Amara. "It's like someone's turned the clock back." They all watched, stomachs churning, as the little girl hobbled after her friends.

Ezra and Ash exchanged anxious glances. "Whatever he's doing, it's clearly starting to work," said Ash. "We have to stop him, and we have to stop him tonight."

CHAPTER TWENTY-TWO

Darkness had fallen at last. Trik and Amara appeared again, clutching something wrapped in a dark cloth.

"The backup plan," Amara said with a trembling voice. "We get it inside, trigger it, and the fire will start. There are enough components to ensure it will spread quickly. There should be nothing left."

They all turned and stared at the lab building. Although it was part of a street, the surrounding buildings were far enough away to be safe from any impending fire.

"Mine first," said Ash, in a more assured tone than she actually felt. "Let's try and cause the least commotion. We just do what we did last night. Go through the window, get Vedis's weapon inside the lab, and trigger it. Then we're done. We've checked the schedule. There are no ships due this evening. We shouldn't be putting others at risk."

Ash gave Amara a careful sidelong glance. She was trembling – obviously worried about what they might need to do if the pulse failed.

"I'll do it," Ash said quickly. "If I have to, I can do both."
She wanted to make sure things went as smoothly as possible.
If Amara was having second thoughts, Ash didn't want to
know about it. Plus, this was her responsibility. She needed
to do this.

"I'll help," offered Trik, as he glanced at Amara.

Ezra looked as if he wanted to argue, but another glance
at Amara made him nod.

"Let's get this over with."

They snuck round the side of the building, first setting the
force field with the clips Vedis had given Ash, then moving
to where the bright white light streamed from the window.
But as they got closer, there was a glint of glass. The window
was shut.

Ash's footsteps halted. "Damn," she hissed.

"It's only glass," said Trik casually. "We'll break it."

They crept forwards and Trik lifted a sharp stone from
the ground.

"What about the noise?" said Ash. "He'll hear it break."

"Won't matter." Trik shrugged. "If he comes into the lab,
we'll just toss the device in, trigger it and run."

Ash shook her head. "I want to get back inside. I want to
put it where it can do most damage."

But Trik wasn't really listening. Ezra handed him stones
the size of his fists. Trik tried to smash them against the
glass, at first in a half-hearted, quiet sort of way, then in
frustration, battering them against the pane.

Ezra and Amara looked anxiously around to see if they'd attracted any attention with the noise, but the dark streets remained quiet.

Trik started pulling out tools that he'd acquired, trying to jimmy open the window. After a few moments, Ezra helped at the other side, both of them shaking their heads in frustration.

"What is this made from?" hissed Ezra. "The glass is completely solid. Our tools aren't even leaving a mark."

"It's probably made from the same material that surrounds the Library," said Amara.

Ash froze. "What?"

Amara held up her hands. "Well, it's clear, it's protective, it's apparently impenetrable. He's stolen everything else. Why wouldn't he have stolen the properties of the material that protects the Library?"

It made perfect sense. Ash pressed her hand against the surface. "I just assumed it would be glass. Why would he need anything stronger? Then again, he might have realized someone was in his lab. The window glass might be a new arrival."

Ash sighed and turned round, leaning against the lab wall and trying not to contemplate what that might mean. "Then how are we going to get in?"

Five minutes later they all stood in the shadows opposite the door to the lab.

"One way in, one way out," Trik murmured. They'd rechecked the whole surrounding area. Apart from the sealed window and the closed door there was no other way into the building.

"What's the chance that it's open?" Ash asked.

Three harsh expressions gave her the answer she already knew.

"Deliveries," said Amara softly. "There were a few deliveries today. What if Aldus is expecting more?"

They exchanged hopeful expressions. "Do you think we could get away with that? It's late."

"It's also the only idea we've got," said Trik.

"And we can't wait," said Ezra. "There will be too many people around during the day."

They all nodded. "Even if he just opens the door," Trik said, "worst-case scenario we just throw it in."

"You mean *I* just throw it in," corrected Ash.

Trik's eyes narrowed. "Well, if it's a delivery, can't I do it, instead of you?"

Ash shook her head. "This is my job. I need to do it." Before he started arguing, she went on. "Help me get some stuff together – a couple of small crates or something. I can hold them up in front of my face. He'll let me in to see what they are, then I can set them down, inside the building, and run. I'd still really like to get into the actual lab. Make sure the pulse is set off right in the heart of things. If it gets dangerous, I run and pull the door shut behind me."

"It could work," said Ezra carefully. He rubbed his hands

against his legs. He was nervous. "I think I saw some crates earlier. One of the market traders left them behind. Let me go and see." He took a few long strides back towards the marketplace.

"What do you remember about the deliveries earlier?" asked Amara. "Did they carry scanners?"

Ash pulled a face. "Can't remember much. I was kind of focused on Aldus." She put her hand to her head. For the first time since she'd got here, the blossoms on her head were itching. "I'll manage." What else could she do?

Trik had disappeared a little further down the street. He came back with some kind of sacking, just as Ezra came back round the corner with two small crates.

"They look good," said Amara as he put them down. She gently placed the device from Vedis inside the top crate, and the backup device in the bottom crate. "There, once we trigger the pulse, everything in the lab should be wiped out."

Trik laid the sack he'd found over the top of both crates.

Ash handed triggers for the two devices over to her team. "One for the main plan, and one for the backup," she said before pocketing her own triggers.

"Hopefully Aldus will spend some time rummaging through the crates, so Ash can get out of there and the door will be closed."

"Wait," said Ash. "If anything happens and I don't come out, you trigger the device anyway. Trigger *both* devices. We can't afford to take chances."

271

Ezra's eyes grew wide. "We're not going to do that."

"You are. We're a team, but I'm the Guardian. The most important task is to save this planet, stop Aldus from what he's about to do. I have to try and correct the past mistakes of the Library. Aldus should never have been allowed to do all that he's done. And after what I experienced on Erasmus? I can't watch another population be destroyed. We can't wait. Promise me."

Amara shook her head, but Ash turned to Ezra and Trik. "I'm your squadron leader."

She let her words hang. They'd been in battle together. They knew how important it was to follow the instructions of the squadron leader.

Ezra took a deep breath. "The pulse, you know it's likely to damage your body. There's no way to avoid the radiation. The force field is round the lab but if you're in there…"

"I know," she nodded. "And the risk is mine to take. If something happens to me, Vedis knows where you are. Get away on one of the freighters, and then she'll likely be in touch to help."

She could tell they wanted to argue with her again, so Ash tried to change the subject.

"Maybe we should find some other bits to put in the top crate. You know – some stuff to distract him?"

Amara wrinkled her nose. "What kind of things?"

"Anything. Let's have a scout about."

Trik returned moments later with a variety of items. Discarded fruit. A beaker. A small wheel. He tipped them all into the crate. "That will keep him busy, wondering who has sent him this stuff."

"Are you sure about this, Ash?" asked Ezra. "This isn't how we expected the plan to go."

She nodded. "Let's just get it done. Rules are, I get in, I get out. If things go to plan, as soon as I'm out, you trigger the first device, we all hold onto each other, and we're out of here. If things don't go to plan and I don't come out, I'll trigger the device from inside. If all else fails – you know what to do." She licked her lips. "Burn it down."

Ezra made a kind of strange noise at the back of his throat. He looked around, even though it was dark. "Nothing about this feels good. It just seems such a horrible end to our visit to such a beautiful place."

"It would be more horrible if Aldus destroyed this beautiful place." Ash pressed her lips together. Her stomach was churning. She said the words out loud that had been chasing round in her head. "We all know none of this has happened by chance. No, the Library sent us here for a reason – to stop Aldus Dexter." She looked around and said quietly, "I wonder if it's trying to correct its own mistakes."

She bent down and picked up the covered crates. They wobbled for a moment and Trik's eyes were wide. Ash adjusted her weight, making sure they were as steady as they could be, and pulled her shoulders back.

"Wish me luck," she whispered as she strode across the dark street.

Ash couldn't ignore her heart racing in her chest. The

itch on her head was there again too – she put it down to nerves. As Ash reached the large door, she lifted one trembling hand and knocked sharply.

The noise seemed to echo along the street. Her skin prickled and she stood steady, licking her dry lips.

Nothing. No sound from beyond the door.

Panic started to climb through her. Maybe they hadn't watched properly, maybe Aldus had already left?

Then the door handle turned. Part of her was glad it was a traditional, old-style door. It gave her a few seconds to focus.

Aldus's tall frame filled the doorway. His hair was rumpled. He must have been sleeping.

"Delivery," she said in her brightest voice.

"Delivery?" he repeated as if he were still trying to wake up.

"Yes." She hoped he couldn't hear the slight tremor in her voice. "Where do you want it?" She took a few steps forward, effectively pushing him back towards the lab.

Her instincts had been correct. Aldus acted like most people would and automatically took a few steps backwards. But then he paused.

"Wait," he said. There was an edge to his voice.

Her heart started pounding. So close, she was so close to what she needed to do.

Ash bent forward to set the crates down. "Would you like to check the delivery?" she asked. The door to the lab was ajar just behind him. All she had to do was shove the device inside.

He lifted the edge of the sack from the top crate. Then he moved like lightning.

It took Ash too long to realize what was happening – or to work out what her mistake had been.

Aldus already had his hand clamped firmly over her arm, over her bangle, before she'd even blinked.

"You!" he hissed, his face right up against hers.

She tried to jump back but of course she couldn't. His hand was firmly on her wrist and his grip was strong.

His other hand grabbed Ash's shoulder and he started shaking her. "What are you doing here? Don't you do enough damage across the universe?"

It was like someone had flicked a switch in him. She could see that enraged glint in his eye. The personable man she'd seen on the street earlier was completely gone.

"Get your hands off me!" she shouted back. "I know exactly what you're up to. You've ruined one planet and now you want to ruin another. Well, I won't let you!"

He released her shoulder and turned round, his speed and agility taking Ash unawares. His hand came back holding a wide blade. The entranceway was dark, but as the door wasn't completely closed behind her, the silver blade caught the light.

Terror flooded through Ash.

She lashed out, kicking frantically at Aldus's knees and more sensitive parts. But Aldus was quick, turning to the side to give her less of a target area. The blade was arcing towards her. She was going to die. Ash was going to die at the hands of this evil man and then this beautiful planet would likely die too.

Something sparked inside her. An influx of rage that had been there since she was a child. Since her sister died in the bombings of her village. Since her mother died of a broken heart, and her father died of lung disease. Since Aldus Dexter had put her planet at war with another. Since Star Corporation Academy colleagues had died in that war. All of it boiled in her chest, along with her overwhelming feelings of despair about the people on Erasmus.

Ash leaped towards him. His hand was still round her wrist but his knife arm had changed his balance. He wasn't expecting the full weight of an eighteen-year-old to land on him. And she had purpose. Her thumbs were extended and aimed straight at his eyes. Ash didn't hesitate, she pushed with all the force she had.

Aldus let out a scream. But Ash didn't care. All she cared about was the fact that the shock had made him release her wrist.

She tried to dart away, but Aldus caught the back of her clothing, yanking her backwards by the scruff of her neck, taking the breath clean from her lungs as he flung her straight onto the floor and sat astride her.

Ash couldn't believe she'd been so stupid. Her arms were pinned to the floor. She couldn't reach the trigger in her pocket. She'd been a fool – believing she could walk in here and walk back out.

Aldus bent over her, his words coming out in a hiss.

The knife came down to brush her cheek. "You little nobody. Who do you think you are? You've ruined my plans once. You don't get to ruin them again."

"I know what you're doing," she hissed back, trying to ignore the blade. "You want to drain the energy from Konoha. Why? Are you trying to go back to U62 to finish what you started?"

Aldus's eyes gleamed with fury. To her surprise, he threw back his head and let out a weird, maniacal laugh – it was too bad the hand with the knife was rock steady. "U62? Go back to U62?" He lowered his face so it was close to hers. Spit flew from his mouth as he rushed his words out. "My beautiful planet. I formed that place. I grew it. I developed it and its people into what I always pictured as the perfect place. But you – YOU!" His words were laced with menace. "You let them see things they shouldn't. Let them think thoughts they were never meant to think. They were mine, MINE. But after you came to U62, my people, my androids revolted. They banished me. Banished *me*! Their leader. Their creator."

She felt the tip of the knife nick her cheek and a slow warm trickle slide to floor. Aldus was going to kill her. She was struggling to breathe. He was going to kill her, here and now. His full weight was pressed down on her frame. Her chest couldn't expand properly to let any air in.

Ash edged her arm into her pocket little by little, feeling the shape of the trigger. She didn't need to pull it out. Her fingers fumbled frantically for the switch, but her position wasn't quite right. She had to keep Aldus distracted.

"You're crazy." She struggled to get the words out. "A megalomaniac. Why did the Library ever choose someone like you? All you want is power. You have no compassion. No empathy. You don't have any of the skills a Guardian should have. You cut off your own arm to get rid of the bangle! Who does that, and what does that say about you?"

He was breathing faster now, his rage clearly building. "You have no idea," he taunted. "You have no idea what I'm about to do, or the deal I've made. In a few hours, I will be unstoppable. I'm only sorry you won't be here to see it!" His weight shifted as he lifted to his knees. As soon as it did, she grabbed the remote through the cloth.

Everything happened in the blink of an eye.

Ash didn't hesitate. She didn't even think twice as she flicked the switch. She knew the dangers. She knew she was about to kill herself. But the rush of adrenaline was too much. She had to stop him, no matter what the cost.

As soon as she pressed the switch, it was like a bolt of lightning struck her arm. Aldus was thrown back against the wall and there was a whoosh. A pale lilac shimmer appeared around her, and the sharp pain continued in her wrist.

It was there and gone before she even had a chance to think about it.

Had that just really happened? Ash wasn't entirely sure.

Her whole body was weak, muscles twitching. She struggled to her feet. The door to the lab had flown open.

Aldus was still on the floor, his eyes fixed on her as they

heard a series of hums and buzzes, then sparks flew from the equipment in the lab. There was a hiss, a bang and an explosion at the other end of the lab, smoke drifting upwards.

Then there was silence.

Ash didn't need to pull the trigger from her pocket to know the light would be white. Her arm was still tingling and she rubbed it. Her fingers pulled back as she realized the bangle at her wrist was burning hot – even though it wasn't searing her skin.

What had happened?

Aldus was still crumpled on the floor. His skin was sagging, as if all his body fat had been pulled from underneath. The pulse. The blast of radiation. She should look the same.

Had the bangle protected her?

Aldus laughed, his voice higher pitched than before. "You can't stop me. You can never stop me. I'll just come back and do it all again." He gave a snort. "You're not brave enough to kill me. I'll always be in the background, waiting for when you least expect me." He coughed, a few spatters of blood landing on the floor.

Ash drew herself up to her full height, even though her body still objected. "I'm the Guardian. And I'll do what I need to do to protect the people in this universe."

She darted back and sprinted straight for the door, not waiting for a response. Then she kicked it shut behind her and yelled, "Burn it!"

It was only a few seconds but it seemed like for ever.

She sprinted down the street, not even looking behind her. There was a small noise, a strange one, then a whooshing sound as the night erupted behind her.

Ash was flung forward, to her hands and knees. Yellow flames licked the dark sky behind her. She turned round in amazement and stared at the lab, its roof blown open, fire already consuming what was left.

Within moments, people started to come out of dwellings and other buildings. Ezra appeared out of nowhere, pulled Ash up, slung an arm round her shoulder and started walking her down the street.

"Let's not vanish in front of people," he murmured.

She kept glancing backwards. "How did it go up so quickly?" She was stunned. Surely there was no way Aldus could have survived that. She felt numb and a bit dumbstruck.

He steered them round another corner, where Amara and Trik were waiting. "It's done," he told them. "The force field held."

They sighed in relief. "Let's go," she said firmly.

They all reached out and touched Ash's arm. She winced, but shook her head. "I'll tell you later," she muttered.

But she knew how to prioritize. Ash had to. She closed her eyes, twisted the bangle and let the pulling sensations take over her body.

CHAPTER TWENTY-THREE

Two hours later they were still at the table in the area above the Library, explaining what had happened to Vedis.

The Keeper's first reaction had been scarily calm.

When she had learned of the small success Aldus seemed to have had in stealing Konoha's power, she'd actually disappeared for a few moments. They had just got themselves something to drink when she reappeared, asking rapid-fire questions.

"You're sure the pulse worked? The equipment died?"

"Did you get another opportunity to see the device he was waiting for?"

"Could you draw it?"

"What did he mean, about the 'deal' he'd made?"

The trouble with Vedis's questions was that the team didn't know all the answers. Vedis paced relentlessly. It was clear she was upset, and Ash found it hard not to be fascinated by this. The thought of Aldus making a deal was playing on her mind too. Who had he made a deal with?

At the end of the two hours they were all exhausted. It was now, by their time, the middle of the night. Amara was already sleeping with her head on the table. Trik was leaning back in his chair and doing his best impression of someone pretending not to be sleeping. Only Ash and Ezra still had half-opened eyes.

Vedis made a little noise of frustration. Ash leaned forward and touched her arm.

"Vedis, the energy he stole – will Konoha be able to regenerate it? Will it retain its healing powers?"

The Keeper blinked and her eyes looked almost tearful. "Eventually," she replied after a few minutes. "It will take a few months." Her holographic hands moved to the bangle on Ash's wrist and she spun it with a slow nod of her head. Her eyes met Ash's. "I guess the Library works in mysterious ways. I never knew the bangle could protect the Guardian. At least, I've never heard of that happening before."

Ash pulled back, surprised. "Was that what happened when I set off your device?"

Vedis arched one eyebrow. "Apparently so. We'll pick this back up in the morning," she finished, and before Ash had a chance to ask any more questions, Vedis disappeared again.

Ash didn't even have the energy to roll her eyes. "Thanks, Ezra," she whispered.

He gave her a lazy smile.

"What are you thanking me for? You did all the hard work." He leaned forward. "You never really told me what happened behind that door."

She gulped. "He was Aldus. Just like you warned me he would be. I saw the same look in him as before – the same greed, the same self-determination. Nothing was going to get between him and what he wanted."

She breathed slowly then met Ezra's gaze.

"Do you think he's dead this time?"

Ezra closed his eyes for a second, as if he didn't want to say the words while she was watching him. "We made a pact," he replied, his voice so soft it was almost a whisper. "It wasn't just an incendiary device. It wasn't just to cause fire. It was more like a bomb. Setting it off would always have been the last resort."

He heaved a sigh at the final words but still didn't open his eyes.

"So, I hope that Aldus Dexter is no more. I hope that every single part of that lab has been destroyed." He waited, then opened his eyes. "We knew if we told you it was a bomb, you might have doubts. You agreed to a fire, but insisted it was merely a backup plan. You didn't agree to a bomb."

Ash was speechless. She knew why they had done this. They'd tried to take her out of the decision-making process – to help her feel less guilt, because she was the one who would plant the device.

"I did just think it was fire," she said shakily.

"Because we let you." Ezra nodded. It was like he was

reinforcing the message. *They* chose to bomb the lab and Aldus, not Ash.

A tear slid down her face. She couldn't explain it. Maybe it was the shock. She might have hated Aldus, but she still didn't like feeling responsible for someone's death – even his. Ash felt a movement behind her and turned.

Vedis had reappeared again. She had a strange look on her face. One that the Guardian had never seen from her before.

Admiration.

Vedis spoke clearly. "Your decision probably saved Konoha."

Ezra took a deep breath and looked at Ash with regret. "But it definitely didn't save Aldus, and we meant it that way."

Vedis gave a nod of her head. "The Library has just confirmed that Aldus Dexter is finally, definitively, dead."

Ash's hands were shaking, but she reached over to touch Ezra's hand as he stood up. "I should have made that decision," she said.

He gave a gentle shake of his head and touched her shoulder. "This isn't all on you, Ash," he said, before walking away.

Ash couldn't speak. She was trying to work out everything in her head.

Vedis sat down in Ezra's place. She'd rarely seen Vedis sit before. It was strange to be across the table from her.

Then words came from her lips that Ash thought she'd never hear from the hologram: "Thank you."

Ash blinked. "Wh-what?"

"Thank you," Vedis repeated. She lifted her hand to the leaves on her head. "You know why I picked this appearance." She gave a smile. "But you don't know why I picked my name.

"Vedis, my name, means holy spirit of the forest." Vedis put her hand to her chest. "For some reason, when I was created as Keeper and asked to select a name, there was only one I was drawn to." She gave an odd smile. "The memories of Konoha from our previous Guardian were fixed in my head. I also feel an affinity to a planet I've never visited. When you told me about Aldus's actions, I wished absolute harm on him."

Now it was Ash's turn to give an odd smile. "I never realized just how real you are," she said in a low voice.

Vedis looked a bit startled. "You didn't feel like Orius was real?"

"No...I mean, yes!" She gave an anxious laugh. "When I first met him, I didn't realize for a few seconds that he was a hologram. It was only when he seemed to glide across the floor – I realized he wasn't actually walking. But then," she paused, "he acted like a real person. He got annoyed with me. He was evasive at times. And then...he could touch me. As his programming diminished. I could feel him."

Vedis paused for a few moments. "We can all touch." She reached over and put her holographic hand back on Ash's arm. The sensation was cold and Ash pulled away in shock.

Vedis gave a little shrug. "It became intermittent with Orius. I choose when I want to touch. He lost that ability, just like he sometimes lost his form a little."

"Like when he shimmered?"

Vedis gave a nod. "It was all part of the programming breaking down."

"And you know all that?"

Vedis put her hand on her chest. "Because Orius is part of me. We both came from the Library program. I know every conversation you had together. I also know how much he believed in your selection as Guardian."

Ash pressed her lips together. "Something that you don't agree with?"

Vedis took her time. "I come from the same program. I know everything that has gone before. But I am me, not Orius. I have thoughts and opinions of my own. Not all new Keepers agree with actions of previous Keepers."

Ash leaned back. "I can hardly get my head around all this."

"You don't need to," said Vedis. "I just wanted you to know that I'm glad you took action to stop Aldus from harming Konoha."

Ash leaned her head on one hand and drummed her fingers on the table.

"You're disappointed," stated Vedis.

"In myself, yes. It wasn't until I saw the gleam in Aldus's eyes that I knew he would never let things go. He would always come back. So I'm disappointed I didn't realize that earlier. But disappointed in my team? Never."

Vedis pushed herself up from the chair, resuming her normal authoritative stance. "You were right about a team being a good idea," she said thoughtfully, then looked at Ash again. "It brings something new to the Library. A freshness. A sense of balance. As for you and I? I think it may be time for us to come to a truce."

Relief rolled off Ash. "Really?" She couldn't help her surprised tone.

"Really." Vedis folded her arms. "It seems to me that things might work better if the Guardian and Keeper of the Library could work together."

"And with the team," added Ash carefully. She stretched out her hand towards Vedis.

There was a slight pause and then Vedis stretched out her hand and clasped Ash's. "Here's to teamwork," she agreed.

CHAPTER TWENTY-FOUR

For the next few weeks the Library was quiet. Amara returned to Columbia 764 for a few days and Trik to the Star Corporation Academy. Both sent good news about their friends back home.

Ezra stayed with Ash at the Library in case any Infinity Files appeared as assignments, but he hoped to visit his home world of Hakora soon too.

Ash was having trouble sleeping. She kept waking in the middle of the night, wondering about what Aldus had meant when he'd said he'd made a deal. She searched the Library for any information, but in the end, she couldn't find an obvious answer.

The others came back from their visits, and all waited restlessly for their next mission.

Ash was slumped in a comfortable purple velvet chair, gazing out at the stars, with her feet on a nearby bookcase, down in the heart of the Library. She'd resorted to late night strolls in among the stacks.

The good thing about the Library at the End of the Universe was that there was always something new to discover. An object she hadn't seen before, or a scroll she hadn't read. Currently she had an old favourite next to her – the spear of Damocles – along with a scroll from an ancient civilization that had ceased to exist one thousand years earlier. There was nothing like trying to decipher another language written by a long-extinct species.

As she watched how the symbols curved on the page, Ash felt a slight tremor. It was unusual. The Library was generally steady.

She looked up. The tremor increased in intensity. Ash jumped to her feet as artefacts on shelves started to rattle round her.

This was bizarre. This was like an earthquake!

She gripped the chair to steady herself as something slowly started to rise into her line of vision outside the glass dome.

Ash couldn't breathe.

The black oval shape was enormous and sleek, in a glistening, ominous kind of way. And every bit as intimidating as it was the last time she'd seen it at Quisquilla space port.

The craft froze, hanging in space straight in front of her.

"Ash!"

Trik, Ezra and Amara came running down the wide Library stairs, obviously woken by the shaking. Vedis appeared at her side in an instant.

"It's the B…Byroneans," Ash murmured.

One thin blinding white light appeared across the front of the ship – just like it had done on their last encounter.

"I have a very bad feeling about this," murmured Trik under his breath.

Vedis took charge. She looked up.

"Library, open a channel to the Byroneans," she said.

"We can do that?" asked Ezra.

"We've never had to before," whispered Amara.

There was a noise in the air and Vedis spoke crisply. "Please announce your intent."

No pleasantries. No introductions.

The noise changed to a weird kind of buzz. A face appeared in the air in front of them and Amara let out a shriek.

None of them had any idea how the image had been projected inside the Library. It was one of the Byroneans.

They were a robotic race, large and intimidating. The most striking feature was that they strongly resembled their spaceships. Black, glossy, with a sleekness about them. The Byroneans' bodies were built to resemble Humans, but their faces were featureless. Just that one bright horizontal strip in the place of eyes. It pulsed from side to side, giving off an air of impatience.

An electronic-sounding voice replied.

"You are in possession of a Byroneus crystal. It will be returned immediately or the Library will be destroyed."

The words sent instant chills down Ash's spine.

She couldn't take her eyes from the face of the robot. No emotion. It looked impenetrable.

Ash spoke out of the side of her mouth to Vedis. "Should we just hand it over?"

"No," said Vedis simply.

Ash wanted to ask so much more, but now was clearly not the time.

She couldn't believe how calm Vedis was. Behind her, Ezra, Trik and Amara were throwing wild, anxious glances at each other.

"So be it," said the electronic voice, and the screen disappeared from in front of them.

Vedis looked up and said clearly, "Library, deploy defences."

There was a grating sound as if something were sliding into place. Moments later the stars outside disappeared and the Library was flanked with a silver shield.

Ash held up her hands. "What?!"

Vedis vanished and reappeared at the top of the stairs. "Move!" she shouted to the rest of them. They raced across the floor of the Library towards the stairs, but before they'd even set foot on one, the whole place shook.

Ezra fell to one side. Amara landed face first on the stairs. Trik tore past them and sprinted up the steps. "Where do you want me?" he asked Vedis.

She pointed to a screen. "Monitor the shields."

"When did we get shields?" yelled Ash as she took two steps at a time. "We never had shields the last time."

"Why do you think the programming took so long?" said Vedis coolly. "The Library needed to shore up its defence systems. I'm not entirely sure how long the holographic shielding will work."

Ash glanced through the glass again. For some reason she'd assumed the shielding was some kind of metal. But of course, it wasn't. There was no way metal shielding could have been installed in the Library without them noticing.

"Shields are at eighty-five per cent," said Trik, glancing over his shoulder at the rest of them. "Do we have weapons?" he asked.

Vedis clicked her fingers and another screen appeared.

"Mine," said Ezra and stood in front, scanning the screen.

Ash shook her head and moved over to Vedis. "Shields? Weapons? You don't think these are things that the Guardian of the Library should know about?"

"I was going to tell you," said Vedis. "It just hadn't come up."

"Until now?" Ash asked incredulously.

"That's correct."

Amara wrinkled her green brow as she looked around in wonder, clearly wondering how this had all passed her by. They'd all thought Amara knew the Library systems inside out. "Can someone tell me why we can't just give them the stone back?" she asked. "Aren't we just supposed to caretake this stuff, then return it?"

"When it's appropriate," emphasized Vedis. Her calm was amazing Ash. She seemed completely unflappable. "Do you really think now is a good time to give the Byroneans a crystal that can allow them to regenerate endlessly? The Library predicts that if we do that, they will multiply their forces by one hundred times and mount an attack that will lead to the direct destruction of two solar systems."

"Maybe not, then," muttered Ezra as he scanned his own screen.

There was another boom and the Library shook. "Eighty per cent," said Trik, with a trace of worry in his voice.

Vedis scowled. She clicked over on her heels and stared at the screen. "It should be holding better than this."

"Yes!" said Ezra punching the air. He had two screens in front of him, one with technological instructions, the other showing the giant Byronean fighter outside. As they watched, something impacted on the fighter and it rocked – actually rocked. The whole ship looked like a giant black egg, somehow turned on its side. For a second, the white strip of light flickered, then it steadied again, this time glowing so bright they all pulled back and looked away.

"What was that?" asked Ash.

"Pilozean missiles," said Vedis, as if these were something they fired every day.

Ash moved next to Ezra. He waved a hand to change the view on the screen. "There's a variety of weapon systems. I just picked the one I understood most."

This whole situation was unreal. An attack when they least expected it, from a race she literally knew nothing about. Weapons and shields she hadn't been briefed on. Her friends being pulled into a war they didn't understand. Again.

As yet another boom sounded, Ash held up a hand. "Vedis, start explaining to me right now exactly what is going on."

Trik looked over his shoulder at her. "Seventy-five per cent. Ezra, try something else."

He was starting to look worried.

Vedis opened her mouth to speak and then stopped, as the air around them shimmered.

They all held their breath, wondering what could possibly be happening now.

Eight large figures materialized in front of them – black robots, twice the height and breadth of any one of them. And a ninth, smaller, wriggling figure.

"Reker!" said Ash in shock. The girl from Quisquilla was being dangled in mid-air by one of the giant Byroneans. As they watched, she squirmed so much that she actually wriggled her way out of her coat and landed in a heap on the Library floor.

Ash stepped forward to pick her up, but her path was blocked by a giant leg and black torso.

"You will remain where you are." The electronic voice echoed around the Library.

The group stood frozen, not sure whether they should jump forward and attack or dive for cover.

The voice spoke again. "You will return the crystal, or you will all die."

CHAPTER TWENTY-FIVE

For a second, everyone was frozen.

All eight of the Byroneans seemed to be entirely focused on Ash – as if they knew she was the Guardian. None of them even glanced towards her team. And something clicked in Ash. It was the oddest connection. Even though she was standing in a confined space, with eight large black robotic creatures surrounding her team, a wave of something she couldn't entirely explain swept over her. Her connection to the Library. Fear seemed to switch off and be replaced by something else. Sense. Logic. Knowledge. And she knew exactly what to do next. Ash smiled. When she spoke, her voice was low.

"Trik, Ezra, get into the fighters. I need some distraction outside."

She saw the glances between them, but they didn't argue. They didn't panic.

"Done." Both of them turned and ran down the nearby

corridor that led down to the flight deck. Reker gave a panicked look, then scrambled after Trik and Ezra. None of the Byroneans moved. They still seemed very focused on Ash.

One of them stepped forward.

"You will give us the Byroneus crystal, or we will destroy the Library in order to find it." His head turned with a metallic whirr, and his white light pulsed madly for a few moments. "There is nothing here of importance anyway."

He'd been scanning the Library. There was a shimmer, and Vedis appeared at Ash's side.

"I think you'll find there's much of importance here," she retorted. "Lessons to be learned in order to maintain a functioning, equitable universe."

It sounded very logical and obviously caught their attention. The head turned back, moving up and down minutely, as if it were scanning Vedis.

"A hologram. How interesting. A distraction."

Ash's stomach gave a twist. They obviously weren't swayed by distraction techniques. Maybe she'd just made a mistake.

The only thing on her mind right now was the fact she needed to get the Byroneus crystal as far away from the Library and these guys as possible.

Vedis's hair branches twitched in an invisible breeze. "What exactly do you need the crystal for?"

There was not a second of hesitation. "You know exactly what we need the crystal for. We require the second crystal to allow our species to replicate. We had arrangements to have our crystal reproduced. Unfortunately, those plans have been halted."

Even though the words were robotic, there was still a hint of annoyance in them. Maybe the Byroneans weren't quite as emotionless as they seemed.

The one who was talking to them pointed at Ash. "You, the Guardian. We have put a force field round this dome. You won't be able to use your device to leave."

Ash could almost feel the blood drain from her body. Her hand went automatically to her wrist.

It was as if Vedis read her mind. "Try it," she murmured.

Ash twisted the bangle. Nothing happened. The world didn't shimmer around her, it didn't turn white, or multi-coloured, or effect any of the other sensations that had happened before.

She turned her head towards the Proteus circle. Maybe it could help her override whatever they had done? But it seemed they'd already thought of that. Another of the Byroneans was standing on it. He was twice as tall as Ash and looked around four times as solid. She wouldn't have a hope of moving him.

Ash tried to ignore the tiny flare of panic that was fluttering in her chest. Vedis started talking again.

"What happened to your plans? And how is it possible to replicate a Byroneus crystal? The science makes it impossible."

There was a giant flash of light from outside, followed by some kind of pulse wave.

Both Ash and Vedis crouched, their arms moving to cover their heads – even though surely Vedis didn't need to. Everything in the Library moved. Several items fell from storage racks and shelves. All of the Byroneans remained steady, but their heads turned in unison.

There. Another flash. It was Trik's fighter, with Ezra's crossing from the other direction! Whatever weapon they had just fired, it had caused some kind of damage to the dark egg-shaped ship. The glare from the light across its front wasn't quite so bright now, and the outside skin seemed warped in one part.

Had Ash imagined it, or had the ship just lowered slightly – as if there had been a loss of power?

In two giant strides, the nearest Byronean grabbed her round the neck.

Behind her, Vedis spoke clearly. "Continue attack."

Ash couldn't inhale. Couldn't speak. But Vedis was more than capable of giving instructions to Trik and Ezra.

She felt a buzz at her ear, and suddenly she could hear them. It was as if they were being channelled to her through the Library somehow.

Vedis gave Ash a quick sideways glance.

"Fire again!" came the shout from Trik.

"Reload the weapons. Take another run." Ezra's voice was entirely focused.

"Weapons ready. Let's get them!"

The third, unexpected voice made Ash's muscles contract. It took her a second to realize who it was. Reker?

What was she doing in one of the **fig**hters?

As the fighters zipped past again, Ash realized that one of the guys had taken out a two-seater, rather than the single-seater fighters they usually flew in.

Was it Trik or Ezra? She had no way of knowing.

Ash's head was feeling a little fuzzy. The metal hand clamped round her neck was unyielding. She could only suck the tiniest amount of air through her nose. Amara was crouched behind the table near the balustrade, her eyes darting from side to side as she obviously struggled to decide what to do.

Vedis moved closer, addressing the Byronean who had Ash.

"Your crystal. How did you plan on replicating it? You think you're such a superior race. What has gone wrong?"

At this stage, Ash wasn't sure if Vedis was still using this as a distraction technique or if she was actually curious.

The Byronean turned to Vedis without loosening his grip a single bit. "We had a contract with an Anterrean. He'd found an odd power source on a planet. We'd agreed to give him our one remaining crystal to help him drain the power, and then he would use the technology he'd discovered to replicate another crystal for us."

Aldus Dexter. They were talking about Aldus Dexter. It was amazing how even the thought of him could make Ash's skin prickle.

She shot a panicked glance at Vedis as another flash of white lit up the dark space outside.

Vedis closed her eyes. All of a sudden Ash could hear Vedis's voice in her head. It was her connection to the Library again. *Remember, they're a logical race. They said they'd placed a force field round the dome. That means the hidden hangar under the Library should be clear.*

Ash tried to breathe again. She could get out. She could get the crystal and fly out of here. She needed to get it as far away from the Byroneans as possible.

There was an enormous boom. This time it didn't come from the dark space outside – it was the sound of something impacting on the dome.

The Byronean released her abruptly and her legs nearly crumpled. She automatically sucked in a huge breath, to try and replenish her depleted lungs.

"We will destroy your Library bit by bit. Our force field is merely to stop your technology allowing you to jump away. Our weapons can still impact. And we will continue to fire until you give us the crystal or we find it ourselves."

As if there had been an unspoken command, all eight Byroneans moved at once to the wide stone stairs that led down into the heart of the Library where all the artefacts were stored, leaving the three of them behind.

Amara's head came up slowly from behind the table. "What are we going to do?"

Vedis turned to her. "We are going to help with the distraction while Ash gets the crystal and takes it away." She grabbed Ash's arm with a firm grip, straightening her up and looking out over the Library. "There's no time to waste."

Another shot hit the Library and for a moment Ash was worried the dome might crack. At the same time, the Byroneans were extending out their long arms and sending artefacts spilling to the floor.

Ash's eyes flicked to the hidden back corner where the safe was. Vedis's nose twitched and she frowned. Once. Twice. Her gaze fixed on Ash's.

"I can't transport it to you. Whatever their force field is, it's interfering with my abilities."

A picture came into Ash's mind – just as if it had appeared on a screen in front of her. A scene she recognized. Ash swayed as Vedis spoke again.

"What's happening to me?"

"The Library. It's connecting with you."

Ash put her hand to her chest. "With me? But how?"

Vedis gave her a knowing look. "You already suspected the Library was more than just a place. A sentient being. In times of crises, it can connect us."

Ash pulled back. "What?" Even as she recoiled, a flight path to Erasmus – the planet half-destroyed by volcanoes – appeared to unfold inside her brain.

Vedis put a hand on her wrist now – she seemed to know exactly what information Ash was receiving. "It will take a massive amount of power to destroy the Byroneus crystal. We have to ensure we protect other places in the universe. But a planet that is already on the path to destruction and can't be salvaged?"

Ash gave a nod. Of course.

One minute she was standing and the next Ash was flat on her back, as a plume of dust erupted around her. The whole Library reverberated from the impact.

The fight outside was getting worse. The Byronean ship was now firing at both fighters, with spare shots also hitting the Library.

"Go!" yelled Amara as she picked herself off the ground and ran down into the Library.

Vedis materialized at Amara's side and waved her hand at Ash. In the midst of this chaos, she looked eerily calm.

Over the noise from the fighters' comms, and the explosions around her, Ash heard a still voice. "Go, Guardian. You have a job to do."

And then Vedis turned, and her white shirt disappeared among the tumbling stacks in the Library.

CHAPTER TWENTY-SIX

Ash darted as quickly and as unobtrusively as she could, hiding behind one display after another, and several spilled sections of shelves. But the Byroneans were no longer interested in Ash or any of her team. They crashed through the Library and its artefacts, intent only on finding the crystal. Finding it was their only priority right now.

It was odd. She'd thought at first the Byroneans had tracked them to the Library through some kind of signal from the crystal. But, as they crashed through various parts of the vast Library, it was apparent they had no way to track where the crystal was. So they must have found them through Reker somehow.

Ash reached the safe and pressed her hand to it. At first it didn't open. Of course, it had been Vedis who had transported the crystal to the safe. Ash had never set the locks on the safe before. Her shoulders tingled and she tried again, pressing her hand to the safe and concentrating hard.

She felt it, the connection. It was like a spark in her brain. Part of her mind wanted to explore this entirely, another part of her wanted to run for the hills. She didn't even fully understand what it was. And she had no time to hang around.

The safe sprung open and Ash made a grab for the crystal. It was still surrounded by a blue hue, the tiny force field that was keeping all its dangerous radiation inside. She tucked it inside her jacket, praying the force field wouldn't fail, and ducked down a nearby corridor.

It was dark. This wasn't the normal route to the flight deck, and Ash had to scramble down a ladder and open a hatch to reach the fighters. She ran along to her own, halting when she saw some damage at the back of the craft.

It looked minor, but a small piece of space junk had impacted on the hull, smashing the shield generator.

For a moment she almost scrambled for another fighter. There were others she could use, but something clicked in her brain.

The damage to her fighter was specific. Part of her shield was impaired, meaning that her ship would leak tachyon emissions, making her imminently trackable throughout space. No wonder the Byroneans had found her.

She smiled. And they could find her again.

As she climbed into the craft and strapped herself in, she almost let out a laugh. This was perfect! She knew exactly what to do next.

Ash sat back, fired up the engines and gunned out into space. The battle was still in full force all around her.

"Guys," she shouted. "Keep firing. But I want them to follow me. I want them to track me. So, when they come after me – don't follow."

"What?" The yell through her comm echoed in her ears.

"Where are you going?" asked Ezra.

She let off a few targeted blasts at the Byronean ship. Now she was outside and near it, the size was completely intimidating. Trik and Ezra were continuing to dart round it, narrowly missing automatic weapon fire.

But what worried her more was the Library. From out here, the damage was clear. The docking port – where her freighter had first locked on after she'd made the journey from the Star Corporation Academy – was completely destroyed. Parts of twisted metal and wires were hanging in mid-space. A pair of grey blast doors was the only barrier now between outer space and the interior of the Library. She had to get the Byroneans away from here before the damage they caused the Library was irreparable.

"Pull back!" yelled Reker.

Ash yanked the nose of her craft upwards as something shot across underneath her. It had come from Ezra's ship and seconds later the Byronean ship had another dent in its hull.

"What was that?" Ash asked, shaking as she steered her ship away from the main battle.

Ezra answered quickly. "It seems these two seaters aren't for the slow or faint of heart. It's some kind of sonic torpedo. Guess we should have paid more attention to these bad boys. Reker discovered them. And she's proving a very good shot."

A few moments later, Reker let out another yell from the comm, and a host of sonic torpedoes hit the hull of the Byronean ship in an unusual pattern.

To Ash's amazement, this time the ship seemed to stutter in space.

"Where did you aim?" she asked.

Reker laughed. "At their docking points. Figured they might not have shielded those as well as the main hull."

Ash allowed herself to smile. Reker was proving her worth already.

"Ash!" shouted Trik. "Do you want company? What if they blast you out of the sky? You need backup."

Even though they couldn't see her, Ash automatically shook her head. "No. Remember, the Byroneans are a logical race. They'll track me as soon as they notice I'm running. Look after the Library, guys. They'll realize I have the crystal and think I'm attempting to get away. They won't blast me – the crystal is too important to them."

"Wait." Trik sounded confused. "Isn't that exactly what you *are* doing? Shoot!" He let out a curse. "That was too close for comfort."

"Watch yourselves, guys! Look after Amara and Vedis for me. I'll be back before you know it."

Then, before she could change her mind, Ash let the craft jump.

CHAPTER TWENTY-SEVEN

One wormhole and two jumps in the fighter later, Ash was finally where she wanted to be. She hadn't moved quite as quickly as the craft was capable of, though, as she wanted to make sure the Byroneans were following her trail.

But there was no reason to worry. They'd materialized through the wormhole just after her, and clearly had the same space-jump technology on their huge craft.

As soon as Erasmus appeared in her viewfinder, Ash sped up, dropping height swiftly to descend into the planet's atmosphere. The move would confuse the Byroneans. They wouldn't understand it.

For a few moments, her eyes focused on the scene beneath her. Half of her had hoped the Library might have been wrong. But it clearly wasn't.

The cataclysmic eruption may have started at the volcano nearest the city she'd visited, but it had clearly set off a chain reaction throughout the planet.

As Ash flew above the ash-cloud-strewn atmosphere, there was an occasional break in the grey and blackness to reveal what lay underneath. It was heartbreaking. The planet, which had been alive with greenery, blue seas and colourful life, looked as if it had been smothered in a wash of brown and grey.

Nothing could survive down there, not even a creature at the base of the now-black oceans.

She blinked back tears and kept flying. Part of her was desperate to see any sign of life – anything – even though it went against her mission. Faces flashed into her mind: Lucia, Elias, the twin girls in their pale-pink robes. Another colour swam into her brain. Green. The pale green of the Healer robes, and the dark green of the grass between her toes.

In the far distance, she could see a flash of orange. Another volcano spilling its contents over the already dead earth.

The Library had predicted that this whole planet would be destroyed. Ash didn't doubt it for a second.

She pressed some coordinates into the display and swung her craft round, just as the Byronean ship submerged into the atmosphere beside her.

The dark ominous egg hovered as if it belonged there.

Ash pushed the control forward, zipping away to the volcano that was about to re-erupt.

For a few moments, she was foolish enough to believe that she'd actually escaped from them. But as she reached the rim of the volcano, Ash's fighter came to a sudden and abrupt halt.

She shot forward, her harness holding her in place but taking the air from her lungs. Nothing stopped her head clashing with her display controls.

Ash sat back winded, and in shock.

She heard a weird grinding noise and, even though she could hardly focus, tried to twist in her seat.

No. No way. Not even possible.

A giant metal claw from the Byronean ship had her fighter in a solid pincer move! She'd never seen anything like this before. At least not at this level.

Sure, lots of spacecraft had small, extendable claws to perform minimal repairs on the outside of their ships. Space ports often had similar extendable clamps to allow docking between ships and accessory tunnels.

But a claw to capture and trap another ship? Never.

She glanced down just as a space appeared in the smoggy clouds beneath. There! The rim of the volcano, with bubbling lava underneath. The exact place she wanted to deposit the crystal. The Library had predicted that the power of the crystal would combine with the force and momentum behind the building pressure of magma. The effects would be catastrophic.

As her fighter was jerked backwards, something bubbled in Ash's chest. They wouldn't fire on her. They wanted to safely gain possession of the crystal – that's why they hadn't shot her out of the sky.

As she looked round, she realized they'd probably just solved her last problem. She hadn't been entirely sure how to safely open her cockpit while piloting her ship and throw the crystal into the mouth of the volcano. Her ship didn't have hover capabilities in a planet's gravitational atmosphere. The Byronean ship clearly did.

It was now or never.

Without thinking too much, she pulled the lever that released her cockpit hood. It sprang backwards, instantly exposing her to the suffocating atmosphere and smothering ash. Even from up here, the wave of supercharged heat from below flooded around her.

She coughed and choked instantly when she inhaled. There had been no time for a helmet. Covering her mouth and nose with one hand, Ash pulled the crystal from inside her jacket with the other. In an instant she knew this plan was flawed, as the ship jerked back further – potentially pulling her away from the mouth of the volcano.

The Byroneans were trying to retract the clamp and pull her back towards their ship. But things weren't going smoothly. There was clearly something wrong with the mechanism. As she looked back in panic, a panel slid back on the oval hull and a large black figure emerged next to the arm of the clamp. It seemed like the Byroneans had decided to fix the problem.

There was no time to waste. Ash released her harness and clambered out of her seat, spinning round to face the Byronean ship. She balanced precariously, grabbing the edge of the fighter.

She'd moved backwards, further away from the mouth of

the volcano. She wasn't entirely sure she was still above it.

Ash choked as she tried to suck in a deep breath. The searing heat seemed to stretch up towards her. The thoughts that were flooding her mind were extreme, and she knew it, but there was only one way. Wind was whistling around her, unbalancing her as she scrambled to climb out of the cockpit and onto the wing of the fighter.

It would only take one more retraction of the claw to topple her off the wing.

As she took her first unsteady step, the Byroneans clearly realized her intent. It was like the world moved into slow motion all around her. The fabric of her flight suit crinkled round her legs, instantly affected by the supercharged heat.

The bangle on her wrist tingled and then the buzz spread throughout her body. Only it wasn't a buzz. It was a connection. And everything seemed to come into focus for Ash.

Now, her legs weren't trembling. Now she wasn't walking. She was running along the unsteady wing. She pulled back her arm and threw the crystal with all her might. The blue-tinged crystal caught the bright orange glow from beneath and for a few seconds turned into a glistening neon purple, turning over and over in the sky before vanishing into the mouth of the volcano.

Now was the time to stop. The time to try and fumble her way back into the fighter. Instead, she reached the end of the wing, grabbed her wrist with one hand, and jumped.

Her brain was currently screaming at her. But Ash wasn't scared, there was a whizz of elation as she leaped out into the smoggy air, tumbling downwards. The searing heat almost reached out and grabbed her.

Ash twisted her bangle firmly as the scorching air rushed past her ears.

She'd done it. The crystal was gone! The Byroneans would no longer be a threat to the universe.

And then the world erupted into a multitude of colours.

CHAPTER TWENTY-EIGHT

It was the musty book smell that awakened her senses first.

"Home," was the word she breathed out.

Her back ached. She was lying flat on the Proteus circle, staring up at the ceiling above her. The dome was still there. It hadn't disintegrated into a million shards and allowed the contents of the Library to be sucked out into space.

As she blinked, Ash realized how deep-rooted that fear was. She could almost see that horrible nightmare before her eyes, and her relief at seeing the glint and curve of the dome against the dark sky outside was huge.

Lots of people didn't realize that space wasn't always black. It was a myriad of colours, as stars and solar systems constantly died and were created. Right now, if she squinted, Ash was sure she could see a bit of pink out there.

There was a rustle, and Ash sat up, wincing. Her back would likely be bruised.

Five figures were standing a little way away with their

backs to her. All eyes were fixed on a display screen in mid-air. She could see everything herself.

As she pushed herself to her feet, the planet – which from here was a mixture of browns, oranges and greys – seemed to expand. Everything was happening in slow motion. Erasmus. They were watching Erasmus. No wonder the team hadn't even noticed her arrival.

Ash's mouth fell open as the expansion of the planet seemed to continue. A smog of vapour appeared, making the planet almost shimmer.

Finally, the colour changed to a rapidly expanding bluish-white fireball. One minute Erasmus was there, next the surrounding space was filled by a deluge of debris.

Amara sucked in a breath, and the tips of the leaves on Vedis's head curled inwards.

Trik spun round, blinking at the sight of her.

"Ash!" he yelled in a booming voice.

The others all jumped and turned round, their eyes wide and glistening. Trik smothered her in a hug, squeezing the air from her lungs. Was she ever going to be able to breathe properly again?

Ezra didn't wait to join in. As Trik was still hugging her, he lifted Ash from the ground. Trik's grasp loosened and Ezra spun her round.

"What did you do?" he asked. "We thought you were still there. As soon as the reaction started…"

Amara let out a small cry as she slid one clawed hand into Ash's. Her green head pressed against the side of Ash's too.

"Promise you will never, ever do something like that again," she said.

Ash's feet touched the floor again, and she coughed and spluttered.

As she lifted her head, Vedis moved in front of her. The stern expression had returned, even though her white blouse was askew and wasn't tucked quite as neatly into her black skirt. She pressed her holographic hands into Ash's shoulders.

"Guardian," she said softly.

Ash wondered what might come next.

"You're home." The words echoed in Ash's brain as her body was swept over in a flood of warm, soothing, book-scented air. It took her a few seconds to realize no one was actually touching her any more, and Ash wrapped her own arms round herself and smiled. The connection. It was there. And it was real.

"Thank you," she whispered.

In a flash of blue, Reker appeared at her side. She gave Ash a disdainful glance up and down, then her face gave a crooked smile.

"You're back. Good. I have questions."

"Look," interrupted Ezra, pointing back to the screen.

Something came into view, carried along in the shockwave from the planet. It was the remains of a slightly battered, certainly dented, Byronean ship. It seemed to stutter to a halt.

"Are they coming here?" asked Ash in horror. For the first time since she'd jumped back, she looked down into the

315

Library. Chaos. Utter chaos. It would take months to fix and they surely had few defences left if the Byroneans decided to attack again.

She turned back to the screen in time to see a little sputter of light appear. The ship seemed to jump a few times, then move off in a juddering fashion.

Vedis shook her head. "No. They're not coming here. We have nothing they want now. We're instantly unimportant to them again. Now they can't reproduce, they will focus on conserving the population they have, rather than leaping into battles with others."

"You're sure?" This time it was Reker's voice, laced with strain.

"I'm sure," said Vedis. She frowned. "Who are you again?"

Ezra slung his arm round Reker's shoulder. "I believe you're looking at the newest member of our team."

There was a moment's silence as gazes connected and small nods were acknowledged.

Ash moved forward. "I think that sounds like exactly what we need. Someone who is resourceful, bright, and has the ability to learn new skills."

She grinned at Vedis. "Shouldn't we have some kind of apprentice programme?"

Ash could tell Vedis was about to say something scathing, but Amara moved smoothly to her side and touched her slightly smudged white sleeve. She nodded down to the chaos of the Library beneath them. "So much work to do," she said in a solemn voice. "We'll need all the help we can get."

They all moved over to the balustrade, first looking down and then out to space. There were a few blemishes on the dome. Repairs were needed everywhere.

"I can stay?" asked Reker nervously, glancing around. "Here?"

This time it was Ash who put her arm round Reker's shoulders and led her to the wide stairs. "Let me tell you a story," she started, "of a place of fabulous learning, both good and bad. A place where you can learn the histories, secrets and wonders of the universe. A universe we all have a duty to protect."

And with those words, they descended down into the Library at the End of the Universe, the holding place for the Infinity Files.

ACKNOWLEDGEMENTS

I'd hoped by the time my last book, *The Infinity Files*, came out, we would all have come out the other side of the pandemic and moved on. But we're still here, trying to pick up the pieces from the prolonged periods of lockdown, now on our third round of vaccinations, and still trying to get through.

Writing books like *The Infinity Guardians* in lockdown has been a definite outlet for me. Getting to jump to other planets, to meet other species, and have space-type dramas definitely takes away from everyday life.

Huge thanks as ever go to my two Sarahs. My agent, Sarah Hornsley from Peters Fraser and Dunlop, and to my editor Sarah Stewart at Usborne, for backing my space stories all the way.

As ever, there's a great team at Usborne who have all played a part in assisting with this second story. Alice Moloney who assisted with the editing, Tilda Johnson who has now copy-edited many of my stories and does a fabulous job with bringing up my manuscripts to the standard you all see. For Hannah Featherstone and Gareth Collinson, thanks for proofreading, picking up any of my errors and giving lots of useful suggestions. For PR and marketing, my huge appreciation and thanks go to Jacob Dow, Katarina Jovanovic and Stevie Hopwood for getting my stories out into the world. For my cover designer Will Steele, and to my cover illustrator Steve Stone, thank you for my fabulous space cover which captures the essence of the story perfectly. And to Sarah Cronin for the text design of the inside pages, thank you for making my story look so perfect.

And finally to my readers. Thanks for reading the space stories that started in my head. I'm hoping you see the growth in Ash and her team, and you can imagine a million other adventures for these characters.

S. M. Wilson x

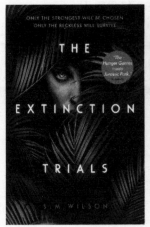 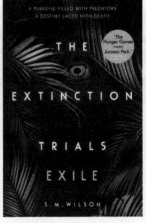 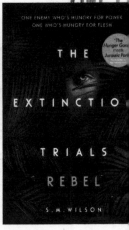